BLOOD TIES

SUI LYNN

Dreamspinner Press

Published by
DREAMSPINNER PRESS

5032 Capital Circle SW, Suite 2, PMB# 279, Tallahassee, FL 32305-7886 USA
http://www.dreamspinnerpress.com/

This is a work of fiction. Names, characters, places, and incidents either are the product of author imagination or are used fictitiously, and any resemblance to actual persons, living or dead, business establishments, events, or locales is entirely coincidental.

Blood Ties
© 2014 Sui Lynn.

Cover Art
© 2014 L.C. Chase.
http://www.lcchase.com
Cover content is for illustrative purposes only and any person depicted on the cover is a model.

ISBN: 978-1-62798-699-1
Digital ISBN: 978-1-62798-700-4
Library of Congress Control Number: 2014944021
First Edition September 2014

Printed in the United States of America
∞
This paper meets the requirements of
ANSI/NISO Z39.48-1992 (Permanence of Paper).

Readers love the *Changing Moon* series
by SUI LYNN

A Royal Bind

"Ms Lynn made this a dynamic world and left open plenty of avenues for the next book in the series. I can't wait to jump into the next story because after this one? I'm definitely getting the first… and relishing the idea of the next."

—Mrs. Condit & Friends Read Books

"I will recommend this to those who love shifters, vampires, paranormal, strong love, hot sex, developing characters, a great story and being left with a desperate hope that the next book will be published soon."

—MM Good Book Reviews

The Pauper Prince

"Romance, fast paced action, and an intense plotline are packed within Lance and Andrew's tale. I Joyfully Recommend The Pauper Prince."

—Joyfully Reviewed

"The author's writing style is lush, simple, and eloquently concise, with a fresh twist on an average storyline. There isn't anything I dislike about this story, and the HFN ending leaves me eagerly looking forward to the next installment in the series. I really enjoyed reading this fascinating tale, and if you're looking for a shifter story that is a fantastic start to a new series, then I can recommend this book to you."

—Mrs. Condit & Friends Read Books

By SUI LYNN

Blue Rose

CHANGING MOON
Book One: The Pauper Prince
Book Two: A Royal Bind
Book Three: Blood Ties

ELEMENTS OF LOVE
Book One: Adel's Purr
Book Two: Nico's Fire

Published by DREAMSPINNER PRESS
http://www.dreamspinnerpress.com

ACKNOWLEDGMENTS

I WOULD like to thank all of those who had a part in getting *Blood Ties* to be the story it is today. It has undergone many transformations, and I couldn't have done it without the help of my beta readers Julie, Susan, and Yvette. With your help, and the wonderful editing staff at Dreamspinner, *Blood Ties* is a work I can be proud of, and one that I hope the fans, who have been waiting so patiently, will enjoy.

Thank you,
Sui Lynn

PROLOGUE

A Night in Andrew's Bedroom

Seventy-four years in the past....

"Mama... Mama... Mama... Mama... Mama...." Andrew giggled and ran through the house, down the hallway, and into the kitchen, dragging a stuffed wolf along by the tail in his wake.

"I'm in here, little cub." Laura Reed turned from the sink. She wiped her hands on the dish towel, having finished the cleaning in the kitchen, and then focused on the naked young boy who had wrapped his arms around her knees.

"Love you, Mama!" Andrew smiled up at Laura.

Laura reached down and pulled the boy up to sit on her hip, his arms draped over her shoulders and the wolf toy dangling down her back. "I love you, too, but aren't you supposed to be in bed? Where are your pajamas?"

The sound of slow shuffling footfalls coming down the hall preceded Max as he entered the kitchen. He appeared a bit frustrated and tired. "I thought I heard voices in here. The little hooligan escaped when I turned my back to get his pj's from the dresser. I turned around. He and Scruffy were gone, except for the sound of giggling and the thumping of running footsteps down the hallway."

Laura laughed softly. "Your son is as stubborn as his daddy when it comes to wanting things his way. But, cub, it's time for you to be in bed and go to sleep."

Max wrapped his arms around both of them, nuzzled his wife's neck, then gave her a kiss on the cheek and a gentle hug before accepting the handoff of the child back into his arms.

"But I don't want to go to bed. I'm not tired, and Scruffy wants to play outside." Andrew frowned, his bottom lip sticking out in a decided pout.

"It's dark out and time for cubs to sleep," Laura insisted. She ruffled her son's hair.

Max turned and walked from the kitchen, a squirming Andrew in his arms, Laura following close behind.

"I don't wanna…," Andrew whined.

"Too bad. Boys go to bed when they are told," Max huffed, obviously getting tired of his son's incessant complaints.

"Mama…." Andrew began to fake cry, rubbing his eyes with his little fists, as if trying to make the tears flow.

"You heard your father—to bed." Laura chuckled at her son's antics. "But once you are there, you may have one story, then lights out and time to go to sleep."

"Yeah! A story!" Andrew cheered.

Max flinched, pulling his head away from his son's screech of joy… right in his sensitive ear. "Tell me again, why did we want children?" Max grumbled as they walked into the powder blue playroom, scattered with carved wooden toys and a table covered with crayons and paper.

"Because you wanted a son and I wanted a family. Now hush," Laura scolded Max. She pulled the covers back and watched as her son leaped from his father's arms onto the bed. He dutifully held his arms up, and Max grabbed the pajama top and tugged it down over his son's extended arms and then his head. Max handed him the bottoms. Andrew frowned as he inserted one leg through at a time with great care and concentration before pulling them up over his rump and scrambling to lie down with the stuffed wolf at his side. Laura draped the blankets over his little body and tucked him in before sitting beside him.

Max stepped back to stand by the door, as if guarding his most precious treasure, his small pack.

"Now, what story would you have tonight?" Laura asked as she brushed Andrew's bangs to the side, away from his bright blue eyes.

"The First Prince!" Andrew begged.

"That old story?" Max watched his mate and his son.

"It's kind of scary. Are you sure it won't give you nightmares?" Laura frowned and glanced at her husband, who shrugged.

"The Prince… the Prince!" Andrew chanted.

2

"All right. But after this, it's straight to sleep, my little cub." Laura tucked the covers a bit more snugly around her son and grinned down at him. "Well, the story, as it was told to me by my mother, begins…. Long ago there were four magical races. Can you tell me what they were?" Laura prompted, knowing her son liked to answer that question.

"Shifters, vampires, the honored dwarves, and fae." Andrew nodded solemnly.

"That's right. Our people and the vampires were friends with the dwarves, but the fae were evil and manipulative. They wanted to rule the entire supernatural world and make humans their slaves. In those days, although we lived with the other tribes in peace, there were no governments, no rulers. The Vampire Council didn't exist, nor had the royal family of the werewolves come to power. We were all just a bunch of clans, pressed up against each other for control of a territory and of the humans we hunted."

"We used to eat people? Ewww!" squealed Andrew, giggling.

"No. We did hunt humans—they were looked down upon. Many of our ancestors felt humans were less than us, merely animals who could speak and reason." Laura smiled down at her inquisitive son.

"We hunted them for sport and status. They made good prey because they were smart and were a challenge." Max leaned against the doorframe, his arms crossed over his chest.

"But now we know better and it is against our laws to hunt humans. We hunt animals to let our wilder, animal side out. For us, it isn't the blood we crave, but the excitement of the hunt and the kill our beasts need in order to be whole and balanced. Vampires, on the other hand, require human blood in order to live, but do not desire the thrill of the hunt. So both our species have found ways to exist alongside humans."

"But not the fae?" Andrew shook his head.

"No. The fae were vicious and blood crazed. They weren't content with the land they controlled. They wanted more power and began trying to take it from everyone they encountered. First, they destroyed all the humans within their borders for the energy and power the blood gave them. Then they began attacking the villages of the dwarves and the wolves living along their borders. Nobody was prepared for the attacks, and entire villages were destroyed as the fae feasted on their blood, growing stronger and more deadly."

"Nobody escaped?" Andrew's eyes had grown wide, his voice a whisper in the quiet of his bedroom.

In reality, the first attacks had no survivors. It wasn't until long after the fae had grown bolder, attacking large towns, that some were able to escape in the chaos of the fighting and raise the alarm. But for her son's bedtime story, Laura skipped that part as she had no intention of giving him nightmares.

"Of course, some always escape in the chaos of a fight. They warned the others in the surrounding villages, who didn't believe until they too fell victim to the fae's fangs and claws. The lure of blood and power is such that the more you get, the more you want, and for the fae, there would never be enough. So the attacks became more frequent and more deadly.

"After a rather large town was attacked and destroyed by the fae, a group of vampires, dwarves, and wolves from the largest families met to decide what could be done. They decided the fae would destroy them all if left alone, and so they devised a plan to create a barrier, a place separate from everyone else where the fae couldn't cause any harm to anyone but themselves. There they could live out their lives, fight their wars, and all without destroying the other peoples of the earth. It would take the power of all four of the magical races to create the barrier, but in the end, only three would be free to find a way to live in harmony with humanity and each other without preying upon one another senselessly."

"What happened?" Andrew gripped the covers under his chin with his tiny fists, his eyes darting from his mother to his father and to all the dark corners of his room, as if expecting the fae to jump out at any moment.

"The dwarves dug deep into the center of the earth and brought forth a lodestone. They blessed it with great powers and sacrificed many lives in setting it in the proper place, so it stood on a ley line on the border between two realities. Most of the time, we don't see other dimensions. If we do happen to come across a ley line, we feel a slight tremor—humans call it déjà vu. But with the lodestone in place, we see a curtain of power shimmering between the dimensions. It glistens at night, a slightly translucent barrier between our lands and those beyond, allowing us to see through the veil to the lush and green land beyond. Humans see nothing."

"If it was so pretty, why didn't we go there, instead of sending the fae there?" Andrew frowned, obviously thinking hard.

"Well, because at that time, both our people and the vampires were still dependent upon humans in one way or another. We didn't want to leave them behind. The dwarves don't require blood, as they have a different type of magic altogether. Their magic ties them to the land, and they need to have a connection to it in order to flourish. But of all the races, theirs was the most powerful. Dwarves created the veil that connected the realities, and with the blood of the shifters, the vampires, and the fae, the veil would be locked, preventing the fae from escaping back into our world ever again." Laura grinned down at her son.

"So what happened?" he begged.

4

"Well, the vampires, dwarves, and shifters all sent fighters to be part of an enormous army and, when the fae attacked, they were ready for them. The battle took a very long time. Some say days, some say weeks, some say it was months of nonstop fighting and bloodshed. But in the end, the fae were subdued and forced across the veil, with the few remaining dwarves acting as guards. By this time, because of the organization needed to create the armies, our peoples had become much more centralized and, for each, a form of government was born. The vampires devised a council, which today governs us all. For us, our animalistic nature will submit to only the strongest and most alpha male among us. That man became king. His name was Henry the Gray."

"But what about the prince?" Andrew giggled.

"Well, you see, now that we had the fae on the other side of the veil, the dwarves needed to return before the portal sealed and the fae regained their strength and tried to return. The fae are nothing if not tricky, and the elders were in a hurry to lock down the entrance quickly to prevent them from finding a way to escape. They gathered around the lodestone and began the ceremony, casting the spell that carved the words into the stone, which would seal the fae away for eternity. As the last drop of blood sizzled down on the stone, they realized there was a problem. The dwarves were coming back toward the barrier, but they seemed to move in slow motion, as if time itself were preventing them from reaching the boundary between the worlds.

"Prince Atol had become good friends with one of the dwarves named Ventall. In fact they were mates. When the veil began to crystallize into a solid form and disappear from our world, Prince Atol threw himself at the barrier. He reached through it with both hands, trying to grab hold of Ventall, to yank the dwarf back into our dimension. The two screamed that they would not let go. They would not be separated. The barrier could not be stopped. Atol's father, the king, seeing that the barrier would cut his son in half before the dwarf would be drawn through, grabbed Prince Atol by the waist. He threw himself back, forcing his son away from the fading barrier. Prince Atol screamed and fought his father, but the barrier vanished from this world, taking Ventall, the dwarves, and the fae with it.

"Prince Atol snarled that he'd never forsake his love and would wait for Ventall to return. He'd guard the stone forever, and, one day, the barrier would come down and they'd be reunited. That was the last time anyone ever saw Prince Atol. It's said that on nights when the moon is full, if you see a lone black wolf and you hear mournful howling, it is Prince Atol crying for his missing mate, still waiting for the day the veil falls so he can be reunited with his love and the dwarves are freed from the fae."

"Will they ever be free?" Andrew mumbled, his eyes drooping sleepily, as his father flipped the light switch off by the door.

5

"No. The veil is forever," Max's deep voice whispered from beside the door. "Now, go to sleep, pup. Tomorrow is another day." Laura rose to her feet and joined her mate. He wrapped an arm around her waist and ushered her out into the hall.

"I can't figure out why he likes that old story. He asks for it every night. It's so depressing." Laura frowned as they stepped into their own bedroom, and she felt her husband nuzzle her neck.

"Who knows what prompts children, but it's the story he likes to hear and I see no problem with him learning our history. We were a proud, strong people once. We were an honorable race before…. Well, it doesn't matter now. Let's just go to bed." Max sighed and rubbed the back of his head.

"Stephon?" Laura asked.

"Yes and no. He's there, listening in, but it's not like he's protesting or anything. I think I need to shift and go hunting soon. My wolf is restless," Max mumbled as Laura rubbed his back and the two settled down for a nice quiet night.

CHAPTER 1

Present Day

"ARE WE there yet?" I mumbled from under the blanket, curled alongside Andrew, my head pillowed on his lap as he drove toward Denver. The steady thump of the windshield wipers kept time with my erratic nerves and heartbeat, as the miles whirred by beneath the tires of the Dodge Ram. We weren't alone, of course. My vassals, Charlie and Tim, were following close on our heels, protecting us as they always did. They gave us whatever privacy they could, but were never far from sight.

"No, Lance. Just try to get some rest. I'll wake you when we get there." Andrew brushed his fingers through my hair under the blanket I'd pulled over my head, his touch soothing the itch to bolt and run. He could always settle me. Regardless of how badly my nervousness grew, a simple caress grounded me more surely than chains.

The plan was to live with Lord Basil, my grandfather. Thinking of him as my grandfather was going to take some getting used to. I had family of my own now… family besides Andrew.

Swish-swish, swish-swish.

After my party, Stephon disappeared. Andrew told me he did this every year, something about a yearly sabbatical, which he usually returned from in poor spirits. Nobody could tell me when Stephon's birthday was. Seems the old—and I do mean ancient—vampire, for all his talk about birthdays and parties, refused to celebrate his own. So Andrew and I threw him a party he would never forget.

Damn weird, though. I knew he was prissy and stuck on propriety, but he appeared to enjoy the orgy it ended up becoming. Then Stephon disappeared into the maze early in the evening. No one saw him come out. The following

7

morning, after he inspected the grounds to make sure we hadn't messed up his impeccable gardens, we were packed up and sent to Grandfather.

Swish-swish, swish-swish.

Since I'd mated with Andrew, our mind, experiences, and understanding had become one. The time he spent at university with Stephon pursuing various interests and hobbies, all the years of his life, it's all in there for me. He saw my loneliness and isolation, my will to survive and determination to live regardless of what the humans had told me. He experienced it all as if he were me. We're two bodies, but our thoughts and spirit are one. Before, I was alone. I was good at protecting myself. Now, there was more to fight for. More to protect. More to love. More reason to live. I refused to fail him or any of them. They deserved my best, and they would get it.

Swish-swish, swish-swish.

I was used to fighting to keep myself safe... to stay alive. I had only ever risked myself, but when others are involved, it becomes more complicated. I wasn't exactly comfortable with the responsibility of caring for others, but I was a prince and my people were being persecuted. I had freed Andrew, but his family and our people as a whole remained veritable slaves. I was the means to their salvation... no pressure there.

The big question was how to free our people while attempting to keep Andrew's connection to his family hidden? In truth, it might not be possible to do so for any extended period of time. I wasn't looking forward to stepping outside my comfort zone and making myself a target. I didn't want to paint a bull's-eye on my mate's back either, but it was unavoidable. I needed everyone focused on me, on us, and not on the others supporting me behind the scenes. The only way to do that was by making the biggest spectacle of myself possible. But what would come next? What would it cost? In my experience, being the center of attention always came with a price.

Swish-swish, swish-swish.

"Sit up. Seat belt. Now!" Andrew hollered, pulling me from my contemplation back to the present. I threw the blanket onto the floor, sat up, and peered around as he floored the gas and the truck lurched ahead. The unmistakable squeal of tires braking hard and the crunch of metal on metal had me staring out the back window.

"What's going on?" I scooted over to my seat on the bench and buckled, turning to glare out into the murky gray of morning. A black car was trying to run Charlie and Tim off the road, clearly trying to drive the larger SUV into the ditch. As I watched, a Jeep joined in the chase, jumping the median from the oncoming side, barreling down the interstate after us.

"We've got company." Andrew stepped on the gas, trying to put as much distance between Charlie and Tim and ourselves as he could.

"We can't leave them behind! If they have an accident and the weather clears, they're toast out here in the open!"

Andrew glared at me briefly before returning his attention to the road, and letting off the gas a bit. "I'll keep them in sight. Call your grandfather and have him send out help. We're in his territory by now." He took his eyes off the road for a second to meet mine. "I am not stopping, and Charlie would thrash me if I did. You are the priority. We're being attacked because they want to get to you. Charlie and Tim are just in the way." I cringed as the sound of metal on metal assaulted my ears, and I gawked back seeing Tim had forced the SUV into the car.

My phone started ringing where it lay on the dashboard. Tones of "California Gurls" by Katy Perry filled the cab, and I smiled despite the situation. Charlie was calling. I'd chosen the song specifically because the woman was always dressed in black leather... well, almost always. She resembled a cross between Catwoman, Lara Croft, and Xena, with black vampire-drone eyes and white skin. But Charlie was far deadlier.

I grabbed the phone and answered. "Yes, my guardian angel."

"We'll take care of them. Don't you dare stop, you selfish bastard," Charlie yelled into the phone.

"Now that's no way to talk to your prince," I griped back. I was just being stubborn. I didn't want to leave them. I worried about them. They were my friends, and I couldn't spare any of them.

"Andrew, once you're gone, they'll let up on us. They're after you, not us. We'll catch up with you. We know where you're going. Hopefully they don't." Charlie knew both of us would hear, despite the phone not being on speaker. Even without our mental link, shifter ears are sensitive enough that we could both hear her. Of course, drone ears were practically as sensitive, and she could hear both of us just as clearly.

"I understand. Be careful, you guys. You know Lance will never forgive me for leaving you behind if you get hurt. As it is, he's pissed as hell." Andrew's smug snort as I hung up the phone had me wanting to snarl.

Yeah, he was right. I was pissed and worried. I stared as the SUV slammed into the black car. The scream of metal had me cringing as the car was forced against the metal guardrail and head-on into the cement barrier of an off-ramp. The car tumbled, back end over the top of the car, to flip off the interstate and down to the crossroad below. I hoped no one was driving below for them to land on. It was one thing for vampires to go through a car crash. Short of beheading, they could heal from almost anything. Humans were another matter entirely.

Andrew was already accelerating. We were leaving the SUV, now battling the Jeep, behind us. I held back a panicked gasp as I watched the door to the SUV open and Charlie climb out onto the roof. One of the people in the Jeep— another assassin, sent to kill me—climbed out onto its roof to meet her. I hated leaving her to fight my battle. Yes, she was my bodyguard, and as a trained warrior drone, she was the essence of deadly, but I would never get used to that.

"Just don't kill yourself, Charlie. I need you." I wasn't sure she could hear me, since we hung up the phone, but the fervor of her attack seemed to become even more aggressive.

"Call your grandfather. He can send them help." Andrew placed a hand on my thigh and squeezed before returning it to the steering wheel.

Taking a steadying breath, I dialed the number my grandfather, Lord Basil, had given me before he'd left Stephon's after my birthday party. We'd spoken every day since our introduction, and I was growing to like the man.

"Lance?" Grandfather's voice flowed over the line.

"Hi, Grandfather. We've had a bit of trouble out here. We are a couple miles west of Denver. Andrew's trying to get away, and I'm scared for Tim and Charlie," I babbled into the phone, staring back at Tim and Charlie, who were getting smaller as we sped away, leaving them behind.

"Are you all right?" Lord Basil asked.

"Yes, but Tim and Charlie are trying to keep our attacker busy so we can escape. I think they are going to need some help."

"I'm sending out guards as we speak. Just keep coming. Don't stop." Lord Basil spoke calmly, but the sound of moving air and running belied the tone. "It will be all right. My men will be there very soon to help, so don't worry about Tim and Charlie. They are my two strongest children. They will be fine."

"Okay. Thank you, Grandfather." I disconnected the call as Tim and Charlie disappeared behind us. Turning back around in my seat, I drew my feet up to rest on the edge of the bench, and rested my forehead on my knees. This was the part I hated most about my new life with Andrew. Someone out there wanted me dead... and that someone was Brad.

THE EARLIER rain had given way to a sun-filled morning as we pulled into Denver. The air had a fresh, clean pine scent to it, reminding me of the pine forest surrounding our cabin in the Black Hills of South Dakota. It was the only similarity as we drove deeper into the city and away from the natural world we were comfortable with. The industrial world of concrete and steel lined the roadsides until even the mountains were blotted out by human industry. A claustrophobic sense of dread took hold as I scrutinized the sterile concrete of the parking garage. We'd made it this far. We would survive this.

We arrived at Grandfather's penthouse in Denver within the hour. Charlie, Tim, our guards, and two others who had to be Lord Basil's men arrived within a few minutes of our pulling into the parking garage. We could have gone up to the penthouse without them, but after all the excitement, it was good to have a couple minutes of quiet before my nervous breakdown.

Charlie was right. We were the target. She'd called and informed me that when Grandfather's guards had arrived and it was obvious we'd left them behind, the attackers had cut their losses and escaped. It was obviously lucky for them because Charlie would not have taken prisoners. As it was, they left without their dignity but still had their lives.

CHAPTER 2

Stephon's Unbirthday: Part one.
Two weeks ago

AT THE back of his property, Stephon stepped out of the shiny black lacquered horse-drawn carriage. It wasn't that he didn't have cars—or trucks, for that matter—but when he came home after traveling, he enjoyed the slow ride through his lands in the old-fashioned carriage. Of course since he was a vampire of means, he'd had the carriage completely outfitted with all the modern conveniences, including a state of the art sound system, heat, air-conditioning, and XFM radio. He'd only been gone a week, but his home was not as he had left it.

"Maurice, what's going on?" Stephon stared dumfounded at what should have been the gates to his estate and the peaceful, neatly clipped yards beyond, but wasn't.

His yearly sojourn had gone as it always did—poorly—and it left him feeling bereft. He had wanted to come home to peace and quiet, where he could lick his wounds alone. With the chaos before him, it was clear that wasn't about to happen any time soon.

"I'm not sure. It kind of looks like someone is at the house and they are throwing a party."

"Thank you, Captain Obvious. That much I can see," Stephon sniped and swatted the arm of his burly drone.

Two more of his drones stood at attention in what appeared to be poorly copied Roman gladiator costumes. They wore red tunics that clearly were not wool. The body armor was some sort of silver plastic with a fake leather cingulum no self-respecting Roman soldier would be caught dead wearing. Drawing himself up straighter, he took a deep breath, grabbed hold of his temper, and tried not to notice the horrible costumes. Just because his emotions were a bit frayed was no reason to take it out on his drones, especially when they didn't know any better. They hadn't been alive to see what a real centurion wore.

"Someone needs to speak now and explain what the hell is going on in my home before I completely lose my temper!" Stephon growled, his eyes flashing and fangs dropping uncontrollably, as they hadn't done in years.

Both drones dropped to one knee and bowed their heads before their maker in complete submission. Stephon sighed. It hadn't been his intention to throw that much power at his drones. They were his family, and it clearly showed how stressed he felt that he was hurting his own, even unintentionally.

"We're sorry, my lord, but Lance and Andrew insisted," the guard on the right practically whispered, his eyes on the ground.

"They ask that you wait here just a moment and they will be out to explain. They are on their way now, my lord." The other guard visibly trembled as he spoke.

"I'm sorry, my sons. It appears I am more on edge than I imagined. I didn't mean to take my agitation out on you. Evidently I am the recipient of some sort of joke...."

The lights glowed from behind the billowing white canvas of the pavilion tents. They stretched along Stephon's black wrought-iron fence to the gates in front of the woods to both the left and the right. Suddenly everything went dark except for the lights illuminating the canvas opening to the tents that blocked his way. A chorus of snickers and hushing sounds rippled from behind the canvas.

Stephon could only sigh with tired frustration. Whatever was about to happen, he told himself he wouldn't be angry. LB and his Poodle must mean well; the mated pair was like family to him and would never intentionally hurt him. He just felt so bone weary. His mate still avoided him even after centuries of patience and waiting. Of late, he'd begun to doubt his complete control and sanity. He wasn't sure how much longer he could last before he lost his mind entirely. Of course, none of that was Lance and Andrew's fault, so he schooled his features to reflect an emotion that said annoyed and not homicidal, like he felt.

Lance and Andrew walked out from behind the canvas, and Stephon's jaw dropped to his feet. The two men were nude except for the small black Speedos they wore. He was used to seeing his shifter friends either clothed or nude, but the tiny black Speedo seemed indecent in its teasing, seductive nature.

Lance seemed to take in the tense stance of the irritated vampire, walked forward, and wrapped his arms around Stephon. "I'm so sorry. If I had known you were this unnerved by surprises, I never would have suggested this."

13

"I told you... he gets tense this time of year and goes on sabbatical to be alone." Andrew stood with an arm propped on his hip.

"Well, yeah, but I thought when he came back that he'd be relaxed and ready for company, not even more wound up than before he left," Lance pouted. "Nobody touched the house, I can have everyone close everything down, and we can all disappear like we weren't even here." Lance took ahold of Stephon's shoulders and stared into the eyes.

Stephon took a deep breath, and forced himself to relax. It felt so good to be held, to be touched by someone who cared about him. It was a luxury he only had with these two. Of all his children and friends, only Lance and Andrew ever touched him. He didn't think he was unapproachable, but there was some barrier between him and others that nobody seemed willing to breach, and he was starved for affection and touch.

"Of course not. You went to all this trouble. Tell me about my surprise." Stephon reached forward and tweaked Lance's chin and tried to give him a relaxed, mischievous grin.

"You aren't fooling me, you know, but I think this might help." Lance grinned back and took Stephon's hand in his. He led Stephon through the canvas and into his yard, which was suddenly filled with colored lights.

"Surprise! Happy Unbirthday!" was hollered from the men spread out around the large yard. They were all dressed similarly to Lance and Andrew, in swim trunks of various types and colors. The hard bodies of drones appeared pale in the light, intermixed with the golden bodies of a few male shifters whom Andrew and Lance had obviously brought with them.

"Victoria called your usual party list and invited the eligible, unmated males. We brought a few available friends from the men who volunteered to become part of Lance's guard." Andrew spoke from just behind them.

"Unbirthday?" Stephon couldn't help his bemusement.

"Well, of course. You won't tell anyone when you were born. So we decided to celebrate your unbirthday, which can be done on any day of the year that isn't your birthday. It isn't your birthday today, is it?" Lance teased.

"No." Stephon laughed, looking out over his lawn at the expanse of muscles and skin on display.

"So, first of all, you need to be properly attired... or should I say... less attired." Lance laughed and led Stephon to one of the many white cabanas that ringed the yard.

"What kind of unbirthday party have you thrown for me?" Stephon's voice rose to an unnatural tenor in alarm. The white tent was strewn with fairy lights, which flickered gently, giving the room the private feeling of a spa. It was more like an upscale hotel room instead of a tent in his yard.

Andrew untied a knot, releasing the canvas flap that closed the cabana off from the rest of the yard. There was a clothing rack against one wall, a small table with red roses in a small vase, and a colorful bag with a bow. The center of the tent was taken up by a beautifully dressed double bed in burgundy and blue satin.

"The best kind there is. An all-male party." Lance nodded to Andrew, who picked up the bag from the table.

"You threw me an orgy?" Stephon started to laugh. In all his long life and all of the parties he had thrown and in turn attended, nobody had ever done something like this.

"In a manner of speaking. I guess so." Lance smirked. "Now off with the clothes."

"We have your designer-label outfit all ready for you." Andrew held up the paper gift bag by the string handle on one finger, letting the bag swing slowly back and forth.

"You expect me to run around as unclothed as the rest of you?" Stephon tried to act affronted, but he could tell he wasn't fooling anyone.

"Stephon, you used to attend frat parties in togas with nothing underneath. A Speedo is not going to embarrass you." Andrew taunted good-naturedly. "Besides, if I remember correctly, you have a beautiful body, so why not flaunt it? You never know, you might just find your mate."

It was like being doused with bucket of cold water, but Stephon tried not to let the hurt show. "My mate isn't among the men out there, Andrew. But that doesn't mean I can't still have a good time."

"How do you know? He might be out there. Don't give up hope. If I had ever given up… before I met Andrew… I could have died on the street a long time ago."

Stephon paused. He'd heard Lance's story and knew what the young man had been through. It was amazing he wasn't more damaged than Stephon knew him to be. And it wasn't that he didn't have hope. It was hope that kept him going year after year to the same place for his sabbatical, just in case…. But the man he knew to be his mate had yet to come for him, despite what he'd said all those years ago. The sabbatical had become his yearly self-flagellation of the spirit, but he couldn't stop going, and seeing Lance and Andrew together in happily mated bliss was just one of the reasons he continued to try.

Still, all spanking aside, Stephon refused to let his missing mate suck the joy out of life. His mate might not want him, but that didn't mean he couldn't have company and enjoy the friends he did have.

"Okay." Stephon nodded and began unbuttoning his coat.

"Really!" Andrew's jaw dropped.

"See, I told you he'd play along." Lance's eyebrows rose as he gave his mate a cheeky grin. "You owe me a blow job."

"But I was sure that he'd never…."

"What's that old saying, 'Never say die'? Well, I decided there was too much handsome man flesh out there to be a stick in the mud." Stephon took off his suit jacket and walked over to the clothes rack. "But you two are going to have my lawn spotless when all this carousing has reached its finale, and that means replacing the sod if all this activity destroys the grass. I won't have my gardener paying for your little surprise with extra work."

"You got it." Lance grinned and leaned in, kissing his mate before going to Stephon and playing butler. Stephon was meticulous about his clothing. Lance took each piece as it was handed to him and hung it so it wouldn't get rumpled.

"Here." Andrew handed Stephon his bag before he took off his Calvin Klein underwear. "You'll need this. Come out when you're dressed." With a growl, Andrew grabbed Lance's arm and led him outside.

"Some mates." Stephon laughed as he heard Andrew possessively snarl something about not seeing any man's underwear but his. Stephon was actually surprised he could laugh, since he'd been in such an awful mood when he'd arrived. There was just something about being around Lance and Andrew. The pair relaxed him and made him happy. Sure, he still longed for his mate. But he refused to dwell on it, so the closest thing he had to that kind of happiness was when the pair shared theirs.

"I must have lost my eternal mind," Stephon mumbled to himself as he checked out the contents of the bag. He couldn't believe what he saw. He pulled out a hot-pink spangled Speedo with the words "Unbirthday Boy" on the little bit of material on the back. Accompanying the Speedo, a few accessories had been added to the bag: a tube of ID Glide lube, a hot-pink butt plug with what appeared to be a glass ruby in the end, and a pack of chewing gum so he could be minty-fresh for whoever struck his fancy.

Stephon dropped his Calvin Klein's and put on the Speedo. *The things I do for my friends,* he thought. He wasn't about to use the butt plug or any of the other accessories. Well, maybe the gum, but it tended to stick to his fangs in strange places. It wasn't his favorite thing to chew.

Bag in hand, he stepped out of the pavilion, and Andrew and Lance each took an arm and led him into the menagerie of colorful tents. A carnival-like atmosphere filled the air, the scent of popcorn and candy, as well as hotdogs and hamburgers charbroiling on the grill, had Stephon smiling. Shifters would never neglect their stomachs, and an event like this was primed for a barbeque, regardless of the fact that probably over half the guests were drones and wouldn't be able to consume food. Some tents held games of chance, some had tests of strength in what could only be arm wrestling, and others were ring-toss and shooting galleries. The prizes appeared to be a range of adult toys, from lube to vibrators and dildos, to a range of restraints, hoods, gags, ticklers, paddles, and whips.

"First up. Wet, Wild, and Twister." Andrew pointed to the left as they walked past a giant inflated Twister board where a group of men were playing wet, bouncy Twister. One guy was calling out colors while another was spraying a constant stream of water over the players. The whole thing was ridiculous and fun as the participants stretched and twisted into a near-impossible knotted mass of laughing, wet and slippery men. Lance burst into a fit of giggles as the caller shouted another color and players attempted to keep from falling or taking out as many others as possible when they collapsed into a heap of arms and legs.

"I think I'll save that for later." Stephon couldn't keep the grin from his face. He wasn't interested in playing, but the enjoyment he saw Lance having as he watched the players was contagious. LB was truly having fun, and the young man had experienced very little of it before finding Andrew.

The three proceeded down along the row to the next attraction. "Okay, here in the middle we have the Naked Jell-O Pool. Hop right in and let the Jell-O ease your way to a brighter tomorrow." Lance motioned to the ladder at the side of the pool. Speedos littered the little deck where guys had obviously ditched their trunks before joining in on the fun.

"A strong possibility, but I don't think I'm ready to take the plunge." Stephon ducked as a handful of green goo flew over his head, tossed by one of the drones.

"Keep the Jell-O in the pool!" Andrew yelled at the men currently participating in a Jell-O fight, flinging the sticky green glop at one another. "I told you we needed to put up some sort of barrier to make sure that stuff didn't end up all over the yard. But oh no, you were sure nobody would be careless enough to throw it beyond the deck," Andrew teased Lance.

"We do have plastic tarps down, so most of it will be easy to clean up. Besides it is just Jell-O." Lance shrugged, and the trio continued on down the makeshift midway.

"Next up is the Bouncy House of Ill Repute." Andrew motioned toward a deep red- and black-striped bouncy castle. It wasn't open so you could see what was going on inside, but you could easily guess. Small black mesh windows showed dimly flashing lights in various colors, and the whole house rocked erotically. If that wasn't enough of a hint, the sound of moans and the overpowering odor of sweat, sex, and blood poured from the building.

"Holy mother of orgies." Stephon laughed and smacked Lance on the shoulder. "You definitely know how to throw a party."

"I didn't originally intend it to go quite like this, and some of it has clearly gotten out of hand." Lance winked at Stephon. "But everyone does appear to be having a good time."

"Last but not least, the maze." Andrew led them to a blacked-out building and handed Stephon a glow stick. "You might find what you're seeking at the center of the maze."

A vaguely familiar shadow at the edge of the rows of pavilions detached itself from the darkness and disappeared into the maze. The breeze carried the faint scent of something tantalizingly familiar, and then it was gone.

"One never knows for sure, I guess," Stephon mumbled. He plastered a grin on his face and gave his loving, well-intentioned friends a hug, before facing the maze. "Guys, I'm going in!"

"We'll see you on the other side… unless you find something worth staying for in the center." Lance waved as Stephon gave his glow stick a shake, ducked around the corner into the maze, and disappeared from sight.

The maze was a simple and fairly uncomplicated affair of lefts and rights. There were little secluded side areas clearly set up for chance meetings between the men wandering through the maze. The scent of sex was heavy on the air as he reached out and brushed the pine bough-covered lattices that stood over seven feet tall. They created a nice mobile fake hedge maze that could not be seen through, but did nothing to diffuse the sounds of the hookups or the scent of lube, sweat, semen, and testosterone-driven sex.

Stephon avoided the occupied alcoves easily enough, following the alluring scent left behind by the shadow that had entered the maze before him. He turned a corner, knowing the owner of the scent was waiting for him, standing in the center. There was an elegant three-tiered bubbling stone fountain with a rack standing nearby. The soft glow of light from the fountain showed an alcove with a wide padded bench—and there he stood.

Lance and Andrew would not have invited this particular vampire to the party. Neither of them had met the man… yet. Even during all the years he'd

18

imagined himself being in love with Andrew, deluding himself that something might be possible, but knowing Andrew could only ever be his friend. He'd never revealed the existence of the man before him, who stared at him like he was the one being betrayed, instead of the other way around.

"What is all this, Stephon?" The man flung an arm out as he snarled.

"You have no right to say anything. You forfeit that right every single time you betrayed me by refusing me year after year, decade after decade. Hell, I get to start counting the years of your betrayal in centuries." Stephon crossed to the rack. He no longer felt secure in his near nudity. He felt cold to the bone, and his heart physically ached in his chest. For the first time since Lance had disconnected him from Andrew and his family, he was grateful, because the pain he was currently feeling would have sent the shifter family into a panic. They would've rushed to his defense as quickly as possible. Right now he wanted privacy. He refused to let anyone know how wounded he was because of his mate's rejection. He took a bathrobe from the top of a pile of supplied towels, washcloths, and soaps conveniently provided for the couples to clean up after their romp in the maze.

"My betrayal? My betrayal! Never once since the day I met you have I been with anyone. I have never loved another. I have never...."

"You have never! Why should I care if you do or don't, Quinn?" Stephon spun to face his mate and realized Quinn had silently crept closer when he had his back to him. Stephon hissed a warning, his fangs dropping and dripping venom, his arms flung out to his sides in an attack stance, claws curved viciously from his fingertips. Quinn stood before him, and even though Stephon knew he was his mate, he was also an uninvited born vampire male invading his territory, behaving in a hostile, aggressive manner.

"You would attack me?" Quinn's voice was soft, barely audible even as close together as they stood, no more than two strides apart. "You see me as a threat to your territory? God, what have I done to you?"

Stephon's head fell forward, and he let out a wail of pain and anguish as he crumpled to his knees. "What have you done? You don't know? How can you not know? Don't you feel the daily mind-numbing pain our separation is causing?"

"I... I feel it. I hoped it was only me, because this is my fault. I don't want you to hurt, Stephon." Quinn moved closer, reaching out a hand toward Stephon.

"Stay away!" Stephon screamed and covered his face with his hands. "Please, Quinn, you are already too close. Unless you are here to acknowledge our mating, you cannot stay. I cannot bear it."

Quinn stopped, his hand dropping to his side. He stood breathing deeply as he watched tears of blood dripping between Stephon's fingers onto the grass. "D-don't cry, babe. Please. You know I want you."

"Do I? How? How am I supposed to know you want me? When in all the centuries since we met, the day your father introduced you as his heir to the council, have you ever told me that you wanted me as your mate?" Stephon sobbed, his hands covered with the bloody tears from the centuries of rejection.

"I truly am a fool." Quinn got down on his knees. "Please, Stephon. Let me hold you, so you know how much I do want you. God, how could I let you think that I don't want you? That's the furthest thing from the truth."

"I've been… to the lodestone every year since you told me to meet you there. You've never come, not once. If you want me so much, why haven't you come?" Stephon beseeched Quinn, hoping he had some kind of answer, but saw only the pinkish tinge of unshed tears.

"At first, I couldn't come. When I told my father you were my mate, he told me I had lost my mind, and if I kept up with this nonsense, he would have me killed as an abomination. He would not stand for me ending our family's line and abandoning our position on the council by taking a mate who could not produce an heir." Quinn eased himself forward on his knees toward Stephon. "I was barely of age when we met. He still controlled my actions as I had yet to break away from his mental control completely. The psi bond between him and most of his drones is never completely broken. It took me decades to be able to keep him out of my mind."

"And whose fault is that, hmmm? If you would have come to me, I could have protected you. I could have broken you away from him!" Stephon snapped, flashing his fangs and pushing to his toes in a crouched position. "Do you have any idea the kind of power I hold? There isn't a vampire in your family line who can come close to rivaling me!"

Quinn drew back, slowly lifting his hands, showing his clawless fingertips and tipping his head to the side in submission. "It's my fault. I know, Stephon."

"Your father, Rufus, and grandfather, Philo…. That pompous ass. They weren't even born citizens of Egypt. I was there! Rufus was born in the slave quarters shortly after his parents, Philo and Gwenore, were brought before the pharaoh in silver chains." Stephon's lips remained curled back from his fangs, his words slurring slightly as he spoke around them. Venom dripped from the corners of his lips, a clear, dark fluid that sizzled as it struck the grass between his knees. "They were recognized as vampires and were to be sacrificed to Sekhmet, the blood goddess!"

"They were slaves?"

20

"My father and I were known to be vampires," Stephon ranted, ignoring Quinn's obvious confusion. "We were priests of Sekhmet. Believed to be her children and blessed with her bloodlust and eternal immortality in the eyes of the Egyptians. I was young, only a couple hundred years old, but I understood we could save your family or have them destroyed. My father, Caius, petitioned the pharaoh for their lives, and your family was handed over to the priests as slaves and eventually released instead of being put to death."

"I didn't know. My father never told me any of this." Quinn folded himself over his knees in complete supplication, his hands lying palms up, his arms flat on the ground alongside his legs, his forehead touching the grass in front of him. In this position, he was completely at Stephon's mercy. Even the fastest-moving vampire would not be able to avoid a killing blow from an attacking adversary at such close range. If Stephon wanted him dead, his actions showed an acceptance of that fate.

"Of course he wouldn't tell you any of this. It wouldn't do for you to know you came from slaves. The great line of Philo has stood as a pillar of vampire society since the creation of the all-powerful vampire council during the reign of the Romans more than two millennia ago." Stephon stared at Quinn. The man was beautiful bowed before him. He even had his head cocked to the side, bearing his neck. The power Quinn just handed to him, touched his icy heart as nothing else the vampire could say. Breathing deeply, trying to master his slipping control Stephon clenched his hands, his nails biting into his palms. He allowed Quinn's scent to soothe him as nothing else could. He closed his eyes. Regardless of how angry and betrayed he felt, he had no desire to physically hurt Quinn. He needed to focus on trying to talk to his wayward mate. Maybe there was a chance the young vampire—well, young in comparison with his three-millennia-plus age—could be convinced that acceptance was a better choice.

Quinn was only two hundred eighty-eight years old, still quite young by vampire standards. The male drove Stephon to distraction. His heart pounded a heavy, quick rhythm, which unnerved him a bit, making him feel hot and out of control. It was a sensation that occurred only rarely in a born vampire's lifetime, as normally their hearts don't have a regular beat. A born vampire's heart will beat when they feed, spreading the life-giving blood to all their vital systems, but after that, the rhythm becomes slow and sporadic, moving blood only when their body requires more sustenance. The last time his heart had raced like this was the day he had met his mate, and Quinn had rejected him, walking away.

"My grandfather was murdered when I was very young. I wasn't even an adolescent by human standards. I don't remember much about him, other than disliking him a great deal. Father was intolerable under most circumstances, but when Grandfather was around, the man became completely impossible. Mother made my life bearable. Then I met you, and God, you probably don't even know what happened that day." Quinn shook his head, the grass rustling around his ears, as he had yet to rise from his bowed position.

Stephon trembled, desire to wrap himself around Quinn's prostrate form softened the edge of his hurt and anger. He knew some of how Quinn lived his life. Just because his mate didn't want him, didn't mean he didn't keep track of the man. Quinn was his mate. He wasn't the oldest vampire for nothing. There were few places his influence didn't touch. Maybe not significantly, but Rufus couldn't keep him out completely. Stephon shook his head, part of him said this was pure folly and he was simply a glutton for punishment, but he could not bring more pain to Quinn. If his lot in life was to be damned to madness because fate had screwed up and he couldn't reach Quinn to save them both, then he deserved to be slaughtered and sacrificed to his goddess for his failure. It was obvious they had much to discuss. Even though he wasn't sure he could forgive him for all of the pain in his soul, he needed Quinn almost more than his next breath.

"Stop that. You'll get grass stains on your forehead," Stephon mumbled. "Sit up. I like seeing your eyes when we talk, not the back of your head, even though you do have nice hair."

Quinn slowly lifted his head, and when no hissing or other aggressive sounds came from Stephon, he sat back on his heels. "I really am sorry, Stephon. I know you probably won't believe me, but I do want you. I need you… want you so much. God, I want this to work so badly, I just…. How are we supposed to make this work, Stephon? Please tell me how?"

"Sometimes great sacrifices are required in order to show the goddess how determined you are to correct a wrong. I long ago gave up my seat on the council. And it wasn't just about the shifters, but because the very people chosen as the best and most intelligent of our kind, to protect and teach the generations yet to come—the high council members themselves—had forgotten the rules under which the vampire council was first forged. I have at times regretted my decision, and yet again I am much more often thankful that the headache of trying to guide so many is no longer my responsibility. But the goddess has not relieved me of the duty, and so I draw the youthful here with parties and the promise of fun. When they are here, I subtly mold them and try to ground them in morality as I always did, even in the courts of the pharaoh." Stephon took a deep breath and felt a heavy lethargy weighing down his consciousness. "I have seen a great many sacrifices in my lifetime, but never have mates sacrificed the life they could lead together for anything, and yet you have squandered our time."

"I-I…." Quinn stammered.

"For two hundred and seventy years, Quinn, you've stayed as far from me as you possibly could. Tell me, why have you chosen to come here and kneel in supplication before me today?" Stephon's eyes narrowed to hard violet unfeeling stone.

"I'm not entirely sure. Partially to ask for forgiveness I don't deserve. The rest…. I don't know anymore whether there is anything I can say or do that will fix what my father and his master have broken." Quinn stared into Stephon's eyes.

"Let's start there, because I'm not entirely sure I can give you an answer about forgiveness, Quinn. There is very little I have not done or been able to achieve, so tell me what this is all about and what kind of master Rufus would bow down to." Stephon stood and motioned for Quinn to follow him away from the celebration and into the large colonial mansion Stephon called home.

CHAPTER 3

Present Day

I COULD imagine how odd we looked to anyone passing by, or even on the security cameras in the underground parking garage. There just was no way to make a drone appear normal. It was even worse when they were accompanied by shifters. I was on edge, and each time the elevator chimed as the car descended to our level, it added to my mounting anxiety.

The door opened and we got on the empty elevator. Two members of my guard would remain in the garage, while Tim, Charlie, Andrew, myself, and the other two guards went up to Grandfather's home in the penthouse. When the elevator carrying us stopped and the door opened, Charlie motioned for my guards to take positions in front of the elevator doors. She obviously wasn't taking any chances that Brad might be somewhere inside, ready to ambush us.

The four of us proceeded down a well-lit hallway to a desk at the end. It appeared to be more like a reception area at an office instead of someone's home. A rather ordinary, brown-haired, doe-eyed human woman in her late twenties, dressed in a business suit, sat behind the desk.

"Timothy! It's so good of you to come. Lord Basil will be so happy to see you. And you brought Charlie this time. How wonderful! It's been too long." She stepped out from behind the desk and took Tim's hand and smiled at Charlie, who merely nodded at her as she continued her constant visual sweeps of the room.

"Brenda, it's nice to see you too. Is he in?" Tim patted the woman's hand as she gazed up at him adoringly.

"Why, yes, and he's expecting you. This way, please." Brenda paused only a moment as she tried to inconspicuously search Andrew and me for clues as to who we were. I could tell she suspected we weren't human or vampire. She didn't seem to be afraid, just curious.

"Thank you, Brenda." Tim followed the brunette as she led us into a large living room. It had very clean lines, but didn't feel cold or austere with its vaulted ceilings and dark hardwood floors. The colors were simple: ivory brocade drapes and soft brown sheers accented with touches of jewel tones, sapphire blue and ruby red. The furniture was dark leather while throw pillows gave the room a homey lived-in feel. The room was beautiful.

"I'll tell him you've arrived. Please make yourselves comfortable." Brenda glanced again in my direction as she left.

Andrew and I walked through the room to a dark-brown love seat. I dropped onto the soft cushion with a grunt, wanting to curl into myself and make it all go away. Andrew sat down beside me, taking my hand. The physical contact was an instant balm to my fraying nerves. Tim chose an armchair on our left, while Charlie took a seat near the entry so she could watch the hallway. Charlie nodded slightly to Tim just before I heard approaching footsteps.

Grandfather entered from around the corner. He appeared every bit the sophisticated, high-powered businessman, with his close-cropped brown hair, slate pinstriped business suit, dark-blue shirt, gray silk tie, and black polished Gucci shoes. But his eyes were still the beautiful crystal-clear green I remembered from the ball. We all arose from our seats as he entered with his arms outstretched.

"Welcome home! Oh, it's so good to see you. It has been far too many years, my children." Lord Basil pulled Tim into a warm embrace. "You don't need an engraved invitation to visit your father, you know," he scolded gently as he released Tim and held out a hand toward Charlie.

"Father, it is so good to see you." Tim grinned and ducked his head like a wayward teen.

"I have missed you both so much. Just because you're adults, there's no reason you can't visit." He wrapped his arms around Charlie, who remained stiff at first before melting into the embrace. "Always the strong woman, my girl."

"I missed you too, Father." Charlie rested her head against her father's shoulder, smiling serenely at the older man.

"Lance, I'm glad to see you. I wasn't sure you would come. You honor me. Thank you." Grandfather took my hands and gently pulled me into his embrace. He was so careful with me. It was as if he was afraid I'd shatter if he moved the wrong way or hugged me too hard. But I was a shifter, after all—I wasn't fragile. I shook off the thought as a shivery spike of cold slid along my spine. His touch was frigid, the same as all the vampires I'd met. Funny thing was, you could see the desire in his quiet heart. It was a nurturing need to love his family.

"Thank you. We don't want to be a bother...." I tried to hedge, to give him a chance to change his mind now that we'd invaded his home and his territory.

"Nonsense. My home is your home." Grandfather held me at arm's length with his hands on my shoulders, examining me with a critical eye as if memorizing every part of me to make sure he never forgot. It was odd for me. I wanted to fidget, rub my nose, scratch my balls, something... so I could avoid knowing how important I was to this man. That I was part of his family and he was recording my every detail so I would never again feel like an invader in his home.

"I'm glad we came." I stared into his eyes, and a connection sparked. Just for a moment, I sensed an overwhelming feeling of total acceptance and love, as well as loss, before his eyes closed, hiding the emotions from me.

He cupped my cheek gently and patted it softly. "You are so like your mother." The words he said were barely a whisper, and had I not been right there in front of him, I would have missed the near-silent comment. He inhaled deeply before he turned to focus on my mate. "Andrew. Welcome. I trust you are well." Grandfather took Andrew's hand and shook it while placing his other hand on his shoulder.

"I'm fine. Thank you." The warmth and gratitude radiating from my mate made me realize how much I desired this man's acceptance.

"Father... is Brad here?" A bit of ice crept into Tim's voice as he paced away from his father and taking a seat in the armchair he'd occupied before Grandfather had arrived.

"No. I sent him to check on the condition of Nathaniel's holdings weeks ago when I first learned of Lance's existence." Grandfather paused, his gaze darting between Tim and Charlie. "You seemed hesitant to want his involvement, so I thought it was better if he wasn't here when Lance arrived. Brad hasn't been back to the penthouse since you contacted me. I assume he's preparing the house and securing the grounds. I get regular daily updates from Brenda on his progress." Both Tim and Charlie relaxed noticeably, as though a weight was lifted from the room. "Why do you ask?"

We all followed Tim's example and returned to our seats, while Grandfather chose an armchair to my right. I was immediately dissatisfied with the arrangement. Lately, I'd been discovering a new touchy-feely side of myself. It was the animal in me needing physical contact with its family, its pack. I could only imagine generations of my people, all growing up together, knowing each other as well as Andrew knew his brothers, sister, and cousins.

My beast craved that connection with a family of my own. Instinct dictated my desire for physical contact with my grandfather, but also a very human longing to connect with a father figure who'd long been denied me. I wanted to

26

imprint my grandfather on my soul. My wolf wanted to claim him as my family. Not in the sexual sense that Andrew and I had claimed each other, but to have our scents mingle, become one. I wanted him to carry my scent. To be a combination of our essences that at its core would tell all paranormals we were one family.

Andrew nodded to me, knowing my feelings without words.

I stood. "Would you sit with us, Grandfather?" I was a bit hesitant. Vampires weren't a tactile bunch, but I took a chance and held out a hand to him in invitation.

"I'd be honored." He took my hand and sat down on the love seat next to Andrew. My wolf practically purred with contentment as I squeezed between them. It was uncomfortably close. Three adult males squished onto a love seat, we were definitely in each other's personal space. But as Grandfather's scent wrapped around us, mingling with mine and Andrew's, he became family.

Tim frowned, appearing to be somewhat confused, while Charlie rolled her eyes. My behavior rarely surprised her, or at least that was the impression she gave.

Grandfather reached over and clasped my hand in between his. His cool skin felt far different from Andrew's warm touch, yet it was him, just like some people had black hair. It made my grandfather special but wasn't a barrier between us. He seemed stunned by the level of acceptance and trust I gave him. He knew my history and clearly had expected suspicion and maybe even fear, but I could feel his sincerity. The man truly wanted me for his grandson.

I inhaled deeply, my wolf's senses cataloging every nuance of what made up Lord Basil, everything his scent could tell me about him, even what he'd recently eaten, that he'd handled freshly printed paper, and a host of other things. He would be imprinted on us. I'd know his scent among thousands and be able to follow him anywhere.

Tim anxiously cleared his throat. "Father, much has happened since Lance appeared at the Reed farm. There were things that could've been done differently or better, but the biggest mistake was mine."

"What are you trying to say, son?" Grandfather frowned as Andrew and I stared at Tim in complete confusion.

"I should've listened to my instincts as you always told me to. I should've brought Lance to you as soon as I even guessed who he might be. But the worst thing I did was to tell Brad about him." Tim hung his head. He was so distraught, as if he had failed me. But there was no way he could have known. "Shortly after that, the attempts on Lance's life began. It's all entirely my fault. My bad judgment has caused him to be in jeopardy time and again. I'm so sorry, Father."

My jaw practically hit the floor; I was so stunned. "You can't say that. You can no more predict what someone else is going to do than I can." I scowled at

Tim, who stared back at me, his submission to my judgment clear. Yet I knew the forgiveness he sought wasn't mine. "You've done so much for me. You kept me sane when my life was coming apart, before I accepted Andrew. You taught me about who I am and this new world I'm part of. I owe you everything, because without you I could've destroyed everything before I'd even begun." I tried to reassure him.

"Tim, I believe that my grandson has the right of it. I don't blame you, son. Although I do wish you would've brought Lance to me right away, for my own selfish reasons. I do believe the environment at the farm benefited him much more than I could have." Grandfather faced Andrew and nodded slowly. "He needed to be with other shape-shifters to learn about what and who he is. But you're here now and I am so pleased to have you staying with me."

"Brenda, can you come here please?" Charlie called down the hall.

"Yes, my lady?" Brenda stood in the door, smiling warmly, fearlessly.

"Father has need of you." Charlie nodded in Grandfather's direction.

Brenda was clearly dumbfounded as she studied us. Three grown men sitting on a love seat must have made quite a strange sight when there were other seats vacant.

"Please inform the staff that my grandson, Lance, and his mate, Andrew, will be staying with us. Have the suite across from my own prepared for them. Charlie and Tim's apartments will need to be refreshed." Grandfather nodded in the direction of the guards at the elevator. "Their entourage will also need rooms in the guest quarters. My grandson, his mate, and my children are welcome in any part of the house. They have come home. Be discreet, Brenda. I do not want anyone who is not currently in this building knowing that they are here. Am I clearly understood?"

"Yes, my lord."

"Good. That will be all for now, Brenda. Thank you."

Brenda nodded respectfully and disappeared back down the hall.

"So, children, tell me how this all began. I realize Andrew must have found you, somehow in his territory, and the two of you fell in love. I know from Tim's reports that you had a rather traumatic childhood among the humans. I am so sorry. Had I known, I'd have prevented that from happening. I'm obviously in your debt, Andrew."

"No, I'm just lucky he was able to let me into his heart to help him heal." Andrew gave me a slight nudge with his shoulder and grinned. We began telling Grandfather our adventures—of how we met and everything that had happened, the good and the bad—with Tim and Charlie jumping in to fill in their parts of the story.

"So you are here. Andrew is free, but his family is not and does not wish for freedom, if I understand what transpired correctly." Grandfather frowned, shifting a bit on the love seat.

"They're afraid of the repercussions from the rest of the clan, possibly imposed by other benefactors. They could be cut off from the rest of the family, and we don't want that for them." I bit my lip as I couldn't quite keep my frustration from slipping through.

"Ah." Grandfather nodded. "A wolf without a pack is alone and vulnerable. Andrew's father would not want his family to be without the support of the pack."

"No, sir." Andrew shook his head solemnly. "It was a hard decision, but they chose to remain as Stephon's beneficiaries in the hope that we will be successful."

"And what do you hope to attain?"

"We—well, I, really—hope to be able to prove 'The Right to Rule' and free my people." I trembled a bit, hoping Grandfather would understand.

"Is the beneficiary system so bad? Do you think, from what you've witnessed of Stephon's treatment of Andrew's family, that he's mistreated them?" Grandfather frowned, his eyes flashing and unreadable for the first time since I'd met the man.

I took a deep breath. "I don't like it, Grandfather. Being raised by humans and having grown up exposed to their freedom and the importance of choice, I know this is wrong. Humans really didn't do me any favors, but they taught me that there is an inherent truth that all men and women have the right to determine their own lives. Humans with their short life spans have accomplished great things, while my own people are slaves and have no say in the direction their lives will take. They are allowed an education only if their benefactor allows it. They don't have the luxury of deciding where they will live, or even who will be the mother or father of their children. We're more like pets than individuals. Why should my people's lives be worth less than a human's? Especially when most vampires view humanity as food."

"But this is how our society is. Who are you to decide it's wrong?" Grandfather pressed. "We take care of each other and prevent those humans who are unaware of us from discovering and hunting our species. Isn't that more important than worrying about an education, love, or romance?"

I frowned and tried not to get angry. If I couldn't convince Grandfather, what hope did I have of convincing anyone else? "When Andrew and I discovered we were in love, I realized I needed to find a way to be worthy of him because I was just street trash. A nobody. No bloodline, past, education, or future." I smiled at Andrew, who sighed in disgust.

"That's hardly the case, love. It's I who needs to be worthy of you and not the other way around. You're the prince, remember?" Andrew played with my ponytail, running the hair through his fingers.

"But, in the beginning, I was just a throwback. An unclaimed mutt. I was so afraid Stephon wouldn't allow me to be with Andrew because I had no bloodline. There was no reason for Stephon to agree to anything. I had no standing in any pack, much less the paranormal community. I had no rights and no means of reprisal if Stephon said no. There was nothing to prevent him from outright killing me if he so chose."

"But he didn't."

"No, he didn't. Although I think it was touch and go there for a bit. We were able to prove to him who I am and that we are mated."

I tried not to blush as Lord Basil smiled, raised my hand to his nose, and took a deep breath. "I knew your mother and father well. Your scent and facial structure are very much like hers, as are your eyes." He sat back a bit, releasing my hand, and studied me closely. "But you have your father's coloring. I see him in the hue of your hair and the tone of your skin. Your height comes from his side of the gene pool. Your mother was a rather petite woman."

"That's when we found out I was a pureblood and royal." I sighed in frustration. "The bottom line is this. I believe everyone has the right to decide their own fate as long as they're not hurting others in doing so. My people have become matriarchal in nature. The women hold the land while the males are swapped among the vampires like trading cards, used for stud until they find a woman who accepts them as mate, or are forced to remain unmated, unable to continue the search for their mate. I've heard stories about young men who disappear when taken and who are never heard from again. Nobody knows what happens to them. Occasionally humans are brought in and forced to breed. We're told it's to temper the beast, keep it more manageable in the next generation. We become weaker and have gone from an existence of near immortality, similar to your own, to a near-human life span."

"If it were simply a matter of keeping the animal from being aggressive, then we should be seeking out ways to strip the beast from ourselves. Your kind did not start the war alone. It was greed on both sides." Grandfather raised a hand to his forehead, closed his eyes, and for a moment, appeared much older. "This fact has never been contested by the council. Enough of us remain on the council that we will not allow it to be forgotten."

Tim shifted uneasily in his chair. "Brad did me one favor before becoming my enemy. He explained how the beneficiary system was not set up to benefit the shape shifters, but to control them and prevent purebloods from returning." He met my eyes and then checked with his father as if for confirmation. Lord Basil gave a slight nod, and Tim continued. "Stephon doesn't seem to believe in the current system, although if he were discovered to be strengthening Andrew's family, he'd be branded a traitor. He hopes by releasing Andrew, he will delay any scrutiny or inquiries, at least until Lance is declared Prince by the royal family. Afterward, it shouldn't matter as the council will have little choice but to allow Lance to choose the 'Right to Rule.'" Tim hesitated only slightly. "Right?"

Grandfather nodded slowly. "You're right to be cautious. Our people will fear this, especially those who weren't born among purebloods. It's the only way open to you. The other would be another war, and I have to believe you'd prefer not to have blood on your hands."

"No, I don't want to start a war. In fact, were my people to tell me they don't want this change, I'd drop it. Andrew and I would live our lives privately, happily. It may not be what I want, but if they are content and choose to remain dependent, then so be it. I won't contest the will of my people."

"If you choose the 'Right to Rule' clause in the treaty, to free the shape shifters, allowing them to pursue their own destiny, you'll be setting yourself up for a battle. I was against the beneficiary system when it was first installed. Both sides were so tired of war and vengeance that I believe peace could've been achieved without such diabolical measures." Grandfather gave my hand a squeeze, and his lips set in a grim smile. "I will support you, child, in your bid for freedom. I know of quite a few others who will join us."

"Thank you, Grandfather."

"There are still a few old vampires like myself who remember fighting alongside the pureblood shifters, who could do the things you can. It was through cooperation of our species that we barely survived the Blood Wars against the fae. We sealed them behind the veil together."

"That's something left out of our history lessons." Andrew stared at Grandfather as if he'd dropped a bomb. "We know the stories that have been handed down through the generations, but it isn't something that is encouraged."

The silence grew as footsteps from down the hall drew near and Brenda stepped into the room. "Sorry to interrupt, but it is close to three o'clock, my lord. I was sure you would want to—"

"Ah yes, my lady awaits." Grandfather grinned, but the smile didn't reach his eyes. It seemed decidedly mournful.

"Mother… is she?" Charlie stood so suddenly there was an uncharacteristic touch of panic in her eyes.

"Oh no. She sleeps like all the others. But it's odd. Lately, on the day of the full moon, she becomes restless. At noon she will begin to shake as if having seizures, which by now will have subsided. She is drawing me to her—she needs to feed. For a brief, wonderful moment, I can touch her mind before she slips into

31

sleep once again." Grandfather's voice had become soft as he spoke, his breathing increasingly labored before his eyes flashed an odd sallow yellow color. He abruptly stood, threw back his head, and screamed his pain. It was a ragged sound that spoke of barely contained agony. I could understand why mates caught in the limbo of near death often went insane. Grandfather was truly frightening in his grief before his head fell forward on his chest and Charlie held him in her arms.

"It will get better. It's a good sign that she almost awakens. She's fighting to return to you. We just need to discover how to help her." Charlie rubbed his back, soothing his loss as much as she was able.

"It's just so frustrating. Each time I get so close to drawing her out, only to be left empty when hibernation takes her away. It's all I can do not to follow her into oblivion."

"I know, Father. I know," Charlie whispered. "Why didn't you call and tell us this was happening again?"

"What's going on?" I asked, not wanting to intrude but not liking the pain and suffering I heard in my grandfather's voice.

"Years ago a plague struck all the mated pairs of born vampires. The females became sick and slipped into hibernation. They've never awoken. Many different cures have been tried over the years to awaken them, but nothing works." Tim spoke, his tone clinical. Grandfather shuddered, and Charlie seemed to clutch him tighter to her.

"We have lost many of the older generation who have not been able to adjust to being without their mates for such an extended period of time," Tim said. "But something has been changing with Illiana. The last couple of decades, she has come close to awakening."

"I just wish I knew what was doing it or how to draw her to consciousness. I miss her so very much." Grandfather stroked Charlie's hair and kissed her cheek. "I must go, see to her needs."

"May I meet her sometime?" I asked Grandfather, not at all sure if it was proper that I do.

"Of course. I know she would love that. This will not take long. I will rejoin you soon. Brenda, please see to some refreshments for my family." Grandfather excused himself and disappeared up the stairs.

CHAPTER 4

Stephon's Story—Egypt
May 1504 BC

IT WAS rare for the pharaoh to summon his father these days. He was far too interested in the Greeks and their growing empire that threatened the Egyptian borders to concern himself with the priests of Sekhmet, even if she was the goddess of war. Stephon had always found it a bit ironic for a vampire to be a priest to a shape-shifting goddess, but the lioness-headed goddess of war—as she is portrayed on the walls of the Egyptian pyramids—was more bloodthirsty than any vampire he'd yet to meet. Her followers, mainly citizens in the pharaoh's army, made sacrifices of blood and fermented beverages, food, and beer, which kept her priests content. There was little the goddess' servants desired that wasn't freely bestowed upon them, and to the vampires in particular, as they were considered the blessed children of the goddess.

Stephon followed his father through the golden gates and into the sunny, warm courtyard. The bubbling of water in a shaded pool demonstrated the opulence of the pharaoh's palace, and a number of his harem wives reclined about it, their slaves and attendants seeing to their every comfort as they amused themselves with games. A prickly sensation of unease flowed over his skin as they approached the throne room. Stephon had to clench his fists to keep his claws from sprouting. A nasty hiss could be heard from the room ahead, followed by a loud crack and the sound of a body hitting the floor.

"We have company, my son. Do not display your fangs or claws if you can help it. It will help the vampires in the room ahead control their nature," Caius whispered as they passed through the golden gates, and the guards bowed in respect as the head priest of Sekhmet passed.

"Yes, Father," Stephon hissed softly, trying to control the growing urge to fall into a defensive crouch and approach the invaders of their territory with all the fighting skills he'd been taught as a child of the lioness goddess of war.

They approached the throne from the side. The pharaoh's private gardens annexed the throne room, allowing them to arrive unseen. The invaders were below the dais, having entered from through the main hall, which opened out to a lower public courtyard and the city beyond.

"Ah, Priest Caius. So good of you to join us. I see you have brought your lovely sun-touched protégé with you." Pharaoh Thutmose III nodded to Caius.

They entered and bowed, showing their respect to the man both Caius and Stephon had watched grow up from boyhood. Mortals had such remarkably short lives, even these who were thought to be the god-king children of Ra. Stephon was considered a juvenile among his vampire family, and yet he'd already seen many pharaohs come and go in his short two hundred summers of life. His father had seen many more come to power and fade over his lifetime.

"My Pharaoh, how can we be of assistance?" Caius regarded the audience chamber, and the two vampires at the bottom of the steps. They appeared to be a mated pair from the woven hair mating band the female wore about her neck and the male wore about his upper arm. Manacled together by heavy silver chains, the female lay unconscious and pregnant. The male crouched over her limp body, attempting to shield her. They were malnourished, obviously slaves or prisoners of the gray-skinned, white-haired fae merchant whose men guarded them.

"This is merchant Legithian the White, of the light fae. He claims to be an emissary of the light fae court, and that these two creatures were members of the prior royal household. There appears to have been some sort of power struggle, and the new royalty does not approve of blood drinkers. They wish for us to dispose of them, as they cannot directly take life and they do not wish to keep them as slaves for fear of them scheming to take revenge against the current ruling family." Pharaoh Thutmose gestured to the captives.

"They want us to do their dirty work for them. I am not comfortable destroying kinsmen for any reason. Sekhmet may be a war goddess, but she is also a goddess of healing." Caius tipped his head to the side as he noted the pair. The male vampire hissed and snarled, his fangs and claws distended, although he wavered back and forth over his mate, clearly at the end of his endurance.

"It isn't so much doing our dirty work, priest, as ridding the world of an evil blight. We, the light fae, prefer to preserve life if possible. We have learned to control our baser urges. We do not kill. We hold great reverence for life, because from it we draw our own existence." Legithian all but snarled. His upper lip curled into a mockery of a smile, flashing his jagged, deadly teeth.

"Oh, this is the first I've ever heard of fae from either court demonstrating any kind of restraint." Caius placed a hand on his son's shoulder. Stephon tried to remain as calm as possible, but he knew his father's baiting of the fae was dangerous business.

"As your people have evolved, so too we must learn to adapt. Our new royal family is taking steps to teach this to us." Legithian scowled as if put upon but continued, ignoring the insult. "These two have done great harm to our people by preaching a separatist doctrine that would have all paranormals at each other's throats. They attempted to place themselves in positions of power within the royal house, whispering their lies and deceit in an attempt to undermine my people. They succeeded in starting a civil war among the light fae. We have been fighting for the past several decades, and sadly, it is far from over."

"All that. A war. Caused by two vampires living among the fae, and you haven't put them to death?" Stephon asked incredulously.

"No. We have punished them as far as we are able. But we must abide by our own laws, not to cause death." Legithian glared down his long, pointed nose at the vampires lying at his feet. "It is a difficult road we are attempting to follow. To see and honor life, all life, from which we draw strength," Legithian recited as if it were a mantra or an empowering prayer.

"I truly am stunned by this... new attitude the light fae are taking. Your new monarchy must be strong to go against your own traditions and natural tendencies." Caius eyed the two miserable wretches of vampires at Legithian's feet. "I would have expected an exception to be made for prisoners such as these and that the fae don't indulge themselves. I do not understand why you don't just finish off their souls and then feast on their bodies. Every fae I have ever known has carried around bits of teeth or finger bones of their favorite meals. You are telling me this is a practice that is no longer occurring?"

"There was much dissention in the beginning. I will not say this change comes easily or without much resentment. Many of the light fae still see all other species as food and little else." Legithian tipped his head to the side as if considering his words carefully. "Change is difficult, and we must be ever vigilant so we do not give in to our baser natures." The fae hissed through his teeth like a serpent.

"Amazing. I wish you the best at your endeavor to evolve." Caius frowned and shook his head.

"As I have said, the light court of the fae no longer kills. We have fed as much from them as we dare, enjoying their especially strong life force. If we indulge ourselves further, we would kill them, and then we are no better than our dark brethren." Legithian pointed at the two vampires and sneered. "No, they are of your species, and if they are to be killed for their crimes, then it needs to be done by your hand."

"So it shall be. If those be their crimes, then death is their reward." Caius faced his pharaoh, who nodded his agreement.

Legithian bowed to the pharaoh. "I leave it in your hands to dispose of them. I also warn you that if you change your mind and allow them to live, they will descend upon your court like locusts on a field of ripe grain, causing destruction and deception among your confidants in the pursuit of their own power. Evil like theirs is without honor, and they have no loyalty to any but themselves."

"You lie!" the male hissed.

"Silence, slave!" Legithian punched the male, whose head struck the stone floor, knocking him unconscious.

"I will not allow such an evil to exist in my kingdom," Pharaoh Thutmose reassured the fae and addressed his priests, just as the female began to groggily blink her eyes and attempt to push herself upright. "What say you on this matter? They are of your people. How do you believe we should proceed?"

"As Your Highness has stated, such a blight cannot be allowed to live. They are of my people, children of Sekhmet, and to her they should return. If the fae have left anything of their souls intact, it should be returned to the goddess." Caius yawned, appearing bored as he discussed the fate of the interlopers who had obviously taken on the fae and lost miserably. With Legithian present, he wouldn't be able to question the pair further, but after the man left, he could attempt to see if they were truly a threat.

"So be it. Take them to the holding cells while you prepare for their sacrifice to Sekhmet," Pharaoh Thutmose pronounced the slaves' sentence.

"No!" the female screamed and was backhanded by Legithian.

"Your Highness is most gracious. Would it be all right if I remain to see them sacrificed, so I can report their deaths to my king?" Legithian bowed low.

"Have you brought a food source with you?" Caius asked, eyeing the fae. "These two will be unavailable to you, as they must be put through a purification ceremony prior to their sacrifice to Sekhmet. I cannot let you feed upon a meal meant for the lioness goddess. We can offer you the life force of our beasts, human food, and of course, the blood donated by the priests in our sect."

"Ah... I appreciate your offer, but unfortunately your options are unpalatable to the fae. I do need pure, nonanimal species life force to sustain me. I am only able to feed upon human, shifter, dwarven or vampiric life forces. Our sustenance must be sentient, or it will not renew us. As that is not available, I will need to return to my people. I have no wish to cause any bad feelings and do not wish to feed upon anyone who is unwilling. My party and I shall take our leave. My King may require proof of their demise. If he does, I will return and bring my own food source with me." Legithian's toothy smile had a sinister feel.

"If you return, I will have proof for you," Caius replied. "We don't eat the flesh of our... sacrifices."

"As I told you, we do not eat flesh, either." Legithian sighed as if very put upon. "The dark court still partakes in such barbarous and unnecessary behavior, but we have put those days behind us. Our food supply comes to us voluntarily or, as in the case of these slaves, as a punishment."

"So you say." Caius waved at the guards, who moved in and took hold of the chains of the slaves. "Your proof of their... punishment shall be waiting for you if you return."

"Thank you for your consideration." Legithian bowed to the pharaoh, his eyes sparkling with mischief. He spun on his heal and led his guards from the court, disappearing into the sunlight of the garden just beyond the archway.

"I do not like having dealings with the fae, the light or the dark. Neither one is trustworthy." Pharaoh Thutmose watched as the guards led the slaves from the room. They would be taken to the dungeons beneath the temple of Sekhmet.

"The fae as a species can be formidable, sire. You cross them at your own peril, but the light fae are usually the more stable of the breed. I do avoid dealing with them if I can, but unlike the dark fae, who will start a war without provocation, the light usually need a reason to attack." Caius remarked. "We will pray to the goddess for guidance, interview the slaves, and bring our findings to you, my lord."

"Thank you, Caius. Your counsel is wise and much appreciated." Pharaoh Thutmose smiled and walked from the room, his personal slaves and guards fluttering along behind.

"Is it wise to do something for the fae, Father?" Stephon frowned as he and his father left the throne room from the side entrance they had originally entered.

"All dealings with the fae are regrettable. We must move forward with great care, my son," Caius cautioned as the two returned to their temple. "If something can be done for the unfortunate pair, we shall try. If not, they will be welcomed into the afterlife by Sekhmet."

CHAPTER 5

Present Day

WE ALL stood and watched Grandfather leave. Some of the life seemed to have left his step as he made his way out of the room. Brenda made a cursory glance about the room before she settled her focus on Tim. "Lord Basil requested refreshments. What would you like from the kitchen?"

Tim grinned. "Tea. Earl Grey, if I remember correctly."

I avidly nodded my thanks. We'd missed lunch, and with all the excitement, I'd been too nauseous at first to even consider food. Now that things were beginning to settle down, I was borderline ravenous.

"Sandwiches would be good—whatever the cook can put together quickly."

"And would you like it brought in here or in the dining room?" Brenda seemed oblivious to the complete lack of understanding on Tim's face. My guess was Grandfather didn't have guests often, much less those who consumed something other than blood. It seemed quite comical that Brenda would ask Tim what we should eat—Tim, who hadn't eaten in centuries. As a drone, food was unpalatable to him. His diet had become a liquid one—blood, preferably human, the fresher the better—since the day he'd been turned by Grandfather.

Tim blinked at me, his mouth dropping open slightly. I snickered and answered Brenda. "In here should be fine."

"Very well, gentlemen." Brenda shuffled back toward the desk.

When she was gone, Tim sighed. "You know, I remember a little about those days. Grandfather made me just before the war, so I remember seeing vampires and shifters living together in peace."

"Really? What do you remember?" I found myself curious about Tim's early life.

"Those were different days. No technology. No electricity. I was born a human peasant before I was chosen to become the son of a vampire lord. I can tell you paranormals love their children. Whether from pureblood shifter or born vampire families, all were cherished. I vaguely remember a special ceremony held whenever a vampire child came into this world. The infant needed to be introduced to the community, and the ceremony was to bless the child, and through the newborn, everyone. It was one of the few ceremonies that a newborn drone like myself was allowed to attend."

"You were kept out of most social situations?" I couldn't imagine a time where Tim wouldn't be allowed to any social event. I had heard before that new drones were violent and it took years for them to be able to fully control their thirst for blood, but to envision Tim as anything but the good doctor was almost impossible for me.

"I guess everyone felt there were enough people at these celebrations, that it was safe for us to attend and be part of the family. Of course, before the war, there were fewer drones created. We were thought of as their children as much as the born infants being blessed." Tim had a far-off contented look in his eyes. He appeared to be lost in his memories.

"That's really cool." I tried to imagine those days, believing them to be similar in some respects to my time living alone on the land, before I met my mate.

Andrew put his arm around my shoulder and drew me into his side. "And hard to believe when you think of how things are today."

"There's no way a vampire would have shifters in his home voluntarily these days... Well, a vampire other than Lord Basil." Charlie frowned.

"Or Stephon, so it would seem." Tim chuckled as Charlie tried to cover her laughter with a snort and then peered to the left, down the hallway.

Brenda led in two young women who worked in the kitchen. They brought trays laden with sandwiches and slightly steaming tea sets. The scent of warm blood overpowered even that of the Earl Grey in one of the pots.

"Oh, I'm so sorry!" Charlie started to sputter and wave at one of the servers.

"You haven't had anything either. It's all right, Charlie. We aren't offended." I grinned and nodded, waving the maids into the room. Tim regarded Andrew, who shrugged, nodding that they should continue. *If we're going to live with vampires, we're going to have to get used to the scent of blood. It's not like they have a choice in the matter*, I sent to Andrew through our connection.

You're right, and to be honest, the scent really doesn't bother me. When we hunt, we consume the blood of our prey along with the rest of the kill. What they drink really doesn't smell that much different than what we hunt. Andrew's practical thoughts bothered me a bit, but he was right: essentially, blood smelled like blood. There were distinct differences, but the basic metallic-coppery scent was always there, regardless of the species of the donor.

"You were saying about this ceremony?" I said, wanting to know more. Picking up a sandwich from the tray set before us on the coffee table, and taking a bite.

"It was a blessing ceremony, I think. I haven't been to one in… well, it must be close to a century. I suppose it would be similar to a baptism or a recognition ceremony. The family would bring the infant to the oldest vampire to be blooded. At which point the infant would be recognized as a vampire by its coven and there'd be a huge party." Tim frowned as he struggled to remember.

"They bit the baby?" Andrew asked, astounded.

"Of course not," Grandfather answered. He walked into the room, chuckling, and picked up one of the teapots between Tim and Charlie. "Do you mind?" he asked as he picked up a mug and poured himself a drink, his back to me and Andrew. He appeared a bit pale and tired after having left the group, but showed no other signs of what must have been an ordeal for him. He didn't sit but chose to walk about the room as he picked up the explanation from Tim. "We are not heathens. When a vampire baby is born, for all intents and purposes, it is almost human. Like all born vampires, it has no issue with the sun, and it can consume human food but will eventually sicken and die without a consistent diet of blood."

"So then the first blood meal is this special ceremony?" I nodded my understanding.

"Yes. It's a day of great celebration when the infant is brought to the coven and their fangs are encouraged to drop for the first time. It's painful for the infant, like all babies when they cut their first teeth. The blood that is shed from the teeth cutting through is gathered and saved as the purest blood of the innocent. It's considered a gift of purity to the coven and a blessing. Then the child is given its first blood meal, and the entire coven celebrates a new vampire life. Like a birthday party." Grandfather moved to stand beside Charlie. "I'm about to out you, my dear." Grandfather leaned down and kissed Charlie on the cheek.

"It was bound to come out eventually," she grumbled, scrunching up her face, making a disgruntled *humph*.

Grandfather settled himself on the arm of her chair. "Charlie is the oldest of my children still living. I'm sad to say most of them were killed in the war.

Against the recommendation of my peers, I have chosen not to create any more until Illiana awakens. Choosing to have children was something we always did together. Our drones were carefully picked and agreed upon by both of us before we invested our time in raising them, as well as when we decided the time was right for us to have a child who was genetically ours."

"Can a female vampire control when she is fertile?" Andrew's asked.

"To a certain extent, yes. For a female to become pregnant, her body must have a constant supply of fresh blood. This will trigger her reproductive cycle, and she will become fertile. After conception, her scent will change slightly and she will become ravenous for her mate's blood. She must feed from her mate once a day for the first trimester, which for us is normally...." Grandfather frowned and turned to Tim.

"Four weeks," Tim supplied, "followed by a second and third trimester of six weeks each."

"And Illiana? She's pregnant now right?" I found the whole thing incredulous that a vampire could remain in hibernation for so long and still be pregnant.

"Yes. She was with child, in her third trimester, when she went into hibernation just over a century ago." Grandfather paused and took a drink from his mug. He appeared to be contemplating a very unpleasant task, but one that needed to be done.

"Grandfather, are you all right?" I asked.

His green eyes, full of sadness, focused on me before he smiled. "I'm fine. Just a bit melancholy, I suppose. Nothing to worry about."

Charlie reached up and took her father's hand as he took a deep breath and seemed to steady himself.

"I grew up with shape shifters in my parents' home. We were close, like brothers and sisters. We used to wrestle on the floor, pulling the tails and ears of the nannies who watched over us. As we grew older, we all attended the same classes with my father and other adults, learning about math, the stars, and the proper crop rotation for the seasons before we were given apprenticeships in various vocations. I miss them. I can't tell you how much it hurts some days." Grandfather stood and walked across the room and knelt down in front of me. "Now I have a second chance." He put his hands gently on my knee, and I quickly clasped them in my own. "I can't apologize enough for one of my children threatening to hurt you. I haven't come to this decision lightly. This is one of the hardest things I've ever had to do, but too much is at stake for my son to continue like this. You, Grandson, are proof my son's mate lives, and through her, a piece of my son also exists. I must go and… see… to Brad. You don't need to fear him any longer. I will take care of him." Grandfather stood and walked to the open door. I could tell he was preparing to leave and wasn't happy about the task ahead. He gazed at me with a sadness I'd really only seen in Andrew's eyes.

"Want me to come with you?" I didn't want Grandfather to go alone. He looked like a man walking to the gallows, and I could only imagine his pain at contemplating killing one of his own children. Especially when there were so few left.

"I would not risk your life, just so you can keep me company. No, this is something I must do, and a task I do not relish. I hope you understand. I believed him to be a good and honorable son. Now I fear how many of your brothers and sisters he may have dispatched without anyone being the wiser." Grandfather closed his eyes, and his body seemed to become rock hard, preparing himself.

I can go with Grandfather if you want, love. I'd enjoy getting a claw or two into Brad, and no parent should have to kill their own child, even though Brad is a bastard. Andrew's thoughts whispered through my mind.

"Are you sure you don't mind?"

Andrew gave me an indulgent smile, one he reserved just for me. The one that told me to just shut up already, that he'd do anything I asked just because I asked. There were times I had to wonder how I'd gotten so lucky as to have him as my mate.

"I love you," he whispered in my ear and kissed my temple.

"Take Charlie with you and be extra careful," I whispered back. "I love you too."

Tim, Charlie, and Grandfather stared blankly at the two of us.

"Lance…. Sometimes the conversations you and Andrew have are really hard to follow," Tim said with chagrin.

Andrew rose from the sofa. I didn't want to let him go. It wasn't fear of his getting hurt, but an intense desire to be together constantly. It was very hard to accept this dependent aspect of myself. I'd always been alone and relied only on myself for survival. That part of my life was over. I'd never be completely alone again. Even when he left with Grandfather, I'd hear his every thought and feel his emotions. We needed to learn to temper our instincts, or we wouldn't be able to function in society as individuals. Besides, I needed to protect my new family— Grandfather being part of that—from all things bad… essentially Brad. Andrew had the desire to shred the man, limb from limb. The best way to protect Grandfather from having to kill his own son was to let Andrew do it.

"I understand you feel it is your duty to do this, Grandfather, but could I accompany you?" Andrew requested and tipped his head to the side showing his submission to our Grandfather. He wanted to go, but would abide by whatever Grandfather decided.

I watched Grandfather's posture carefully for any sign of feeling insulted by Andrew's request. But all I saw was a burning rage that had me cringing internally.

"I have a problem with anyone who would dare to hurt Lance. Especially when they come into my territory, into my house, and try to take what is mine from me." As Andrew spoke, the snarl in his voice grew deeper and more vicious.

I stood beside him and took his hand, soothing us both. "Please, go together. If you must go after him, then be each other's backup." I gave Andrew's hand a tight squeeze. "I'm not willing to lose either of you." I said to both Grandfather and Andrew. "He may have set traps, realizing you'd be coming for him." There was only one person I would trust with these two men, the one person who'd have a plan. Charlie was methodical, and she would keep a clear head instead of going in hot with only thoughts of revenge. Focusing on her, I said, "Will you please make sure they both come back in one piece?"

Charlie smiled fiercely at me, her fangs sliding from their sheaths, taking her already badass appearance to a whole other level of lethal. "It'd be my honor to have a chance at killing that deceitful betraying bastard." Charlie faced Grandfather. "May I accompany you and Andrew?" She drew a leather gauntlet from a pocket at her waist and tossed it at Lord Basil, who caught it in midair.

He gave a quizzical look, first at the gauntlet and then back at me, before he replied to his daughter. "Of course, you may both come. But what's this for?"

"I'd suggest you put it on. It's simpler for Andrew to strip here than in the car and birds don't shed. Plus falcons do great recon."

I laughed as Grandfather's jaw dropped in obvious surprise. He quickly shut it and began strapping on the gauntlet before turning to Andrew. "I just remember you saying he was a wolf... but of course you both have several forms now."

Andrew had removed his shirt and sweater, folded them, and laid them on the love seat behind us. He'd waited specifically for Grandfather to turn back toward him before he shifted. The quicksilver took his body, and the rest of his clothes drifted to the floor unharmed. The bird stood beside me on the ground, wings slightly spread, talons laid as flat as he could make them in an effort to not catch them in the carpet.

"Go on, sit with Grandfather. I don't want to have to try to cut your talons from the shag if you get stuck." With a disgruntled squawk, he launched himself at my Grandfather with a single flap of his wings to land with care on his outstretched, gauntleted wrist.

"Now that's something I've missed." Grandfather grinned. "I haven't seen a transformation like that in well over a hundred years."

"You'll be seeing more of it now that we're living here, Grandfather." I held my bottom lip between my teeth. "Be safe, Grandfather, and come back soon. We still have so much to talk about and learn about each other." I couldn't help myself; I had to touch Andrew once more before they left. I walked across the room and stroked under the chin and across the breast of my mate.

Be careful, my love. I nodded at Grandfather and watched as Charlie headed for the elevator, with the rest of us following behind.

I will. I'll watch out for Grandfather. I might even get to destroy Brad. If the coward is even there, which, since he's smart, he probably won't be. I could hear the frustration in Andrew's thoughts. He hated leaving me, but he needed this. Charlie pressed the down arrow, and the doors to the elevator dinged and opened. She stepped in and held the door open for Grandfather, Andrew, and two of the guards.

"We won't be gone more than a couple hours. Your lands aren't far. Once we have this problem taken care of, we need to discuss hunting arrangements and your safety, for the time being at least." Grandfather gave me a brief one-armed hug before stepping into the elevator, leaving me behind with Tim and a confused Brenda.

As the elevator went down, so did I, sliding down the wall I'd suddenly found supporting me until I sat abruptly on the floor. My vision tunneled and began to darken, steel bands snapped around my heart and lungs, drawn tight, and I couldn't breathe. I realized Tim was at my side. I could hear him talking, but I couldn't understand a thing he was saying. He shoved a paper bag in my hand, and my head was shoved between my knees. I didn't need to pass out and upset Andrew any further. He was in as much distress as I was, and the farther away he went, the worse it would get for both of us. Growling both mentally and aloud, I pushed myself to my feet. I was stronger than this. *We* were stronger than this. It wasn't as if he wasn't coming back.

Tim wrapped an arm over my shoulders and guided me back toward the living room. "You'll know everything that happens. It'll be just as if you were there yourself," he whispered.

"I can't be without him, but Grandfather shouldn't do this alone. Nobody should have to kill their own child, even when that child is a greedy bastard willing to kill others." A shiver went down my back, and I glanced over my shoulder to see Brenda standing directly behind Tim.

"Yes, Brenda?" Tim's tone was sharp, making it clear he didn't approve of her eavesdropping.

The pain in my chest was making it hard to think clearly, and I just wanted to rest and send as much energy to Andrew as I could. I sighed and closed my eyes for a moment, leaving Brenda to Tim.

"Your rooms are ready." Brenda huffed, clearly pouting. I could only guess that we were an inconvenience in her neatly run schedule. Well, she would just have to get over it.

"Are you ready for some privacy? I can stay with you if you like, or maybe you'd prefer to be alone and sleep?"

"Rest, yes. Please." I nodded without opening my eyes. Tim led me, an arm about my waist, supporting me as he guided me toward the stairs. "I don't want to be alone. Please stay."

"I'd be happy to. Up the steps now."

"Did Charlie have our bags brought in?" I hoped maybe in the bottom of our trunks Stephon had seen fit to leave me at least one pair of comfortable jeans and a T-shirt.

Tim cleared his throat, and Brenda finally responded. "Yes, your bags have been taken to your suites. This way please." She directed Tim down the hall and to the right.

"Can you have someone pick up Andrew's stuff? I'm sure he'll want it once he gets back," I mumbled as we walked past a couple of closed doors that I assumed were other bedrooms.

"I'm sure Brenda will see to it that the maids take care of Andrew's clothes. Don't worry." Tim spoke softly, trying to soothe me.

When we reached our suite, the two large, black-leather-garbed guards I'd thought we'd left at the elevator now stood outside the door.

Tim questioned the first guard. "Did Charlie take the others with her?"

"Yes. Our orders are to remain and guard Prince Lance." The first guard bowed sharply.

"Thank you." It amazed me that these men were willing to risk themselves for me, even die for me… but I wasn't a street-rat orphan anymore. I appreciated their help and tried to remember to show my gratitude.

"It's an honor to serve, Your Highness." The second guard bowed solemnly.

I imagined the resulting popping sound came from Brenda's eyes shooting from her skull and breaking the sound barrier, as her mouth fell open and her jaw hit the floor. I could see the full Technicolor sketch like something out of an old coyote and roadrunner cartoon. I have to admit it might be a bit sadistic of me, but I really liked taking her by surprise. She'd been getting more and more uppity since we'd arrived, and the guards' treatment of me brought her down a peg or two.

"Close your mouth, Brenda. It's not becoming," Tim teased.

"Lord Basil's private suites are these two doors on the right. Your rooms… ah… my lord… are the two doors on the left. Tim is just down the hall, third door on the left, and Charlie's across from him on the right. Is there anything I can get for you? If you're hungry, I can put in a request to the kitchen for something to eat or drink."

"There wasn't time to really enjoy the refreshments downstairs, would you please bring His Highness a fresh pot of tea. Chamomile, this time, I think would be a good idea." Tim hesitated, waiting for confirmation. I nodded. One of the guards opened the door to the suite. "Have you inspected the room?"

"Yes. We did a thorough sweep of the entire penthouse. Brad is not here and has left no hidden devices that we were able to detect anywhere on the premises," the guard stated. "Security records show he hasn't been here for a couple of days."

The first room was large. It appeared to be both a dining area, with a small oak table and chairs, as well as a sitting area, with a love seat, two overstuffed armchairs, and a coffee table. The focal point of the room was a large stone fireplace with a flat screen TV mounted above the mantel. The colors were masculine and conservative, the carpet a deep brown and the furniture in muted tans and creams.

The outer wall was floor-to-ceiling dark tinted glass. The view of the city, stretching out into the distance and below, was extraordinary. I hadn't realized how much time had passed while we'd sat chatting with Grandfather, but the sun was well past midday. It shone through the glass, dancing around the room. A glass sliding door opened out onto a balcony, hidden by the architecture of the building from below. I had an incredible urge to transform into my falcon and fly after my mate and Grandfather. It took everything I had to restrain myself.

Everything all right, Leannan? Andrew's soft question floated into my consciousness. I loved it when he called me Leannan. He always seemed to use that endearment when I needed to hear it the most.

Yes, I'm fine. This is just a bit more painful than I expected. Don't worry about it. Tim is showing me our suite. It's very nice. I tried to sound upbeat and positive for him. But he ached with me without my saying a word.

Hang in there. Stay at the penthouse with Tim. We're almost at the farm. It won't be much longer and we'll be on our way back. Andrew's tone was warm and loving but strained at the same time.

You have a plan, right? I couldn't prevent myself from asking as I walked over to the windows and pressed a hand against the glass.

Grandfather is going in like he's checking on Brad's progress at the estate this season. I'm overhead, watching for his signal. Then Charlie and I will attack. It'll be quick, for Grandfather's sake. I had long ago gotten used to the slight disconnect from my own mind when I saw things through my mate's eyes. From Andrew's perspective, I could tell that he floated on the thermals above a large house. I assumed it was the one Grandfather had said once belonged to my mother's mate, Nathaniel. It was an immense two-story, stone, colonial-style home with a wide front porch.

It's a nice house, but our cottage was much more homey. I missed our cottage, mainly because it was ours. We had put everything into it.

A building is just that, love. Wherever we are, as long as we are together, we are home. If this house doesn't work out, we'll make another place our own. I understood what he meant; it was just that our cottage was my first home and would always be my sanctuary. He'd made it so, and I would always love it over anywhere else.

I forced myself away from the windows and walked into the bedroom. I was greeted by soothing shades of green. The carpet was a moss green, the walls a deep forest green, and the velvet curtains that covered the floor-to-ceiling windows were a lovely shade of evergreen. The bed was covered in a handmade patchwork quilt done in every known shade of green and brown. It was beautiful and very comforting. Our trunks had been placed along one wall. I went to mine and dug through the neatly pressed and packed designer clothes. Damn Stephon… the vamp couldn't even leave me a pair of comfortable jeans.

"Are you finding everything you need?" Tim asked from the doorway.

"No, but that's Stephon's fault."

"Ummm…."

"The room is fine. I'm just trying to keep busy. Damn snob vamp didn't leave me any jeans. Stuck up, no good…." I mumbled as I hung shirts on the hangers I found in the closet.

"The maids can do that for you." Tim watched me move back and forth from the chest to the closet and the dresser. I could tell that my movements were becoming rougher, and weren't doing the clothing much good either. In my irritation, I forced the material to stretch around the ends of the hangers, instead of unbuttoning shirts, like I should.

"I know. You think I could talk Charlie into picking me up some jeans and T-shirts since Stephon destroyed mine?" I grumbled as I realized I was causing more harm than doing good.

"I'm sure she could be persuaded." Tim walked toward the main room, and from the titter of his laughter at my discomfort, it was clear he was amused by my disgust.

With my tension mounting, I left the bedroom in time to see a maid place a tray on the small table and then Tim escort her from the room. Suppressing an irritated growl at having someone unfamiliar in my space, I struggled to relax. Taking a steadying breath and the animal inside by the scruff, I joined Tim at the table while he poured me a cup of chamomile. I forced myself to focus on the delicate china cup. Picking it up with both hands wrapped around the warm porcelain, I could feel the heat, through the fine pottery, seep into my palms. Inhaling deeply of the soothing scent, I tried to let the warmth radiating from the cup calm me. The liquid was hot. I had to sip carefully to keep from scorching my mouth. But it was a wasted effort as nothing, not even scalding tea and the finest bone china, could distract me from the ache in my chest.

Concentration of any kind was beyond my abilities at the moment. Even though physically I was in our suite, mentally I was with Andrew. The separation was causing both of us a deep physical ache that was steadily increasing to debilitating pain. I was trying to draw as much of it into myself as I could, freeing Andrew to do what he needed to with Grandfather. But the strain was beginning to really make me question whether we could survive being apart this early in our mating. In all the years I spent at the hands of people who physically abused me, the pain growing in my chest, like knives slicing through my sternum into my heart, hurt more than anything I'd previously experienced.

Not much longer now, Leannan. Just hang on for me, and we'll be coming back. It's all right, love; let your wolf hunt with me. The distraction will help, and our joint minds might ease the strain. Andrew's hunger for Brad's blood fired my resolve as my mind slipped into the rhythm of his hunt. The desire to rip Brad to shreds colored my vision. I'd become one with Andrew's beast as he hovered above it all.

"I take it Andrew is letting you in on the action." Tim had taken a seat across from me at the table, and I'd completely missed it. So lost in my own world, I'd become oblivious to everything around me.

I nodded. "He's excited. He's flying reconnaissance." I let myself slip into Andrew's vision to see what was going on. "Charlie just jumped out of the back of the car as they passed a row of hedges. They'd slowed down to turn left off the main road before entering the driveway going up to the mansion, when she exited the car." It was so strange to be sitting at a table with Tim and yet the wind flowed, cold and damp with the humidity of the rains earlier in the day, over my feathers. "They've stopped at the gate."

"The driver's clearing them with the guard in order to get in," Tim explained as he took the teacup from my hands. "You're shaking. I don't want you to burn your fingers."

"Oh, sorry," I mumbled before slipping back into Andrew's mind. "They've gone on into the courtyard. Our guards are taking up positions around the mansion." We tucked our wings slightly, dropped, and hovered over the house. Everyone was in place. Andrew watched the limo. "The driver left the car. He's going into the house. Andrew says he's supposed to get Brad and tell him Grandfather's here to check up on his progress. Grandfather's walking toward the barn. Two men just ran out of the house toward Grandfather. More are coming now, including the driver. No sign of Brad." I practically growled with frustration.

Andrew dove past the men, transformed in midair to his white tiger, and landed between Grandfather and the men from the house. Andrew roared, flashing an impressive set of seven-inch fangs any vampire would envy. His tail lashed back and forth, his posture clearly protective of Grandfather, daring the men to make a move. Charlie stepped from the trees and stood on Andrew's left, also in front of Grandfather.

I chuckled. "I bet Grandfather's a bit embarrassed by all the security. He's pretty much wrapped in a guard cocoon. He has to be the most powerful vamp there, and they have him surrounded as if he were in need of all that protection." I watched as the rest of Charlie's men flanked them. The vampires from the house approached slowly, watching the tiger in front of them with extreme caution. Andrew roared again; the men froze, unsure what to do. Grandfather walked between them, placing one hand on Andrew's flank and the other on Charlie's shoulder.

"Where is Brad?" Grandfather didn't yell or accuse anyone, but the response was immediate. The men fell to their knees, their heads bowed.

"Brad isn't here. He left about an hour ago. He didn't tell anyone where he was going. He just took the young shifter boy you gave him to foster and left." The man who spoke appeared to be a butler, wearing a suit coat with tails.

"I was here, Father, when he left. He took the boy and the boy's things, that's all. He didn't say where they were going. I'm sorry, Father. I'm sure he would've stayed if he'd known you were coming," one of the other men who'd followed the butler from the house tried to explain.

"It's all right, my children." Lord Basil hissed between his fangs. "Brad was obviously warned we were coming for him. Whoever did this has committed a betrayal against me and our family." Grandfather walked among his sons, assessing each one before moving on to the next man. "I will be sending someone from the main house to oversee a reorganization of this property and to check its viability. Any of you who do not know where your loyalties lie, I suggest you straighten them out very quickly. Your life does depend upon it."

"Yes, Father" was heard in chorus from all of the men and women at once. I trembled as Grandfather's power washed through Andrew. It was old power, not that being old made it weak—it was more like age had purified it, honed it to a razor's edge. He demanded submission from his children, and they willingly bowed to his greater strength. It was doing strange things to Andrew, who wanted to roll over and show his belly in the worst way. This was not a time for submission, though, when Grandfather needed us to guard his back.

"You will obey the representative I send, unquestioningly, regardless of whom I send. It is likely to be someone you have never met. I will not tolerate disrespect or disobedience, and the new manager will be reporting to me all infractions, which I will deal with harshly." Grandfather returned to Andrew's side and ran a hand over his head, stroking the fur, relieving Andrew of the need to submit to Grandfather's power. "No one is allowed to leave the premises. A security detail will remain to ensure your obedience. Gerard...."

"Yes, Father," the butler said, staring at Grandfather's feet.

"I want a report of all the goings-on in this household since I relinquished it to Brad. I realize it will be quite the report, as it covers many years. Before you begin work on that accounting, you will tell me everything there is to tell about the child Brad brought here. I did not give him leave to have a fosterling shifter child here to use or abuse. You of all my children here should be very aware of my feelings on this topic. They have not changed over the centuries. Shifters are a noble people and to be respected as such."

"Yes, Father. When he first brought the child, I inquired after the boy but was told it was none of my concern as you were fully aware of the situation."

"That is not the case. Brad has more than likely abducted this boy from his family." Grandfather stared at Gerard, his eyes glowing an eerie yellow green with anger.

"I will speak with everyone who had contact at all with him. He was only a boy, maybe six or seven years old." Gerard stared at Grandfather's feet.

"And nobody thought that by today's standards he wasn't a bit young to be separated from his parents? Really, Gerard, I left you in charge here to keep an eye on Brad. I had discussed with you my concerns and that I felt he needed assistance and supervision years ago. You are one of my oldest and brightest sons. I expected more from you." Grandfather hissed his disapproval.

"I'll get the information to you as quickly as possible, Father. I...." Gerard hesitated and seemed to want to speak further but didn't know if he dared.

"What is it, Gerard?" Grandfather's tone softened a bit, the hard edge easing. "You may ask me anything, my son. I am displeased, but I have never been heartless or cruel, nor do I intend to start now."

"I'm sorry, Father." Gerard seemed to gather his courage, "Brad said you were losing touch with reality, that... Illiana's death—"

"Wait, what?" Grandfather interrupted. "Gerard, Illiana is not dead. My mate hibernates, but she is not dead."

"Father, Brad said you were no longer yourself. That you had become delusional. He warned us to prepare for when you...." Gerard stopped and stared up at his father, blood red tears running down his cheeks, his right hand reaching up toward his father before it dropped back to his knees. "Is she.... Is Mother really alive?"

I could see the pain cross Grandfather's face. His son's obvious misery and disbelief that Illiana was alive, his fear that Grandfather was delusional in his grief, tore at the man. It was obvious he cared about his children and they loved him and his mate. As he mourned her absence in her hibernating state, so did they. Brad used this longing against them, distracting Gerard by telling him Illiana was dead and he was about to lose his father to mate madness. It made perfect sense in a horrible, twisted way. How better to undermine from the inside than to use their greatest weaknesses and fears against them.

Grandfather took a step forward and placed a hand on Gerard's head. "I am not delusional, Gerard. Illiana is as you last saw her, hibernating. No more, no less. She sleeps, my son."

The man reached up and wrapped his arms around his father's waist, clinging as only a fearful child can. "I'm so sorry, Father. It's been so long since she was awake, and so many have died in this unnatural hibernation... I—"

"When things have calmed down here, I think you should come for a visit and see her. She would like that, you know. Just because she sleeps doesn't mean she isn't aware of your presence. You are all welcome to visit anytime you like." Grandfather sighed, running his fingers through Gerard's hair for a moment before turning to Andrew. "We can do no more here. Let's go home for now, Grandson."

There were gasps as Andrew growled, then leaped into the air, transformed in midleap from tiger to falcon, and circled the area once before landing on Grandfather's outstretched gauntleted wrist.

It was over just that quickly. Brad had escaped. He had kidnapped a shifter child, and nobody seemed to care before Grandfather arrived. I was angry, frustrated, anxious for the missing child, but overall I was relieved nobody was hurt and they were coming home.

CHAPTER 6

"I SUPPOSE it could be a coincidence." A tiny crease formed between Tim's eyebrows.

He didn't believe that any more than I did. Someone had warned Brad, and that person was close enough that they knew we'd been coming for him. I was pissed. Anger burned just under the surface, like lava boiling under my skin. The beast in me wanted to hunt the traitor and rip him to shreds.

"It has to be someone here, Tim. Someone in this house is working for Brad and against Grandfather. But who?" I snarled, feeling my jaw ache, and my skin erupted in gooseflesh, warning me I was about to become rather furry if I didn't get a grip on my animal side.

"It would have to be someone very naïve to risk Lord Basil's wrath. I've seen what my father is capable of over the centuries. He is a born vampire. There is no humanity within him. The loving, doting grandfather and father is not the man he shows to the rest of the world." Tim literally seemed to tremble at the thought. "Not that he's bloodthirsty or cruel. He's a fair-minded man. If you deal with him honorably, he treats you in kind. Cross him, and few survive to tell about it. Whether it's a quick death or not depends on the crime." Tim grinned. "You don't live through the Dark Ages without learning how to bite, and he can be ruthless."

"Does he have enemies?" I'd never considered my genial, loving, green-eyed grandfather as having enemies. The kindness and acceptance he showed me so overwhelmed all my barriers, I had no fear of him. The man believed me to be part of his family, and even after feeling the power he wielded at the farm, I knew he'd never hurt me.

"Yes, but it's different now. We don't wage wars and send armies out to do battle." Tim said, sounding every bit the frustrated teacher. I growled, stood, and then restlessly paced about the room.

53

"Most of the world is civilized, and the areas where battle would go unnoticed are so volatile that few of us care to reside there. Blood has become a commodity among our people, bought and sold on our own markets. Just like food is among humans." Tim drummed his fingers on the table.

I glared out the window before turning back on him, my arms wrapped around my stomach. My anger wasn't helping the ill feeling the separation from my mate was causing.

"Are you all right?"

"No, not really." I closed my eyes and rested my arm against the cool glass of the window. I could feel the prickle of quills forcing their way through my skin. I ached to become a falcon and fly after my missing mate. "Andrew's taking some of the pain I'd been holding for both of us so he could help Grandfather."

"But you're all right?"

"I just need to be with him. The animal's a little hard to control right now. I feel like I'm pumped full of adrenaline and there's nowhere for it to go." I pushed away from the window and walked toward the table. "You should leave. I don't think I can stay human, and the state of mind the beast is in won't be pretty."

"You would never hurt me, regardless of how upset your beast is." Tim smiled gently, and I sighed and let go.

Forcing myself into a four-legged form instead of one with wings was one of the hardest things I had ever done. I heard the rip of material as the quicksilver took me, and emerged as my brown wolf. The frustration caged in my body expressed itself the only way it could in my wolf body, my claws clicking on the hardwood as I paced before the windows. Tim spoke softly, soothingly behind me, not that it did much good. My wolf didn't care what he was saying. I wanted my mate.

Stephon's Story—Central Europe
620 AD

THE EERIE light of torches bounced off the grotto walls, reflecting off the wet earth columns made up of mineral deposits that held up the enormous underground ceiling. The firelight made the shadows of columns appear to be living giants moved among the gathered vampires.

Caius had spoken with the dwarves and requested a venue where his people could meet in private, away from the curious eyes of humans. They were given access to an enormous cave, which would protect their drones from the sunlight, as they didn't have their parents' immunity to the deadly star's rays.

Caius had sent messengers to the heads of the families, and they had agreed, some reluctantly, that a formal governing body to make decisions for the growing vampire population had become a necessity, especially as the war against the fae was escalating and becoming bloodier. Whole families were being isolated and wiped out. It was time to get organized, and maybe with the help of the other races, they would be able to protect themselves from the bloodthirsty fae.

The cavern was filled to overflowing with vampires and drones from across the world. Some had human servants; others had brought shifters with them. It was almost amusing to see the pockets of families, as the vampires segregated themselves with their supporters into groups.

Caius mounted some steps to stand on a raised slab of earth in the center of the room. Stephon stood on the step just below his father and surveyed those gathered, both supporters and adversaries alike.

"This is neutral ground." Caius's voice echoed about the cavern. Silence soon fell over the crowd as people hushed each other. When the silence was complete, Caius said again, "This is neutral ground. No life can be taken here in this cavern. It is a sacred place of the gods and the dwarves. If you have to fight, take it outside. There will be no bloodshed here in this place."

"And if we do?" a vampire voice from the far back of the cave echoed around the room.

"According to the dwarves, you and your family and descendants will be damned for all eternity until your line no longer exists. I have seen dwarven curses in action, so it is not something I would recommend anyone challenge," Caius answered with a chuckle echoed by vampire voices around the room.

"Caius, kindly tell us why you have demanded all of us be here. Many have left things rather unguarded in our own territories in order to attend, and I for one am not exceedingly happy about it," a male vampire with bristle-brush red hair said from the left side of the cavern.

"Yes, Caius. Please enlighten us," a female vampire off to the right hissed.

"We are all here because, as a people, we need to draw together to fight our common enemy. In order to do that, we need a unifying government that can consolidate our people, plan for the future, and organize our forces so we can protect ourselves. The fae are a threat larger than can be handled by any single family and possibly greater than our species alone can control." Caius spoke loudly as he addressed the assembly. "We must decide the best form of organization for our people. We must all agree to abide by their decisions absolutely and trust their judgment, whether we choose a monarchy and a king or queen, or maybe we will choose a democracy as the Romans first envisioned, or choose more simply a council of family leaders. Hard decisions need to be made, and we need to choose those who can make them and lead us into the future."

"So, what? Do we fight to be king?" another male voice called from the back.

"Shut up, Johann. You are too stupid and a drone, for god's sake. Your kind have no say here," a female voice called from across the hall.

"I have as much right to speak as he does, Gwenore! At least my family has never sunk to slavery, so disgraceful." The drone Johann growled at the woman.

People's voices started hollering back and forth as clashing groups ignited old arguments and fights. Caius frowned. He had an arm raised and his mouth open as if to speak, but could only seem to watch as the assembly degenerated into shouting matches across the cavern. He turned defeated eyes to his son as Stephon joined him on the dais.

"Please, this assembly cannot slide back into old grudge matches between families. That is why, before entering, you all were sworn on your honor to be peaceful and that all feuds would be left outside this place," Stephon hollered over the crowds. "We will meet in peace, or those who draw the first blood will be left without weapons at the mercy of the fae. You know I will see that threat carried out, on my honor, so be very careful of your next words."

An uncomfortable silence descended. Caius placed a hand on Stephon's shoulder. "Thank you, my son." He faced the assembly.

"I apologize to you both, Caius… Stephon. I lost control. I should not have antagonized the drone. I am above such pettiness as squabbling with a drone." Gwenore cast a haughty gaze down her nose in the direction of where Johann stood.

"Enough, woman! Before you humiliate yourself further." Stephon snapped his fangs, clicking them ominously.

"We will have peace here," Caius demanded. "If we cannot meet in this place of neutral territory, where none of us can claim the land, without bickering and anarchy, our race is lost. The fae will have won. We will have divided ourselves so all they have to do is pick us off one at a time," Caius yelled at the assembly as if they were rabble at his feet.

"So do you elect yourself to be our king, Caius?" The woman called over the assembly. "You who were counsel to pharaohs in centuries past. You who are probably the oldest and most powerful among us." She stepped in front of the platform, and Stephon then realized she was the same Gwenore from his youth. She and her mate were supposed to be dead, sacrificed to Sekhmet years before.

Stephon scowled at his father, who merely shrugged his shoulders.

"I couldn't kill our own just because a fae wanted them dead," Caius whispered to Stephon in answer to his unasked question, before turning back to the assembly. "I have no desire to be king. I have in the past worked in the courts of monarchs and tried to help them serve their people well. The most important thing I learned was absolute power corrupts absolutely. No one man, regardless of how well intentioned, should have complete control," Caius said to the silent room.

"So what would you suggest?" Rufus sneered as he joined his mother, Gwenore.

"I would be in favor of a council of elders to lead us into the future. They can set the laws, write treaties of friendship with other species, settle disputes between families."

"Who should serve on this council, and how long do they serve? Who runs the council?" a vampire Stephon didn't recognize asked.

"These decisions cannot be undertaken lightly. Are we in agreement that we do not want a monarchy, but a council?" Caius asked of the assembly. "All in favor say yea...."

"Yea!" A loud call went up.

"Opposed, say nay."

"Nay." There were a few nays, but the majority was clearly with the yeas.

"The majority has spoken. If this gathering is all right with me leading in this case, I would ask that we all retire to our family leaders and discuss the different council options available to us. If there should be time limits on how long each member can serve and how new members should be added, or even if they should be allowed to be added, and how many people should be on the council. These are all things that must be discussed and agreed upon." Caius placed a hand on Stephon's shoulder.

"These are all good questions, Caius. I agree they need to be discussed, but we cannot afford to wait too long," Basil said from where he was leaning against a wall. "The fae are amassing along the northern borders of my land. I cannot afford to be here for long and leave my family without my strength or leadership. I say we reconvene with the family heads in order to make the final decisions tomorrow. If the decisions made by the family heads need to be corrected at a later date, then so be it, but right now I need all the help I can get to defend my family. After I leave here, I am stopping in the shifter villages close to my land. I must have their assistance or without question, we will fail."

Murmurs of both concern and disbelief were heard about the cavern. "Surely things are not that desperate?"

"Yes, I am that desperate. I'm willing to ask for any help I can get in order to protect my family," Basil snapped, his fangs glinting in the torch light.

"You are not alone. Many of us are asking for assistance from our shifter neighbors." Caius nodded. "Stephon and I have also enlisted their help in holding our borders. They are resilient and iron willed when it comes to protecting their families. I hold them in the highest regard and respect."

"It is good to know that I am not the only one who carries no prejudice against others." Basil narrowed his eyes, daring others to challenge his comment.

"I can assure you, I as well as many others want these proceedings to move forward as quickly as possible," Caius said.

"Well, I for one want to go back to my family and discuss these questions. Until tomorrow. Gentlemen." Gwenore's skirts swished as she headed toward the entrance of the caves.

CHAPTER 7

Present Day

I WANTED to howl and cry, but instead I lay down by the windows and closed my eyes. I focused internally, taking in Andrew's view. I could hear Grandfather's voice as clearly as if I were in the car with them.

"Charlie, have the driver stop the car. We're just outside the city, and Andrew can get to Lance faster if he flies, while we deal with the traffic." I felt the car roll to a stop and watched as Grandfather pressed a button and opened the sunroof in the ceiling of the limo. "I know you are both in pain, even though you are good at hiding it. Thank you for wanting to relieve me of this nasty burden. I appreciate your sacrifice on my account. Now, go to your mate. Charlie will keep me company the rest of the journey." Grandfather ran a finger gently along Andrew's feathered breast, petting the falcon. "It's an honor to have a shifter of your caliber at my side, and I'm pleased to call you family."

Andrew bobbed his head and clucked, then eased his way to the end of Grandfather's gauntleted wrist as he held it up through the opening. With the downstroke of outstretched wings, Andrew launched himself into the afternoon sky. I could feel the wind flow over his feathers as he pushed himself as fast as he could go. His calls echoed across the city, reflecting off the surface of the buildings as if they were wild canyon walls. He was coming. The relief was not quite instantaneous, but knowing he was on the way made me feel more in control of the situation. My wolf rose and trotted into the bedroom, where I shifted and dressed, chuckling to myself at how horrified Stephon would be that I'd ruined one of his carefully selected outfits.

I walked out of the room and tried to smile at a rather upset-looking Tim. "Andrew's on the wing. He'll be here in a few minutes. Grandfather let him out

59

of the car at the edge of the city. Said he could fly here faster than they could drive through traffic." Standing in front of the glass door that led out onto the veranda, I could feel Andrew closing in on the penthouse quickly. I could feel the muscles of his chest pump and his lungs expand to draw in oxygen as he flew. Grasping the handle, I opened both the door and screen so Andrew could fly straight into the room. The outside air was cold, but Tim wouldn't care. Drones didn't feel the cold like we did.

"You're feeling better." Tim sat back in his chair, relaxing for the first time since we'd come upstairs. "I was worried I'd have to defend the household staff from you after you chose to devour them, if they took much longer."

"Sorry. Being separated is physically painful. We're so connected that sometimes, when I wake up in the morning, I'm not sure which body is mine anymore. There were days I almost believed I was the one sitting through classes, dealing with Stephon's mood swings, and that it was Andrew who had the unfortunate family life." I walked back to the table as Tim stood.

"I had no idea the connection ran so deep. I mean, shifters talk about being one, but I always thought it was temporary. It's mind boggling to think about the ramifications of having your lives become so enmeshed...." Tim seemed stunned. "Do you know how long this condition is supposed to last?"

"We really don't know. Andrew's father, Max, seems to remember stories of mates where the joining lasted a lifetime. He and Laura mentally link during the full moon, but it doesn't last long—anywhere from six to twenty-four hours, at the most." I rubbed a hand across the back of my neck, the tight muscles loosening as Andrew drew nearer. "It was more intense and lasted longer when they were young. Maybe the connection will relax once we've grown accustomed to one another. Or it could remain as it currently is throughout our lives." I rubbed my hands up and down my arms as gooseflesh arose on them from the growing chill in the room.

"It's just fascinating. There are so many differences between yourselves and the rest of the shifters, and yet, at the same time, you're the same species." Tim seemed to be warming to the subject. "Are you glad of the connection, or is it unnerving knowing you have no secrets, no privacy from Andrew?"

"To be honest, I like the connection, most of the time. Today... not so much. There were times I felt as though our connection was stretched so thin, I was being ripped apart. But Andrew is very close, and I'm... more whole. I feel more like myself again."

"If you don't mind my asking, I'd like to document some of the differences between your connection and the connections between shifters of mixed blood. If there is a correlation between the strength of the bloodline and the strength of the connection between mates, it would be good to have a reference for the future." I couldn't help but be pleased with Tim's enthusiasm. The good doctor was always more than willing to help. "Will you let me know if you feel the connection changing, or if it ceases? I know it's intrusive...."

Tim backpedaled a bit, realizing how personal this was getting. There were so few people around who knew anything about pureblooded shifters like myself that he took every opportunity to learn more. I'd do whatever it took, including talking about my connection to Andrew if it could further our understanding of what our limits were and what we were becoming.

"Sure, I guess we can do that." I sighed with relief as Andrew glided in through the open doorway, landed on the back of the chair next to me, and pressed himself against me.

"I'll give the two of you some privacy. If you need me, I'll be just down the hall." Tim excused himself as Andrew transformed to his beautiful, wild-eyed human self.

My mate stood tall, proud, and naked beside me. He had no sooner become a man than I was surrounded by his arms, his lips crashed against my own, demanding my submission to his desire. He trembled as I slid my hands around his waist and up his back, pressing the length of my body against him. I did not see or hear Tim leave, but when we broke apart to breathe, he was gone.

Stephon's Story—Northern Europe, what today would be part of Siberia
614 AD

"IS THIS really necessary, Father?" Stephon complained as they waited for admission into the court of the dwarves. "Why can't we just let the fae handle their own problems? Sure, they are taking a toll on the humans, but that race is so proliferate. Their propagation rates, if left unhindered, could overwhelm the planet. Surely we needn't be so overly concerned about the wellbeing of our food."

"We've discussed this. The dwarves have abstained from interference. The human population has even named the killings after the dark fae, calling it the Black Death." Caius put a hand on his son's shoulder. "There are whole villages of people who have been obliterated, corpses with black hands and feet, black around the lips and nose.... What do these signs point to?"

"They've had their souls consumed. The black marks are the last points of contact the soul energy had with the body as it was violently removed." Stephon grimaced and gave a shake of his head. "Horrible way to die."

"Yes, it is, but it is how the fae feed. We require blood to survive. Shifters require the adrenalin rush of the hunt to satisfy their bestial nature. The dwarves draw energy directly from the earth beneath our feet. The fae feed on soul energy." Caius stated much more matter-of-fact than Stephon could have ever imagined his father being where human lives were concerned.

"It is still a distinctly horrible way to feed." Stephon stared off into a dark corner of the stone-walled room in which they sat. It was more the conversation that made the room feel heavy and claustrophobic than the actual room itself. The warm earth-toned walls, deep green moss-colored handwoven rugs covering the floor, and the chairs, hand-carved from ancient dark woods and comfortably upholstered, made the room inviting.

"We and the fae are not so different. We both have the potential to kill. But it is the dark fae who take greatest pleasure in the total obliteration of their victim, feeding upon the soul. Although I do not necessarily believe that the barely sentient living shells of humanity that are left behind after the light fae feed, is necessarily a kinder fate. The dark fae's method is fatal, without question. They also consume the flesh of their victim, which I find disgusting. But death may be preferable to living without—or even living with only a fraction of—one's soul." Caius gave his son's shoulder a reassuring squeeze.

"But what gives us the right to pass judgment on them? By isolating them from their food source, are we not condemning them to death?" Stephon asked, hoping his father had an acceptable answer, but received only silence.

The door opened, and a young dwarf entered. Stephon couldn't tell if it was male or one of the few females their species produced. The squat youth had dark-brown braids to its knees. The darker the hair, the younger the dwarf. Children were born with jet-black hair, and the elderly passed from the world with hair as white as snow.

"Please follow me. King Stauflis and his counselors will see you now." The dwarf smiled, motioning toward the door it had just entered through.

"Thank you." Caius stood and followed the youth to a chamber that could have been a private dining hall as much as a throne room. A long table of a medium height, clearly larger than what the short dwarves themselves would require sat in the middle of the hall. The chairs around it varied in height and width, obviously able to accommodate most anyone comfortably. The dwarves took great pride in being good hosts to all of their guests.

Three of the seats were already occupied. King Stauflis sat at the head of the table with his advisors, Neabu and Bodon.

"Please, Caius, my friend, join us and tell me what has brought you to this court today." King Stauflis motioned to his left.

"Thank you, King Stauflis." Caius stood behind one of the chairs and motioned to Stephon. "May I present my son, Stephon."

"Welcome, Stephon, son of Caius. May the earth always bless you with her bounty, young vampire." King Stauflis grinned, his white teeth barely flashing before being covered by his graying mustache.

"Thank you, Your Highness." Stephon bowed smartly, and Caius nodded slightly before motioning that his son should take the chair to his right.

"We appreciate your agreeing to see us, unannounced." Caius sat down and smiled at his host before leaning forward in his chair. "I admit this is not a social visit."

"If this is about the war with the fae, I am sure you are already aware of my stance on the subject. We will not be involved. We have no love for the fae, but neither do we have any love for the humans over which this war is being waged. My kind have never been prolific. There are few dwarves under the earth, and we have no desire to draw the attention of the fae and die out as a race." King Stauflis frowned, sitting forward and placing his hands firmly on the table.

"I suppose in a roundabout way, this does relate to the war, but we are not asking for your participation. What we require is a way to confine the fae so they can no longer cause any harm to the other sentient races of this world." Caius held up a hand. "The events of the last couple of years, with the fae's continued attacks upon the human population aside, show that the fae's civil war has affected us all, including the dwarves. They kill people of all races indiscriminately."

"It is true. We have had a number of deaths among our people. Children have gone missing, some later found with the telltale markings of having their souls forcibly removed. Others are never seen again. Emissaries to the light court have been returned to us, empty shells of their former lively selves. Some later commit suicide, returning what is left of their soul to the earth mother, unable to live as they are. Those who have been brave enough to approach the dark court are either refused entry or have never been seen again." Bodon nodded in agreement with Caius.

"Yes, but what guarantee can you offer that by participating in whatever scheme you have concocted we won't be dooming ourselves to being targeted by the fae?" King Stauflis let his gaze go from Caius to Stephon and back again.

"Firstly, this isn't my plan alone. The shifters, who have become an invaluable ally in this war and who have taken great losses at the hands of the fae, are in agreement that something must be done to contain them." Caius beamed with pride as he nodded to Stephon on his right. "My son is working closely with the prince. They are coordinating efforts between the vampire warriors and the packs. So far they have had great success in isolating the fae and in some cases evacuating the humans whenever possible."

"The shifters agree to caging another species? I am surprised that they would feel this would be a viable option." Bodon ran his fingers over his white beard in contemplation. "They are such free spirits. I can't imagine they would resort to this type of punishment lightly."

"I agree it is highly unlikely that they would lend their support to this. They are the wildest race and value freedom most of all. Their animal spirits would rebel against the very idea of caging anyone. If given a choice, they would take death over an option such as this." Neabu waved a hand in dismissal. "You must be lying. No shifter would agree to this. Do you think we are ignorant of the ways of others, just because we live beneath the earth?"

"I assure you, councilor, my father does not lie. Prince Atol has discussed this with his father and their advisors at great length. It has taken years of discussion and loss. Many attempted truce talks became bloodbaths as the fae refused to restrain their nature, and the dark and light attacked each other as well as the emissaries of other species. One such encounter led to the death of King Henry's brother, his mate, and young son." Stephon paused and glanced over at King Stauflis. "Even monarchs are not above the pain of losing beloved members of their own families. They are willing and readily back the separation of the fae from the rest of us."

"Well said, young Stephon." King Stauflis nodded. "Royalty is not above feelings. But acting on our emotions can lead to rash decisions we would not normally consider."

"Exactly what type of incarceration are you suggesting, and are you willing to give of yourselves to provide some of the magic that maintains such a boundary?" Neabu steepled his fingers, his elbows on the table as he leaned forward.

"I have been authorized by the heads of the families of the vampires to agree that we will contribute if we can to the creation of this jail." Caius placed his hands flatly on the polished surface of the table. "We will do whatever it takes, but my people do not have the magical abilities either you or the shifters have. We do have the advantage of greater experience, as we generally live longer than both the shifters and the dwarves. So we do ask that your people who are the most magically gifted of the species create a place for the fae. I'm not saying it has to be horrible, but it must be somewhere away from the rest of us. That way maybe they can evolve and learn to control their desires when left to their own devices."

"That is commendable and an interesting idea. What say you, young Stephon?" King Stauflis asked.

"The shifters agree that the fae need to be controlled. They say the fae in their feeding frenzies have destroyed whole forests of life in the north. They have been killing off not only human life, but destroying large populations of animals as well, even though they do not feed from these other species. Nothing is exempt from their appetites and destructive tendencies." Stephon contemplated all the dwarves at the table before directing his remarks to the king. "Prince Atol apologizes to this council for not attending this meeting himself, as he and his father are currently defending the borders of their territory. But they want to reassure you that we have their complete cooperation in finding a way to restrain the fae's feeding frenzy." Stephon focused his attention on King Stauflis.

"Well, it seems we are all in agreement. We will ask the Earth Mother who guides us how best to handle her children the fae." King Stauflis stood, his two counselors standing with him. "Please be our guests tonight before returning to your homes. When we have an answer for you, we will be in touch."

"Thank you, Your Highness, but the night is our preferred time to travel. If you do not mind, we will see ourselves out." Caius grinned and flashed the slightest bit of fang.

"Certainly, Caius. It is good to see you, and I hope that you will visit us again, maybe in a less official capacity." King Stauflis rose and held his arms wide as he walked over to Caius, who bent down in order to allow the four-foot-tall monarch hug him.

"Thank you, King Stauflis. It would be my honor to do so. Thank you for the invitation." Caius patted the king's back before standing to his full height and leading his son from the room, where they were met by a dwarf and led from the underground caverns to where their horses were waiting for them.

"Well, that went better than we could have hoped," Stephon said as he climbed onto his horse.

"Don't assume anything just yet. The dwarves are rarely straightforward. They will be in contemplation with the Earth Mother. That can take anywhere from days to years, sometimes even decades before they have a firm answer and will act upon it. By that time half the population could be decimated," Caius grumbled, urging his horse away at a fast canter. "I'd have been happier if he would have come out and said they would take our request under consideration. At least that has a more limited time frame, that of weeks instead of the possibility of being left hanging for years."

CHAPTER 8

Present Day

"I'VE MISSED you so much." I could finally breathe, and my heart was back where it belonged in my chest. The pain was gone but for a vague memory and the dull ache of chest muscles overused, yet relaxed after a hard workout.

"I've missed you too, Leannan." Andrew slid his fingers through my hair, holding my head to the side. He leaned into the crook of my neck and trailed soft wet kisses along the tendon from shoulder to ear. The greeting was forceful and carnal, our desire so hot it threatened to overwhelm us. Andrew let up slightly, and we stood resting our foreheads together, grasping onto the remains of our control, reveling being in each other's arms. We both needed the reassurance we could get only with a hands-on approach, touching one another, holding each other close. Slowly, the wild, ragged look receded from Andrew's eyes and our touches became bolder, more intimate. A fire of a different kind grew in those sky blue depths, until our breathing became ragged for an entirely different reason.

Andrew growled softly as his newly reformed fingers slid across the mating mark on my shoulder, nuzzling my neck as he held me.

"The others will be here before too long. Our trunks are in the bedroom. I'm sure Grandfather will want to see us when he arrives." I pouted. I couldn't help it. I wanted to keep Andrew to myself. To lose myself in him for just a little while, to curl up on the bed and have Andrew wrapped around me. To feel his hot naked skin caress mine.

"Come on." Andrew took my hand and led me into the bedroom. Everything was as I'd left it earlier; some things were hung, others left piled in the trunks. He pulled out a pair of tailored black slacks and a red sweater, and laid them on a chair beside the bed. With his hand still in mine, he drew me over to the bed and gave me a gentle nudge that had me sitting on the edge. He settled himself behind me, one leg tucked under himself, and the other dangling off the side of the bed.

I groaned wantonly at the feeling of his hands massaging my shoulders, trying to ease the tension keeping me in a stranglehold. I wanted to relax against him but sat rigid beneath his touch. It'd been days since we'd left the cottage, and I hadn't unwound since we closed the door.

"It's going to be all right, Lance. I'm here. We're fine, better than fine, actually."

"Oh, and how do you figure that?"

"We may not have gotten Brad, but there's no longer a question about who our enemy is." He vigorously rubbed my arms and pulled me against his chest. Then wrapping his arms around my chest, he rested his head on my shoulder by my ear and kissed my neck. I leaned into his embrace, liking the feel of his rough five o'clock shadow as it scratched up the side of my neck. I trembled uncontrollably, clenching at his arms, which just held me tighter as I pressed back into his chest.

The stress of everything since we'd left the cottage, which I'd been suppressing in order to be able to think and function, flooded me. A meltdown of epic proportions was headed straight for me, and there was nothing I could do to waylay it any further. The tremors gave way to a short bout of hyperventilating, followed by rocking in an almost catatonic state. Through it all, Andrew was supportive and gentle, doing exactly what I needed. He held me together and coaxed me back from the edge of my manic state. I hadn't felt this panicked since I first accepted our bond and mated with Andrew.

"I keep waiting," I whispered once I could get the words out.

"Waiting for what?" He kissed my cheek and nuzzled the skin beneath my ear.

"For this to be just a dream. I'm going to wake up, and everything will fall apart." I closed my eyes.

"This, my love, is most definitely real." He nibbled on my ear, and every nerve ending along my spine lit up with pleasure. I gasped and clutched at his arm even tighter. "If not, then let us dream together forever." His love surrounded me, flowed through me as it poured through our link, filling my heart until I thought I might burst.

"I love you too." Our emotions and everything that was our being, merged in a moment of complete clarity. Even though we were connected during our time apart, the link demanded total submersion, and in seconds, I felt myself relive Andrew's experience when away from my side, and he received mine. A wave of energy loss swept over us as the merge released us and we once again became ourselves.

"Grandfather seems to understand us almost more than we do ourselves. I think we should ask him what he knows." Andrew rubbed his face against my hair before slowly licking the shell of my ear and kissing down the side of my neck to bite at my mating mark on my shoulder.

"You really believe we can trust him?" I wanted to believe, I truly did. But, after years of abuse, I was hesitant to believe that someone could want me to be part of their family. That was almost as frightening as admitting to myself that I craved a family of my own.

"Yes. He seems to be genuinely fond and protective of you." Andrew's hot breath sent shivers through my body that had nothing to do with my panic attack and everything to do with his stoking the lust burning in my heart for the man. I arched my back and eased my ass tighter into his groin. I could feel his hard-on against the small of my back.

Dangerous… you are just as dangerous as I am, I thought pointedly at him. He gave an amused snort at my teasing and eased his hand down my waist, his fingers gliding along the hardening length of my growing erection. I groaned and felt my hips pitch forward to rub against his hand, seeking the exquisite friction. I tried to continue the conversation but had to struggle to hold my thoughts together. *I want to believe in him.* My thoughts became a bit scattered as I lolled my head to the side, giving Andrew more room to work his magic.

"Tim thinks it's his fault and that he should've brought me here right away instead of leaving me at the farm with your family." Even though Andrew knew my fears, it felt better talking to him about it, voicing my doubts aloud.

"Give him a chance. Get to know him before you pass judgment." Andrew sucked on my earlobe, sending pulsating shivers down my spine with each pass of his tongue over my skin. His hands took possession of my body.

Hissing through my teeth, my eyes closed, all my thoughts evaporated as he plucked at my nipple. I raked my hands over his thighs. Stretching back behind me, I cupped his balls in one hand and held his cock in the other. He gripped my erection and slid his thumbnail along the crease in the hood of my cock as I gasped. "Don't start anything you can't finish. Grandfather will be here soon," I teased.

Andrew growled softly, the vibrations sinking into my body, until I could feel myself groaning with him. It felt wonderful. I didn't want him to stop. "He can wait. We haven't made love since the cottage. And the quickies at Stephon's, the few times we were left alone while he was gone, don't count. I want to feel you wrapped around me, holding me, squeezing me...." Andrew's hands were magic, enticing and seducing, until I could only agree, my need to feel him as powerful as his desire to have me. "Buried so deep inside you, I can feel your heartbeat."

"God, yes," I panted and turned to face Andrew. His lips covered mine, demanding my submission in a passionate kiss full of power and desire. Andrew pulled me around him and laid me back onto the bed. I sighed as he stroked my sides, his mouth latching onto one of my taut nipples. Quick, featherlight licks raised gooseflesh along my arms and legs. Reaching down for him as he crawled up to lie at my side, I wrapped my arms around his neck. The gentle touch of his fingertips stroked along my forehead and down across my cheekbones. His gaze was glued to the skin his touch traced as it followed the line of my jaw, along my neck, and down my body. Rolling slightly to the side, I hitched my leg around his waist and drew him back with me as I rolled onto my back.

We lay pressed together, kissing, with the exquisite feeling of his engorged cock slowly thrusting against mine, pressed between us. With a last hard grind of our hips, Andrew pushed himself up and back, into a kneeling position between my thighs. Lifting my legs up over his shoulders, my butt rested against his abs and my back lay on his thighs. He draped his arm around my thighs, and he settled a hand against my abs, holding my hips still. I whimpered as two of his fingers slid around the edge of my needy hole. I ached to have him inside, and at this point, I'd be happy with even fingers if I couldn't have his cock.

"Andrew!" I begged.

"Shhh... I know." I heard him spit and felt the slip of his wet digits ringing my twitching pucker. My breath caught as he slid his thumb inside and began stretching me open. He pumped it a couple times before spitting again and switching fingers, getting me ready for him. "You are so tight, babe," Andrew moaned. His digits pumped into me as I struggled to meet his movements, trying to push my hips up. But I didn't have the leverage I needed, and with his hand holding me in place, all I could do was feel.

"Need you," I panted breathlessly.

"So tight," he hissed. I whimpered as his fingers disappeared, replaced by his mouth, sucking at my hole. His tongue circled my throbbing muscle, his teeth nipped at me, taunting me. He drew back a bit and spit onto my hole before pressing hard into me, fucking me with his tongue.

"Oh... oh!" I screamed as he slid his fingers inside along with his tongue. I moaned as he twisted and curled them, catching my hot spot.

"No more... I can't.... No... I want...." I slid my fingertips along his sweat-slicked thighs, clawing for purchase.

"What do you want, Leannan? Tell me."

I stared up at Andrew, his blue eyes ringed in wolf amber, pointed fangs glistening from his open mouth. I couldn't answer, spellbound by those eyes filled with lusty desire. Andrew nuzzled my inner thigh before biting sharply into the meat of the muscle. I squealed and moaned; the sharp pinch of pain followed by the warm burn had me arching my back for more. "More... you... inside...."

Lining himself up, he spit into his hand and stroked his cock. He dragged the engorged head over my anus, teasing me, and I felt my hole twitch in anticipation. His eyes met mine as he pressed in, until the wiry curls that encased his balls brushed against my thighs. "You okay?" Andrew held on to my hips as if that were the only thing keeping him from pounding me into the headboard.

"Good...." I managed to get out, nodding quickly. I was burning from the inside out, the heat coming from him sending flames shooting through my body. I needed him to move, and move now!

He threw back his head and clutched my thighs, and began pounding into my depths. I thrust my hips in time with his motions, the slap of flesh filling the room. The waves of passion flowed through us, uniting us in a world where only the other existed. We moved as one in our dance, to music as unique as the beat of our united hearts.

"Gonna cum...." I clutched at Andrew's shoulders, my fingernails digging into his flesh.

"Yes.... Now, Lance!"

"Andrew!" He thrust deeply inside, his body quivering as he filled me with his hot cum, while mine flowed between our stomachs, making both of us sticky. Andrew slid his arms from around my thighs as he fell forward, catching himself on his hands just above my chest before collapsing, half on top of me, half slightly to the right.

"Don't move. Stay with me," I moaned, clenching tired muscles, trying to hold him inside as his limp cock slid from me.

"I'm sorry," Andrew whispered and stroked my hair and gently kissed my lips. "I didn't mean to be so rough."

"It's okay. I just... I like feeling connected to you physically. Even spent, I can feel you and it makes me feel whole." I caressed his face. "I love you so much."

"I love you too. I'll remember... I like being inside you too, so if I move more carefully, instead of collapsing, we may be able to stay joined longer." Andrew snuggled me tighter against him, his nose brushing along the outer edge of my ear.

We cuddled, enjoying the moment of peace in each other's arms, knowing we would have to join the others soon. I wished the evening was over so we could just continue making love. With a sigh I stared into Andrew's eyes. This would have to be enough... for now. I rose gingerly from the bed, feeling the burn of well-used muscles. I held out a hand and Andrew clasped it in his, as we walked into the bathroom. It was a quick shower, strictly kept to the business of getting clean, before we returned to the bedroom and got dressed. Moving through the sitting room, we then left the suite. A guard stood outside the door, watching us as we stepped into the hallway.

"Where's Tim?" I flushed red with embarrassment, wondering how much his very sensitive hearing caught of our recent activities.

"He is in his room, two doors down on the right, Your Highness. He advised me to come for him if you ask after him."

"Thank you. Will you please let him know we're returning to the living room downstairs to wait for Grandfather and Charlie?"

"Yes, Your Highness." He let us proceed down the hall in front of him.

I frowned. I wasn't ready to be addressed as 'Your Highness,' especially as the Royals hadn't acknowledged me. I stopped, Andrew with me. The guard practically stumbled to keep from running into us. Prince I might be by blood, but not by title... not yet, at least.

"Please, can't you just call me Lance?"

"Ah.... No, Your Highness. Um... I could address you as Lord Lance, if you'd prefer." The guard stared at the floor, since to make eye contact with a superior was considered a challenge.

"Fine, I guess." I shook my head, turning around, and headed back down the hall, leaving the guard behind at the top of the stairs. Andrew laughed all the way into the lounge. "Just wait till they start calling you Prince Consort," I reminded him. His chagrin at the thought, and halting laughter, came through loud and clear. "Not so funny now, is it?"

We entered the living room, and Brenda was immediately there. I watched her as she saw Andrew and realized he shouldn't be here.

Her startled surprise shone in her wide eyes before she schooled her features into a stern pout. "Is there anything I can get you, Lord Lance, Lord Andrew?" She stood there, wringing her hands as if she didn't know what to do.

"No, Brenda, we're fine." I turned away, ignoring her. She was a narrow-minded human and seemed to have a grudge against us without bothering to get to know us.

71

Tim came up behind her and placed a hand on her shoulder. She must have been startled because I heard her squeak, and Tim chuckle. "I apologize for surprising you, Brenda."

"Where did he come from?" she demanded of Tim. I saw her waving a finger at Andrew as I glanced over my shoulder.

"Andrew can fly. He doesn't need the elevator to get into the penthouse, just an open window." Tim pushed past her into the room. "Good to see you, Andrew. I take it everything went smoothly, if unsuccessfully?"

"Yes, Grandfather should be arriving shortly. Unfortunately, Brad was gone when we arrived."

Tim stiffened slightly and confronted Brenda, who remained rooted in the doorway.

"That is unfortunate. I wonder what measures Father will want to pursue next." Tim's upper lip curled slightly, exposing a fang.

"I'm not sure. He didn't say anything specific. Just that he would speak to us when he arrived." Andrew nibbled at my earlobe.

"Well, he's sure to have something up his sleeve." Tim closed his eyes as if to restrain is temper before again facing Brenda and hissing. "Don't you have work to do? It's rude to intrude on conversations that do not concern you,"

"When the Lord is out, I watch this house, and I am responsible for what goes on here. Until he returns and tells me that someone is free to appear and disappear at will from the premises, I'm not taking my eyes off him."

The congenial greeting and warm feelings from earlier in the day vanished in a puff of fiery attitude, eliciting a snarl from the vampire drone that should've had the human scurrying from the room. But Brenda simply glared at him without fear, as if he had no power to dismiss her. She viewed him as no threat, despite the fact he could rip out her throat and disembowel her before she could so much as scream. Tim straightened his back and quirked an eyebrow at me. He tipped his head to one side slightly, half smiled, and pointedly flashed his eyes in Brenda's direction, grinning wickedly at me. The gleam of glistening white fangs peeking from between his lips proved just how close the stupid woman stood to finding out she needed to take Tim's warning more seriously.

"You would do to learn your place, human," Tim hissed.

"I am the Lord's personal assistant. None of you dare touch me whether he is here or not." Brenda's frown deepened. I could practically see the stubborn idiocy setting in. If she didn't learn manners soon, she would be a dead human, and I doubted Grandfather would honestly care if his children "accidentally" killed the stupid woman.

"Is there something I can help you with, Brenda?" My vision went from color to black and white, and I stared at her from behind my wolf's eyes. She might not have proper respect for vampires, since living with Grandfather on a daily basis might have dulled her fear. Kind of like a zookeeper in a lion habitat. If they aren't constantly aware of what the animal is capable of, they can forget the power of the beast. If something wasn't done to remind Brenda, she could easily get mauled by a vampire not quite as nice as Tim. Of course, I wasn't a vampire, and the fear she would instinctively feel by my amping up my power and releasing it in her direction would be very different. A vampire, drone or born, gave off a feeling of cold, slow death. I wasn't sure what the feeling of my power was, but because of it, humans had betrayed me all my life. I knew it was strong.

She was used to vampires, but her instincts told her we were a threat. She didn't like our presence in what she considered her home. We upset her orderly world. Unfortunately for her, the penthouse was now my territory. I would not submit to human idiocy anymore. She had an attitude adjustment coming. Of course, it hadn't hurt that Tim had clearly given me the go-ahead to put her in her place.

"No, uh.... Thank you.... Ah.... L-Lord Lance," she stuttered before giving Tim an angry stare before fleeing the room.

"Thank you. For a human surrounded by vampires, she should have more respect." Tim exhaled exaggeratedly.

"I'm surprised she hasn't gotten herself killed behaving like that," Andrew grumbled into my neck, then nuzzling my ear. "You're hot when you're all wolfy, lover."

"Behave yourself," I gently admonished, rubbing my cheek against him before turning my attention back to Tim.

"Father took her on as a personal secretary a few years ago. I think sometimes she believes we belong to her, instead of her just working for us." We all simultaneously looked toward the door, having heard the elevator ping and the automatic doors open.

Grandfather and Charlie had returned with the rest of the guard. The man radiated happiness when he hurried into the room and saw us waiting for him. "Hello, family." He moved so swiftly, almost appearing to glide across the floor without touching the ground. Standing back and taking in the room, the pride and affection that showed on his face stirred feelings of belonging I'd never known. "Come children, we have some decisions to make, and this room is not appropriate for the discussion."

He led us down a wide hallway to a dark mahogany door that opened into a private library. Books of all kinds abounded from floor to vaulted ceiling and from wall to wall. A tall ladder, looking a bit like a steep brass staircase, ran around the bookshelves on rails. The scents of leather bindings, wood smoke from the large stone fireplace, and old paper filled the room. It was wonderful. The knowledge contained within this room would keep me contentedly entertained for months, maybe years. I perused some of the titles on the shelves closest to me.

Tim and Charlie followed us into the library, Charlie nodding to the guard left outside the door. He'd ensure we were undisturbed. Not even Brenda would get past without permission.

Grandfather motioned for us to make ourselves comfortable. Andrew and I relaxed on one of the dark leather sofas. Tim and Charlie each chose one of the overstuffed armchairs, and Grandfather leaned against the dark oak desk that monopolized the center of the room.

"I am sure Andrew told you Brad is still on the loose."

"Yes. What are your plans?" Tim sighed with the frustration we all felt.

"There is a traitor among us. Someone warned Brad that we were coming." Grandfather all but hissed. His eyes had become hard for a moment before his features were once again schooled into normalcy.

"You will have a guard with you or outside your suite door at all times. They will search everything going into your room before it is allowed in, and they will search everyone before they will be able to enter your room." Charlie's no-nonsense tone told me just how seriously she was taking this threat, and how personally she felt about someone besides Brad betraying her father.

"Do you have any idea who it could be?" I asked, hoping it wouldn't be someone I knew.

"It could be anyone. But because of when it happened, there are only so many possibilities. It had to be someone who was here at the time of our conversation, who overheard what we were planning." Grandfather stared at the wall, deep in thought.

"I will get a list of all the employees and drones present that day and try to narrow things down. There has to be a way to figure out who is working against us." Charlie's gaze roved around the room as if to seek out the spies from the shadows they lurked behind.

"Let me know what you discover. Gerard will be watching for Brad at the farm. I do trust him—he is a good and loyal son. Brad preyed upon his love for Illiana, undermining my authority. It won't happen again. There may be others loyal to Brad on the property, but I believe I have a solution to that. Charlie made calls in the car and has her network of warriors hunting for him. He won't remain hidden for long."

I did feel better knowing we were doing something toward finding Brad, but it was unsettling knowing he was out there and had a spy living among us.

"I believe we need to begin to plan for your future. As I see it, first we must take care of your home. You need a territory, and this penthouse will suffice for only so long. The beast will need to hunt. Of course, my son's house and holdings are yours. He gave the house, farm, surrounding forests, and the mountain behind the farm to your mother as a mating present."

"He gave it to her…. Why not just ask her to move in? I mean, if they got married, isn't it pretty much what's yours is mine and what's mine is yours?" From everything I was learning about shifters and their families, this didn't quite fit. Andrew's mom, Laura, had told me their society was matriarchal and women held the land, which was passed from mother to daughter. So it only seemed right that Nathaniel would have moved to Sasha's home.

"Not quite, not in those days." Charlie snorted and laughed. "Remember, we're talking about the mid-sixteenth century here. Women owned nothing legally and had no rights. Of course, our kind were a little less discriminatory when it came to women's rights. Especially shifters, who even then were pretty much a matriarchal society."

"Sasha's father didn't like me, or Nathaniel for that matter. He was very prejudiced against other species and took it out against his daughter and her men. Nathaniel was gifting her with a territory of her own, as Sasha's father had refused to allow her to have her dowry. She should have been allotted a portion of her mother's territory, as was her birthright. Then upon her mother's death, she would have had claim to it all." Grandfather smiled and shrugged his shoulders. "I return to you what belonged to her. It's the land Nathaniel had purchased and set up as a home for them. I hope you'll enjoy it as she did in the short amount of time she lived there. I have tried to maintain it as well as I could. For all I know, she and Henry in their beast form roam the mountains that are part of her territory. I have watched for them, of course, but I've never seen them."

"Are you sure, Grandfather? I mean, we could live on the farm and manage it for you. You don't have to give me the land. It belonged to your son and I wasn't even his biological child." It seemed unreasonably generous of Grandfather to do this. I'd never had anyone try to give something like this to me.

"No, the land is rightfully yours. It was legally placed in your mother's name and would be yours by birthright. I've only been a caretaker, holding it until it could be claimed by its owner." Grandfather shook his head, raising his hands to stall my objections. "I've had my beneficiaries working on the land from time to time, when the animal population needed a proper culling. It's been prosperous in the past, and I know it will do well by you."

"I don't know what to say. Thank you doesn't sound like enough."

"It's more than enough. You've given me a reason to experience joy, an emotion I've not felt in a very long time." Grandfather's green eyes shone with just a touch of bittersweet. Knowing how much he enjoyed sharing his children's lives with his mate, I couldn't begin to imagine the pain of not being able to share this with her. "Andrew, I know that your parents are tied to their territory, but can you think of anyone else you'd want and trust to manage the farm for you? Preferably someone who agrees with Lance's ideas and can defend themselves in case of attack or harassment." Grandfather watched expectantly as Andrew considered the possibilities. I could practically hear the names of people he knew running through his mind as he considered and rejected each.

"I know my dad could do it temporarily, but he'd be unhappy running a farm away from mom and the rest of the family," Andrew said aloud, his mind still circling the ever-smaller number of people he was considering. "There are a couple I would consider capable, fewer that I trust completely with our lives. They may not all have the same benefactor, though."

"There are ways around that. I may have to make a few calls, depending upon who their benefactor is, but usually these things can be arranged. If the vampire is someone I believe could be a potential supporter, it may be as simple as setting up a meeting between the benefactor and the two of you." Grandfather put his hands on his thighs and leaned forward, thinking intently.

"Well, you will need to meet more born vampires eventually, especially those in the council. The more support we can gather before you are discovered, the better," Tim added.

"The only other person I'd trust our lives with is my cousin, Sam Tallman. I am pretty sure his benefactor isn't Stephon." Andrew glanced first at Grandfather, then to Charlie.

"Yes, I can see that. I've met him. He is a strong shifter and seems to be very loyal to you." Charlie nodded her agreement as she absently examined one of the blades she had removed from her belt.

"Sam would be a very good choice, and he'd probably thrive, especially once he's out from under your Uncle David's thumb." I loved the idea of getting Sam away from that pompous waste of space. The man had proven himself in the past to be a bully who enjoyed his job as the pack enforcer way too much. David liked to hurt people. Sam had never admitted to Andrew that he had ever been abused by David, but in my experience, when people like David were given the opportunity to harm others, they did.

"It should be easy enough to find out who his benefactor is. Wouldn't Max or maybe Sandy know?" Tim wondered aloud.

"Dad might, but I'm sure Sandy would know," Andrew agreed.

"Very good. I think we have our new manager, and maybe your brothers could assist him. We may even be able to get some of your shape-shifter guards there under the guise of ranch hands. It's a very extensive operation, after all, and I'm sure your cousin will have the names of men appropriate for the positions," Grandfather said.

"I know he'll have several recommendations to make." Charlie grinned. "He's interviewing them this week, checking their special skills with some drills I'd given him before we left."

"Good. I'd advise making a few calls and getting organized as soon as you can. While you are finding out about Sam's benefactor, ask your matriarch to contact the Royals on your behalf," Grandfather stated, frowning, deep in thought.

"We already have. They sent an emissary to verify my claim. Peter Gray left saying he would return to the Royals with a positive verdict. We're awaiting a call to court. So far, we've heard nothing, even though everything went smoothly during his visit." I couldn't help feeling a bit unsettled by the Royals' lack of response. We'd all expected an answer of some sort by this time.

"Well, that won't do. With your bloodlines, you should be holding court, not waiting on them. Clearly someone is stalling. I'll reach out to a few people who may be able to tell us what the delay is about. I think we need to rally your supporters, and the sooner, the better." Grandfather pensively stared at Tim, nodding slightly.

"Let me make a couple calls and see what we can get started." Andrew reached for his cell phone and began punching in the numbers.

CHAPTER 9

Stephon's Story—Prince Atol and Ventall—Central North America 880 AD

THE NIGHT was silent except for the buzz of insects. The stars shone bright overhead in the depths of the utter blackness of a moonless sky. The dwarf king, Stauflis, his council, Neabu and Bodon, and several others had requested they come to this place, far from known lands of mankind, a place where the power of the earth was at its strongest. The shifters had been invited as well, and from the continual hissing and thrashing, a member of the fae had been absconded and resided in a magical net restricting its movements.

"King Henry, it is good to see that you and your son Atol are well." Caius nodded to the tall, burly shifter on his right. King Henry was a Viking, a god king to the human population. He had a wild golden mane that covered his head and face like the animal he most often was known to shift into: an enormous lion. Atol was young by shifter standards, and his coloring resembled his mother's— his hair was dark, his beard short, and his stature much more lithe and lean.

"Caius, my friend… or should I be calling you Lord Caius? Now that you are head of your Vampire Council." The king approached and embraced Caius, smacking him on the back. The good-natured thumps sounded more like painful blows to Stephon, who stayed behind his father, out of reach of the king.

"That is unnecessary between friends such as us." Caius stepped out of the king's embrace and grinned. "I am glad my information about the last border confrontation your people fought was incorrect. I'd heard you had met your death at the hands of four fae."

"It was a close call. My father was badly injured, but…." Atol began.

"Rumors of my demise were a bit premature." King Henry chortled.

The dwarves soon approached the chatting men, dragging both their captive and what appeared to be a number of large stones across the meadow.

"King Stauflis, do your men need assistance? I'm sure some of my guards—" King Henry waved a hand, referring to the fairly large contingent of men spread out around the circumference of the clearing.

"No, but thank you for the offer, King Henry." King Stauflis waved his men forward. "These stones are very precious. They are lodestones. When set in certain locations around the world, they can be used to form gateways to other versions of our world. Mirror images of this earth, but each unique in its own way. Once attuned to a certain mirror world, it can be held open and we can pass through the gate unharmed, but only as long as the veil is open between the worlds. After it is closed, nothing on either side can pass through until it is opened again."

"So what exactly are you proposing? That we all leave our homes for this mirror place and hope for the best?" King Henry scoffed. "My people cannot leave our territories. We would be adrift. It isn't in our nature to abandon our homes, even with the promise of new lands. We are tied to our territories. We are the custodians of this world, not any other."

"No. That is not what we propose." The small contingent of dwarves entered the meadow's center and then began to spread out, each of the five dwarves dragging their burdens to points about the clearing.

Stephon grinned as he watched his friend and childhood companion, the dwarf Ventall, son of Bodon, haul a huge bolder across the wet grass to a spot obviously predetermined. A large hole had been dug in the ground, and the dwarf was struggling with the stone, which was three times his size, in his attempt to set it upright in the hole.

It was good to see the dwarf again. After the Romans took over Egypt, Caius and Stephon's family had been homeless. Even though the Romans were just as barbaric as the Egyptians, the Romans didn't embrace the blood goddess, and they had been forced to find new territory or be slaughtered. Caius had known Stauflis since before Stephon's birth, and while they searched for a new home, they had been guests of the king. In those days, even though Stephon was full grown, he was still considered a child, and Ventall had been no different. The two became close friends and had found as much trouble as two youths could. He could hardly wait until all of the posturing was over so he could greet his friend properly. He had missed him.

As Stephon watched, he became aware that he wasn't the only one interested in observing his friend. Prince Atol's gaze seemed to follow Ventall with rapt attention. The shifter prince was giving off some heady scents, namely those of confusion and arousal.

Stephon tried to see his longtime friend as the shifter prince might see him, as if he'd never seen a dwarf before. Ventall appeared young, his beard and hair almost as black as the night around them. He was physically fit; his body was muscular and broad. A smattering of dark hair stuck out around his linen shirt and covered his arms in black curly fuzz. He was attractive in a rough and burly kind of way, if you liked that sort of thing.

Ventall was just finishing, packing the ground around the stone, when Atol approached him and began to assist the dwarf and speak to him. The two were unobserved by the others, who were discussing the merits of two worlds, gateways, earth power, and control spells.

Then Ventall leaned back and snarled, then returned to his work, packing the earth about the stone. Stephon tried not to laugh. Something was going on between the shifter and Ventall, but whether it was simply attraction or something more was hard to determine. The mating rituals of dwarves were unlike those of any other culture Stephon had ever been exposed to. They were, in many ways, simply violent and aggressive.

Atol reached over and placed a hand on Ventall's shoulder. The dwarf brushed it off in haste and shoved Atol back hard enough for him to lose his balance and land on his ass. Stephon chuckled—there was definitely something going on between the two—and he was beginning to believe it to be a courtship of sorts between the shifter prince and Ventall. The simple truth was that if Ventall didn't like Atol and he wasn't interested in what the shifter was offering, Ventall would pound him into the ground. Atol's station as a prince of his people would make little difference to Ventall.

Stephon couldn't hold back his chuckle at the prince's expense as he watched the prince get to his feet and sidled up beside Ventall, getting as close as the dwarf would allow before attempting to kiss him. He was almost brutally rebuffed. Ventall stomped on Atol's foot and elbowed him in the gut, before he shoved him back out of his way, and stormed off. Atol seemed distinctly wounded, as if his world had crashed in on him, so Stephon decided to see if he could assist in the romantic foreign relations. Atol definitely needed an interpreter.

"Go after him," Stephon said, walking up to the prince.

"W-what?" Prince Atol stammered, noticing Stephon for the first time.

"I said, go after him. Have you never met dwarves before?" Stephon couldn't resist teasing the bewildered shifter.

"No. I'd never even seen a dwarf before today." Prince Atol watched the dwarf standing with a couple of others, talking and glancing over at them.

80

"He was flirting with you, idiot. He's young for his kind and to my knowledge has never seen a shifter before." Stephon watched both confusion and hope blossom at the same time in the young prince's eyes.

"What do you mean he was flirting? He didn't say anything to me. He just growled at me, stomped on my foot, and pushed me away. He's my mate, and he doesn't want me." Prince Atol's skin seemed to almost quiver, as if he was barely able to keep from shifting and howling his mournful defeat.

"Don't assume that. Dwarves have mates, same as the rest of us. I don't know how they determine who their mate is, but I have seen them courting one another and it's a brutal dance. Female dwarves physically appear no different than the males, other than the fact that they are quite a bit larger. Courtship seems to be a battle for dominance. If the male can physically conquer the female—or more likely, if she lets him win—then they are mates for life." Stephon bit his tongue to keep from laughing at the complete dismay crossing the other man's face.

"No! You can't mean that." Prince Atol appeared to be dumbfounded. "I have to hurt my mate in order to claim him? Will our lives be nothing but a battle?"

"Oh, no. They appear to be very gentle and loving to one another after the courtship and once mated. But before, yes, a definite battle. Pulled hair, black eyes, bruises, and broken bones are all part of their mating ritual. If you believe that dwarf to be your mate, I would suggest taking him and another dwarf aside. I would be completely open about your beliefs and ask the other dwarf to explain things to you." Stephon chuckled. "You'll basically be telling your mate that you don't believe him capable of being nonviolent or patient enough to explain his desires or what their courtship rules are. If I know Ventall, he won't take a challenge to his intellect or control lightly. He will be talking in no time, giving you a chance."

"How do you know so much?" Prince Atol scowled at Stephon as if suspicious of the advice he was being given.

"My father and King Stauflis are very good friends. We lived with them in the caves of the underground city for a time, before my mother was killed by the fae, but after the Romans invaded Egypt. Luckily, my mother was not my father's mate or I would have lost them both that day." Stephon nodded in the dwarves' direction. "Your mate is Ventall, and he is Counselor Bodon's youngest son. Even though I have reached my maturity and we were both considered young all those years ago, he is still considered young. He is about five hundred thirty-five years old. But dwarves age extremely slowly, like the earth itself." Stephon patted the prince on the shoulder and gave him a gentle shove in the direction of the dwarves standing and staring at him. "Heed my advice and go get him before he decides you are too cowardly and not worth having as a mate."

"Cowardly… hardly." Prince Atol snorted and walked across the meadow. His mate snarled and shoved him, but Atol pushed back with the same amount of restrained force. Stephon was pretty sure even though the dwarf was shorter and heavier than the prince, Atol was quicker and definitely stronger. It would be a lovely courtship battle, unfortunately one he probably would not be allowed to observe, as dwarves considered the battle equal to foreplay.

Stephon, his job as matchmaker complete, turned his attention back to the men standing about the stones in the middle of the meadow.

"Okay, so your stones are all in place. Now what?" King Henry asked.

Stephon glanced around, seeing the stones placed in the outer ring were all half buried, while the stone at the center was almost completely buried, with only a third of it sticking out above the ground, its flat surface appearing almost table-like at the center of the group of men.

"Now we consecrate the center stone with the blood of all four species. Then on the full moon, we bring the fae to this place, and when the gateway opens, the fae pass through. We then seal the gate shut, locking them forever on the other side." King Stauflis explained, his advisors nodding in agreement. "Fae are very hard to kill. You can wound them, even think you have killed them, and they still come back. If we banish them through the veil, then they can live there. Maybe they will finally learn to control themselves and find something else to feed on, or the last fae standing will have killed all of its brethren in order to survive."

"So how do you propose we get them to cooperate?" Caius asked.

"Divide and conquer. We can open the gate every full moon. As long as three species want the gate opened, it will answer and open so others can be escorted in. We can go on the offensive, take captives, and send them through the gateway. We do it quietly for as long as possible, but eventually the fae will discover what we are doing, and they will fight back. Hopefully by then we will have most of their forces on the other side of the veil, and we will have the advantage of numbers to keep our people safe." King Stauflis shrugged. "It was the best we could come up with."

"Imprisonment in a different world." Caius nodded. "It just might work."

CHAPTER 10

Present Day

ANDREW AND I stood. We walked, side by side, toward the door. Charlie followed us out. Tim remained behind with Grandfather. He nodded at me as we passed. Charlie saw us to our suite door. She made sure we had guards on duty outside the room before she retired. I wondered what she did during her off hours. Drones didn't sleep. My imagination ran wild, giving me visions of Charlie sharpening her blades, and Tim doing needlework or playing a harpsichord. Andrew busted up laughing as we walked into the main room.

"You have quite the imagination, my mate." Andrew closed the door behind him. "But I don't think Tim's the harpsichord type. Now, a trombone or saxophone, maybe."

The sandwiches had been removed while we were away, and Andrew's stomach growled. We were in the middle of Denver. It wasn't like we could flit outside and hunt. I wasn't sure what we should do. I stuck my head back outside my door in time to see Tim walking down the hallway toward us.

"Tim," I called sheepishly around the guard, who was statue still.

Tim smiled and came when I called. "How can I help you?" He treated me like he was a big brother with a pesky little brother who was always getting in trouble, and I was starting to like it.

"Andrew's hungry. Is there someone still in the kitchen? Where is the kitchen? I figure sneaking out and flying to the edge of the city to hunt is probably not something we should be doing, or something Charlie would appreciate…. Can we call in a pizza?" My thoughts were flowing out my mouth without being censored first, and I really didn't care. I was so tired, and Andrew was hungry and exhausted. We were allowed a bit of mindlessness.

Tim laughed and motioned me into the room. He followed and showed me the panel on the inside of the door. "The red button is the emergency button. It'll bring every guard in the penthouse to your door. The green button is for the kitchen. The blue button will call Brenda at the front hallway. There is kitchen staff on duty twenty-four hours a day. Just push the button, and they'll answer."

"Grandfather has kitchen staff on duty all day. Who exactly do they cook for?" I was tired, but the illogic of a vampire needing to have cooks available all the time had me confused.

"Much of the staff in the penthouse live in the lower levels of the high rise, and very few of them are vampires or drones. Father wanted them to not have to leave the building if they didn't want to, so he provides day-care services and access to the kitchens at all times for those who live in the building and work for him."

"That's actually pretty cool. If you work all day and don't want to cook, you can call the kitchen and they'll do the work for you." Andrew nodded. "I like that."

"They'll make pretty much anything you want, anytime you want it." Tim placed a hand on the doorknob. "I'm sorry. I should've showed you this earlier. When guests arrive, Brenda will buzz your room, announcing them. You push her blue button to answer her. You can go down to them or you can ask Brenda to show them to your suite."

"Well, considering the possible spy in the building, I think it is probably better to have our guests come up here, where we not only have closed doors, but also guards to ensure our privacy."

"I agree. You can always tell Brenda to advise Father and the rest of us, so we know who's going to be in the building as well."

"Thank you, Tim. I really appreciate everything you're doing for me." I reached up and gave him a hug.

"You're welcome. Have a good night." He smiled over my shoulder at Andrew, who leaned against the sofa, grinning. Tim excused himself and beat a hasty retreat to his own rooms. I closed the door.

Andrew came up quickly behind me and grabbed me around the waist, pressing me against the door as he laid his body along my back, kissing me on the neck. He reached over my shoulder and buzzed the kitchen, and ordered us both rare steaks and baked potatoes. He then proceeded to make up for all the time spent apart and in the company of others throughout the day.

Drawing me back with him, he spun me in his arms as he turned us, until he had me walking backward in the direction of the sofa. He took possession of my lips, kissing me, claiming what belonged only to him. Gently lowering us onto the plush, suede leather, Andrew began worshiping my body.

Someone had lit a fire in the stone fireplace across from where we snuggled together. It had me feeling all nostalgic for my sanctuary. Resting, feeling Andrew's lips brushing against my neck, soon had me feeling better than I had all day.

"You, Leannan, are becoming very affectionate. I like it, but when you are affectionate with others, it makes me jealous." Andrew stroked my hair, deeply inhaling the scent.

"I have so much to be appreciative of. So many wonderful people are coming into my life. I feel like I'm able to give all the affection I've been starved for all my life to all the people I've missed, growing up with the humans instead of the wonderful family I now have."

"They all want to love you too. Just as long as you remember you belong to me."

"It's you, my love, who makes me feel the most blessed. You continue to show me every day how to trust others. I feel it in your mind and heart. You give me the courage to keep trying. I no longer wake up wondering if today will be the day I'm betrayed. Because it no longer matters if I am or not. You will never hurt me. Everything else we can deal with together. None of this would be possible, if I hadn't met you." I kissed him gently, showing him all the love in my heart.

There was a knock at the door, and a woman dressed in white brought in two covered plates. The guard escorted the woman in and watched as she set them on the dining table and took the lids off, revealing two large steaks and baked potatoes. The guard inhaled carefully over each plate, then smiled and escorted the kitchen maid from the room.

"What was he doing?" I asked Andrew, shaking my head in amazement. A drone would have no interest in our food, regardless of how rare the steaks were.

"I'm guessing he was checking for poisons." Andrew pulled me up off the sofa and led me to the table. The thought of poison had never even occurred to me, especially in Grandfather's house, yet there was a traitor here and the caution was warranted.

We dug into the steaks, eating our fill before retiring to our bedroom and closing the adjoining door to the suite. Both of us were exhausted from the stress of the day and found solace in each other's arms—between the sheets, in the layers of each other's mind, and from the feel of our bodies entwined. I could spend my life immersed in Andrew's eyes, wrapped in his arms, and never need for anything ever again.

CHAPTER 11

ANDREW WAS first to rise when the light came shining through the floor-to-ceiling windows and forced us to give up on the night. I had no desire to get up, although it wasn't so much the bed—which was nice, don't get me wrong—but spending the night making love had been so spectacular I never wanted it to end.

"Come on, sleepyhead. It's time to move that delectable ass. You know as well as I do that just because there's a guard out in front of the door, Sandy won't be deterred from coming in and getting you." Andrew leaned over the bed and kissed me, drawing back slowly so I was forced to follow his soft lips until I was sitting up.

"If I know her, she'd be reading the guard the riot act for delaying her, and then barging in to tell me how rude I was being to my elders for not being ready to greet her." I sighed and drew the covers back.

"She'd be right." Andrew snorted and walked into the bathroom.

I sat and stared at the wall, listening to him start the shower. I was in a blissful haze and didn't want to think about the people coming to check me out.

I stumbled into the bathroom and found my toiletries bag on the vanity, probably put there by one of the maids or Andrew. I brushed my teeth and then joined Andrew under the water. He washed my hair, and we washed each other's bodies. I couldn't get enough of running my hands over his glorious skin.

"Stop now, or we will never get out of this shower. I love Elder Sandy, but I have no desire to have her see us stroking off in here." Andrew nipped at my ear, sending a jolt through me. Despite our vigorous activities the night before, my body tried to respond, and my cock gave a valiant twitch that had me groaning. Andrew stepped out of the shower while I stayed, letting the hot water pound into my back and shoulders a bit before following him out.

Andrew's towel was wrapped around his waist. His hair, which was getting shaggier every day, was combed and parted down the middle. Even shaggy, he was devastatingly handsome. I soundly kissed him good morning and then dried myself off. He had my comb in hand and began working on my hair.

"You know, maybe I should cut my hair short like yours," I mumbled.

He literally froze the comb in midstroke. "You will not! Please, Lance. I like your hair. I like… this." Andrew finished running the comb through my hair and kissed my temple.

"I'm just teasing. I won't cut it." I snickered as he sighed with relief.

"Please don't."

It was probably wrong of me to tease him, but the distraction eased the building tension for me. As we walked out of the bathroom and past the closet, I glanced in at the designer clothes with disgust. I was going through a serious case of denim withdrawal. I was not going to live without my comfort clothes forever, regardless of what Stephon thought a prince should wear.

Trying not to pout, I realized I currently had no choice but to accept the closet full of beautifully tailored clothes that were beyond the grasp of the street kid I'd been most of my life. Clothes were a necessity, not a luxury, and fashion was superfluous when you wanted warmth for winter. With a twisted smile, I grabbed a pair of chocolate suede pants, a cream shirt with a brown cashmere sweater, and the brown patent oxfords. I pulled my hair back and secured it at the nape of my neck in a ponytail. Andrew would prefer I always wear my hair loose, but it was easier to manage and gave me a cleaner look when bound. It wasn't my jeans, T-shirt, and tennies, but it would have to do.

Andrew came out of the bathroom fully dressed in midnight-blue pants and a sky-blue and black striped shirt. It made his eyes pop even brighter than normal. There would be no jeans in either of our futures.

Andrew swept me into his arms and kissed me so demandingly, I wasn't sure the clothes would survive their first five minutes of wear. The intercom at the door of the suite buzzed, catching our attention and interrupting the kiss.

Growling, Andrew put me down and went to answer the summons. He pushed the blue button. "Yes?"

"There are people here asking for you. Will you be meeting them in the family room?" Brenda's voice crackled over the intercom.

"I'll be right down. We will be in our suite. Will you please let Tim, Charlie, and Lord Basil know that we have guests, so they can join us? Also, please have the kitchen send up refreshments." I watched as Andrew smiled at me, then went out the door to greet his brothers and Sam, who had agreed to come to the penthouse today.

I closed the doors to the adjoining bedroom and went out to the sitting room. Evidently, someone else had also requested refreshments be sent up, as two staff members from the kitchen were just coming in with a cart laden with a pot of tea and a pot of coffee. There were a couple of bowls of fruit and trays of what smelled like fresh baked sweet rolls—sticky and warm.

"Thank you." I smiled at the two women. They bowed and went quickly out the door. I poured myself a cup of tea and added a little sugar and some milk to the dark brew.

When the door opened, Tim entered first, with Lord Basil right behind him. "Good morning." Tim's ready smile was firmly in place.

"Good morning, Grandfather, Tim." I couldn't help but return his good mood.

"You're sure relaxed this morning. I hope you had a good night." My grandfather embraced me before taking a seat in an armchair in the living area, where he could view the door and those who entered. Tim chose to sit in a chair at his side.

"We slept very well. Thank you." I blushed slightly, remembering how we'd made love most of the night. "We both feel very safe and comfortable here."

"I'm very glad you feel at ease."

I immediately recognized the commotion coming down the hall as the sound of the twins harassing Andrew, and Sam ineffectively trying to shut them up. I shook my head and laughed. It was impossible to miss the purposefully loud heckling the twins were giving their older brother. The door opened, and Jack, Joe, Sam, and Andrew poured through the door with Charlie following, rolling her eyes and shooing them along like sheep.

"Wow! Lance, you clean up nice!" Jack said mischievously.

Joe smacked his brother on the back of the head. "Have some manners, you idiot," Joe mocked his brother.

"It's nice to see you, Lance." Sam stepped to my side and shook my hand. "Sorry to have to bring these miscreants into your home."

"I think I need to apologize to you. You had to travel with them." I shook his hand heartily and clapped him on the shoulder, then walked to Andrew's younger twin brothers. "Come here, you two ruffians." I grabbed them each by an ear, giving them a shake for their behavior, as I had numerous times at the cottage. They both laughed as I stared at each of them—first Jack, then Joe— holding up one finger in front of them both. "You will listen to everything Sam tells you to do, and you will do it, or you'll answer to me, and let me tell you...."

The threat was wasted because I couldn't be stern with them for long. I'd missed them too much.

"Aw, Lance!" Joe complained, hugging me back. I could practically feel his eyes rolling behind my back.

"Lance, geezzz!" Jack huffed, but he hugged me too.

I smiled smugly at them both. "Well, don't everybody just hover in front of the door. Come in." I took Andrew's hand, and we sat down on the sofa. Everyone else chose seats around the room. I was startled to see my vampire family on one side of the room and the shape-shifter family on the other. I felt my joy at having everyone together drop. It was all I could do to keep from feeling disappointed. I hoped this wasn't a sign of things to come.

"Well, gentlemen, we do have our work cut out for us." Grandfather's gaze swept the room as he contemplated the new faces. "Sam Tallman?"

"Here, my lord." Sam stood and bowed respectfully to my grandfather.

I frowned. "Wait. Stop." I stood and went to stand between my grandfather and Sam. "This is going to stop before it starts." I studied the room, seeing my family, divided even among ourselves and sighed in frustration.

"Grandson, go on. Have your say. What's the problem?"

I could see the amusement dancing in my grandfather's green eyes. He knew as well as I did what the problem was. There was no way I could free anyone when we continued to behave like a subjugated people, even within my own family.

"In this room, everyone is family. You are all *my* pack—*my* family. In this room, there are no lords, no princes, no masters, no beneficiaries and no vassals." I paced over to my grandfather and took his hand. "There is my grandfather, Basil." Letting go, I proceeded to Sam's side and placed a hand on his shoulder. "My cousin, Sam." I crossed the room again, to where Charlie stood just inside the door. "My aunt, Charlie." I turned to the right to where the twins sat on the floor in front of the fireplace and tipped my head in their direction. "My little brothers, Jack and Joe." Then I returned to the center of the room. "And of course, my Uncle Tim, the inquisitive doctor. Everyone in this room is important to me and has a place in my heart."

Andrew stood and came to stand behind me. "Go ahead, tell them so they understand." Andrew put his hands on my shoulders.

"What we are about to attempt can't succeed if even in my own family there are dividing lines. Vampires on one side—" I swept my arm toward Grandfather, Tim, and Charlie. "—and shifters on the other." I pointed toward Sam and the twins. "If I want to free the shifter people and eventually mend the tear between the vampires and shifters, it has to begin in my family. Eventually, we will have to be an example for our peoples—all of us living as equals, cooperating to make life better for all."

"Well said, Grandson." Grandfather beamed with pride.

"Thank you." I wasn't sure what to do next, but Andrew gave my hand a squeeze.

"That being said, we have a lot we need to do. We have to set up a territory where Lance and I will be safe and able to defend ourselves. Also, as little light as possible must be cast on my origins, to keep the rest of my family from the scrutiny of the Vampire Council and possibly causing Stephon trouble." Andrew led me to the love seat while he spoke, and we both sat.

"Sam, the farm I'm turning over to Lance and Andrew belonged to my son, Nathaniel, before he gave it to Lance's mother. We'd like you to manage it for them." Grandfather steepled his fingers as he spoke.

"Brad ran it for the last eighty-some-odd years. So we suspect he has supporters within the household who may be loyal to him and hostile to any others sent to take over," Charlie grumbled from her spot by the door.

"Although I have every confidence in Lance and Andrew's ability to take over and remove any dangerous elements, with everything else that is going on, I see no reason why we can't help them." Grandfather nodded. "This is not an order from a benefactor. This would be your choice—a way to help out and make a difference." Grandfather stared at the twins as if he were assessing their abilities. "Jack, Joe... I know it's a risk... and the two of you are young. It will be dangerous, ferreting out those who would do your brother harm while trying to run the operation and keep it profitable. In a sense, we're putting targets on you, hoping our adversary will step from the shadows and make a move."

Sam spoke first. "I'm honored Andrew and Lance feel confident in my being able to do the job. I won't let them down." He smirked at Jack and Joe, who were nodding. "Won't make any promises for them, though." Sam teased.

"We won't let them down, either." Jack gave Joe a shove on the shoulder.

"Nobody gets past us." Joe slugged his brother hard enough to knock Jack back a step. The twins just couldn't stand still and behave like the adults they appeared to be for more than a few minutes at a time. The juvenile wolves they shared their souls with just couldn't behave.

"All kidding aside, I'm assuming you'll have the guards Charlie has amassed at the Reed farm moved to this new territory? It'd be nice to have security around, who I feel confident enough in that I can call upon them in a tight spot and know they have my back. I've gotten to know them pretty well."

Sam rubbed his palms together. I could practically see the gears in his mind whirling with dozens of ideas. He was excited and anxious to begin.

"Yes, that is what we anticipated you would prefer. I've been making calls with regards to the people Charlie has named as potential security. Just give me a list of your preferences, and I'll make the arrangements with their benefactors to have them transferred to Lance and Andrew's territory."

"I'm sure between the two of them, Sam and Charlie will be able to make the farm a safe haven for all of us." There was no doubt in my mind in regarding their abilities to do exactly what they planned.

"I would prefer for the time being you remain here. The penthouse is a more defensible position than the farm, and until Brad has been captured, it would ease my mind if you would consider staying. I know you need the physical expanse the land can provide, where you can let your fur down, so to speak." Grandfather chuckled. "The farm can also serve as a good base of operations where you can meet others without my presence hanging over you. The Royals can call on you there, as it will be an independent location, your inheritance from your mother. But...."

"We understand. As long as we can get out and hunt, away from the city so we can let the beast run free for a while, I'm sure we can make it work." Andrew nodded.

"Besides, sticking together is a good idea." I couldn't help it. I wanted to spend more time with my grandfather too. I wanted to get to know the man who was part of my family.

"If Lance and I move to the farm and you remain here, we become two small targets. And regardless of how you try to separate yourself from us, by acknowledging Lance and giving him territory, you're pretty much stating your position for all the world to see." Andrew nodded at Tim.

"He is right, Father. The council will see the steps you're taking as supporting his claims. Granted, nothing you are doing is actually going against any council rules... technically... because he truly is outside the margin, as his bloodline has no benefactor." Tim nodded. "They could still view you as a traitor for not bringing him to them to pass judgment on immediately, or they could target the rest of us to punish you."

"Unfortunately, you are right, my son. My standing as one of the oldest among our kind will carry some weight. But there are those—Rufus and Gwenore are one pair—who will see this as a ploy to undermine the council. The young who've never been exposed to a real pureblood shape shifter will think I've lost my mind to mate fever because Illiana sleeps." Grandfather's eyes went

91

from emerald green to blood red for a moment before righting themselves. If I hadn't been watching, I would've missed it.

"Surely there are others who will know better and will support us?" I couldn't help but ask, once again questioning if this was the right course to take.

"Yes, some will support us, and others will attack us. Me specifically, as they will think that I'm vulnerable and have become an easy target. They will quickly learn otherwise." Grandfather growled.

"If anyone… and I mean anyone… thinks they are going to hurt you because of me, they'd better be prepared. I may be a young shifter, but I've already proven I can bite." I just barely kept myself from snapping at those around me. Andrew stroked his hand through my hair and calm washed through me as quickly as the aggression.

Grandfather smiled. "You will definitely be a surprise for a majority of our people, Grandson."

"Well, then, let's get started. Where's the farm located?" Sam clapped his hands together and rubbed them briskly back and forth in anticipation.

"Charlie, would you mind taking Sam, Jack, and Joe to the farm? You'll need to make introductions to the current staff and begin the changing of the guard." Grandfather nodded at his daughter, frowning slightly, deep in thought. "We have a few more guests coming yet this morning, I believe, do we not?"

"Sure, as long as it's okay with you, Lance, Andrew?"

"That'd be fine, Charlie. We really appreciate everything you do for us." Andrew smiled.

"All right, then, gentlemen, if you would follow me." Charlie stood and led the way out for the guys. We all rose to our feet, and once again I was saying good-bye to part of my family. They were going to risk their lives for us, and I couldn't begin to say how humble I felt and grateful I was to have them in my life.

"By the way, I'll send someone up with those trunks you requested. Andrew said you needed a few things from the cottage. Laura packed them for you. The guys and I did the grunt work." Sam clapped me on the shoulder. "Just so you know, I really am thrilled at the opportunity you're giving me, Lance. Thank you."

"If you brought what I think you brought me…. You will have my undying gratitude for eternity, Sam." I followed them to the suite door.

"Be right back." Andrew walked with Sam, who gave me a wink. The two of them followed Charlie, Tim, and the twins down the hall.

"If you would excuse me, I have a few phone calls to make." Grandfather leaned in and gave me a gentle squeeze before gliding from the room.

The silence that followed was a balm to my irritated nerves. The multitude of things that could go wrong at any point and to any of the people I cared about was almost overwhelming. Yet they risked it all for me. Granted, I would do the same for every one of them. The idea that I had worth to them was still novel, but I couldn't begin to tell anyone how much I cherished knowing people really cared about me.

Turning around in the silent suite, I wasn't really seeing it. I had become lost among my thoughts about the risks Sam and the twins would be taking, rooting out whatever evil Brad had left behind at the farm. Even knowing that the guards going with them would be the ones they were familiar with, who were now staying with them at the Reed's farm, and would be there to watch out for them, I still worried.

I went to the glass doors that led out to the deck, opened the door, and let the mountain air, cold and crisp, clear the fog from my mind. Stepping out into the chilly day, it was obvious there was a bite of frost to the air. The smell of fresh snow on pine needles gave a clean, heavy scent to the day, telling me it was already winter in the upper reaches of the Rockies. I was dying to transform and go hunting with Andrew in those mountains. It wasn't a need or a compulsion, more like impatient restlessness. The wolf wanted to cut loose. It'd be a nice stress reliever. I stood on the deck, longing for the pine-covered cliffs in the distance.

Andrew returned, and Tim came with him. Turning around, I watched as they set a large trunk in the middle of the sitting room, while a couple of the guards carried in some boxes and set them on the tables. A couple of others emerged from our bedroom. I could only guess they must've left another trunk in there.

My wolf sighed restlessly as I resisted my desire for freedom, and went indoors, closing the door firmly behind me. Andrew smiled at me mischievously from where he and Tim sat discussing the farm. I went into the bedroom. Yep, there were two new trunks sitting along the walls. With an attempt to shake the melancholy that was beginning to settle on me, I opened one of them to discover what treasures Andrew had requested from the cottage.

No big surprise really, it was full of the most basic of shifter essentials— sweat pants and T-shirts. I dug around a bit and shoved the cotton aside. Halfway toward the bottom of the chest, there they were.

"Fuck yeah!" I hollered, before slapping a hand over my mouth, grinning, and giggling like a fool. I couldn't help it. There were my beloved jeans. After the time spent in Stephon's "appropriate clothes," I was about to go out of my mind. Yanking on the button of the dress pants, I worked to get them quickly open and off, while trying to do the same to the shirt at the same time. If anyone had come in, they would have burst out laughing as I hopped around with my pants half off, pulling at the buttons of the shirt. They were very nice clothes. I was grateful for them, but I was a jeans and T-shirt person. As I slid the denim over my legs, I sighed, feeling as if I were in my own skin for the first time in a long time. I pulled a T-shirt over my head.

Gods bless my man, Laura, Sam, the twins, and everyone else who got my jeans to me. I'd be in their debt forever. There were no words for how content I felt. Everything faded at that simple kindness. I knew it was silly to put so much worth on simple denim, but truly this was the real me. I was not silk and cashmere, regardless if I was a prince of my people. They would just have to get used to a prince in denim.

I walked into the living room. Andrew grinned, seeing me changed.

"Sam owes me five bucks." Tim chuckled.

"Oh?" Andrew asked.

"There was a pool going as to how long it would take Lance to change clothes once the trunks were up here. I bet under ten minutes. Charlie gave him twenty minutes. The twins actually thought he'd wait an hour for some odd reason. Sam said he wouldn't change until the next day. We all told him he was nuts." Tim and Andrew laughed, and I shook my head.

I walked over to Andrew and, leaning in, gave him a hug. "Thank you so much! This means so much to me." I stood, my fingers itching to rip into the other boxes.

"Go on and open the rest." Andrew waved me toward the table where the boxes sat side by side.

From the first box I opened, I drew out one of my deep red stoneware vases with wolves carved on the rim and the handles. It had been carefully wrapped in paper, as if it were some spectacular piece of glassware. I moved to the other box, opened it, and found one of my large red stoneware bowls. They were two of my best pieces.

"I thought you might like a piece of the cottage brought here, so I asked Mom to send them. They're my favorites." Andrew picked the boxes and paper up from the table and took them to the garbage can in the corner of the room.

"Those are exquisite." Tim examined the bowl, running a finger along the carvings. "Is it a local artist?" He set the bowl down and then picked up the vase, carried it to the fireplace, and then set it on top of the mantle. "What do you think? If we put flowers in it, I think it'd be lovely displayed here?"

"Yeah, I guess." I shrugged. I couldn't believe he wanted to display my stuff. I mean I really was an amateur, and having my work displayed so prominently among the true pieces of art scattered about my Grandfather's home, even though this was our suite, felt good.

"Where did you find such pieces? The craftsmanship is phenomenal." Tim stepped back from the mantle admiring his placement of the vase.

"I didn't find them." Andrew beamed with pride. "Lance made them."

Tim spun round and stared at me for a moment, his mouth hanging open. "You are truly an artist. They are stunning!" Tim nodded to himself as he walked to the control panel by the door, and then pushed the blue button for Brenda. In moments he'd ordered flowers for the vase and fresh fruit for the bowl be added to the daily maintenance of the room.

"You really are an artist. I'm glad I had Mom pack them." Andrew joined us at the table.

"Thank you. You're right. I like having them here. They're a piece of the cottage, a piece of our first home." I kissed him for being so thoughtful. The man always seemed to know what to do to make me happy.

"I'll always try to make things easier for you. I know you miss our home. I miss it too. Maybe by bringing some of it with us, we will never really leave it behind. We will always have the cottage, but...." Andrew sighed into my hair.

I knew what he was getting at. The cottage was on his mother's land, and even though we could go back and visit, it would never really be ours again. Although knowing Laura and Max, they wouldn't touch the cabin. It would remain just for us, as we left it, until we came to visit.

"I know," I told him and patted his arm. I didn't want to think about it.

"Thank you for sharing these beautiful pieces with me. They truly are exquisite. I do need to excuse myself. I have a few more arrangements to make, and I want to check on Father." Tim headed out the door before we could protest. Tim always seemed to be excusing himself and leaving. He was of course making sure Andrew and I got as much alone time as possible. I still felt bad, but I'd talk to him about it later.

Andrew gathered me into his arms, and I exhaled softly, content, leaning heavily against him. There was nothing like it in the world, the peace that came from being held by my mate. As long as I had Andrew, I didn't need anything else, but it was very nice of him to give me the extras.

"I love you." I had no other words to express my gratitude, so I let all the emotions I felt flow through my mind to his.

"I love you too." He kissed my temple before he let go and led me to the sofa. I snuggled against his side, my arms round his neck. He held me close against him, and we simply loved in the moment.

CHAPTER 12

Stephon's Story—Stephon meets Quinn—Vampire Council Chambers
Spring 1728

STEPHON SAT in his carriage, trying to pull himself together. He was still trying to deal with the murder of his father, and now he had to deal with the council. He had no idea how he was expected to lead when he felt so emotionally raw.

Caius had been the one constant in his life. Stephon had never felt his age or felt alone as long as his father remained at his side. Now he felt extremely old, as if he had seen too much and lived too long. He was exhausted, and although he had tried to hibernate, he hadn't been able to reach the deep meditative state required for self-induced hibernation. Besides, with his father gone, who did he trust to watch over his body while he slept? He had no one—no lover, no mate, and now, no family.

He ached all over.

Thump-thump. "Sir. Lord Stephon, you're going to be late."

"All right, Maurice, let's get this over with." Stephon sighed heavily, pulled his dark woolen cloak more tightly over his shoulders, and adjusted his cravat. Caius had led the council with a steady hand and a benevolent heart for over two millennia. Now he was gone, and Stephon had inherited his seat on the council.

He didn't want anything to do with politics or power mongering, which was what the council had become over the centuries. How Caius had gotten anything accomplished with the constant squabbling and self-serving attitudes of the members of the council, he had no idea. Vampires as a whole were just as territorial as shifters. Add in a desire for power, and the beast within the soul of a vampire became very apparent. It was their methods that were different. Shifters were straightforward. If you had something they wanted, they would attack and try to take it from you. If they succeeded, you lost your territory and standing to the attacker. Vampires were underhanded, murderous, and manipulative when it came to something they wanted.

The thing was, his father had been the oldest living vampire. Stephon remembered the stories his father used to tell about his origins. It was always a different story, that he had arrived on the wings of angels, that he had been born of a union of man and beast, that he was a chosen one of the gods.... Stephon imagined his father must either not know his origins or couldn't remember. But the older the vampire was, the more powerful he became. Since Caius was over three millennia old, Stephon couldn't begin to imagine who had succeeded in killing him. Thoughts of revenge haunted him and would continue to plague his heart until his father was avenged. He wanted to be spending his time hunting those who killed his father, not wasting it bogged down with decisions about vampiric society and the good of a people who had betrayed his father.

Stephon walked into the large stone building that housed the council. He was thankful summer was months away, because the building would be stifling hot. With relations with the shifters uncertain, the council would meet only in highly defensible locations. Upon his entrance, drones who served the council came running from several directions.

"Lord Stephon. I am so sorry for your loss," a drone stated. "May I take your cloak?"

"Yes, and thank you for your condolences."

"Your father, Lord Caius, was always kind to me and to many of the drones who staff these halls. He will be sorely missed. If there is anything I can get you, please just call upon one of us, and we will do everything in our power to assist you."

"That is very kind of you." Stephon pulled together as reassuring a smile as he could muster before pushing past the drone and heading toward his chambers. It was all he could do to open the door. Inside was his father's office. There were shelves and shelves of books. His father loved them and so did Stephon. The library was varied and vast and covered just about every topic and language imaginable. He could only stand and longingly wish things were different—trying to decide if he could actually bring himself to cross the threshold.

"Sir?"

Stephon twisted round. His one and only drone, Maurice, stood behind him, having caught him unawares.

Caius had never created more than one or two drones, and they were the staff who had cared for his home. Stephon had never needed more than a driver, as he'd found it was easier to have humans care for his home and, of course, periodically make donations of blood. He in turn gave them a home, funded their educations, and saw to whatever needs they had: food, clothing, and the like. It was a good arrangement that had served him well over the centuries.

"I'm all right, Maurice. I just can't bring myself to go in." Stephon paused outside the door where he could practically hear his father's voice and feel his presence.

"Why don't you go down to the solar or the gardens, my lord. Relax there until you are needed to lead the council." Maurice put a hand on Stephon's shoulder. "I can bring you a carafe of warm wine laced with brandy if you like."

"Yes, I think that might be a good idea." Stephon closed the door to the office and proceeded down the hallway.

"Mother, you know I have no choice!" The yelling voice could be none other than Rufus. Stephon had heard it often over the last century. As Caius's heir, Stephon had often sat in on the council's deliberations. His voice had no weight at the time, and he wasn't allowed to speak, of course. Still, his father had often discussed with Stephon the issues at hand in his chambers for hours, until Caius felt they understood all sides of an issue and all the possible ramifications of their decisions.

"But, Rufus, this doesn't make sense. We can't do what he is asking. The council will never go for it and—" Gwenore argued.

Smack! "Shut up, woman. The damn door is open—you'll be heard." The door slammed.

"Well, what do you make of that?" Stephon frowned and glanced at Maurice who'd been walking at his side.

"Rumor has it among the servants that Rufus had overextended himself financially due to the war. He thought to make a fortune and instead has bankrupted himself. Or so it was believed. A week or so ago, he seemed to have come into quite a sum, as he paid off his debts and paid his employees' wages for the first time in a year," Maurice said in a hushed voice. "I would say he has a new financier, one with demands that Lady Gwenore does not approve of."

"I do agree." Stephon nodded and proceeded down the hallway to where the hall diverged. The solar, a warm peaceful sitting room filled with sunlight and fresh flowers, was on the left while the library was to the right. "I don't think I will be going into the solar. I don't feel much like sunlight and flowers. I believe the quiet and peace of the library is more to my liking, Maurice. Please bring my drink to one of the reading studies off the main lobby."

"As you wish, my lord." Maurice moved on down the hall toward the kitchens, where he could find a blood donor and the brandy.

Stephon entered the well-lit, central library of the council. It was a large affair, donated mainly by Caius, Lord Basil, and a couple of the other members. Walking along the one of the numerous rows of shelves, peering at the titles, he selected a leather-bound book without paying it much attention. He held the book to his chest and moved off to the far right of the main lobby, out of the way of most of the foot traffic. He hadn't been sitting long when a man passing in front of him caught his attention. The gentlemen appeared to be in his teens, a young vampire, to be sure. Stephon had a sudden urge to rise and go after the young man, when he moved to one of the lounge chairs and sat down.

Stephon could only assume the vampire was young. Age could be difficult to discern in a vampire for Stephon himself, who had already lived through a couple of millennia, was told he appeared to be in his early thirties. It was hard to judge his height as he was relaxing in a chair, a book in hand, and he was completely absorbed by what he was reading. The sun shone off his straight jet-black hair that fell to just below his collar. He was impeccably dressed and very pleasingly put together, with broad shoulders and chest, and long legs that were crossed at the ankle, leisurely stretched out before him.

Stephon waved to one of the pages patrolling the library, without taking his eyes off the man.

"Yes, Lord Stephon, how may I be of assistance?"

"Who is that young vampire over there?" Stephon asked, trying to keep his voice even so it wouldn't betray his interest. He was never so glad to have worn a topcoat that covered his engorging wood at the sight before him.

"That is Lord Quinn, Lord Rufus's son and Lady Gwenore's grandson, heir to their estates," the page whispered, keeping his voice soft and low so as not to disturb any of the other people in the library studying. "This is his first time visiting the council."

"Thank you." Stephon smiled at the page, who nodded and scurried off to help another patron. His wood gone at the thought of Rufus and Gwenore but trying to reassert itself, Stephon closed his eyes and shook his head. There was no way he could get involved with such a man. The youth might be handsome, but with a parent like Rufus and a grandmother like Gwenore, he'd have to count the silver every time the man entered his home. Not to mention he would have to make sure he wasn't stabbed in the back while he slept. Yes, the man was handsome, but nothing was worth that, Stephon thought. He dropped his hand and opened his eyes, only to lock on to the most beautiful ash-gray eyes that, for a moment, appeared silver in the golden sunlight. Stephon found him inspiring.

For just that brief second, everything in the world froze. He felt as if he were living a lifetime in those eyes, before a hand fell on his shoulder and Stephon practically leapt out of his skin.

"Are you all right, my lord? I said your name three times before I touched you," Maurice said. Stephon would have snarled, but when he faced his drone, he only saw true concern reflected in the man's eyes.

Stephon took a deep breath to steady himself before answering, "I'm fine." When he sought young Quinn, the discovered that vampire had vanished. "Damn, I must have scared him away."

"Who, my lord?" Maurice frowned, not seeing anyone but Lord Stephon.

"No matter, he's gone now. Have you heard anything about Lord Quinn, Maurice?"

"Very little, my Lord. He is Lord Rufus's oldest son and heir to his council seat and territories. He was a fosterling to Lord Basil for the majority of his life, returning to his home infrequently. He tends to be serious, quiet, and a bit of a loner." Maurice followed as Stephon walked over to the alcove where Quinn had sat, and breathed deeply, inhaling the scent the young vampire had left behind. "From what I understand, Rufus hasn't released him yet. Of course, it's well known that Rufus never totally releases his drones, so I really can't see him letting go of his son, when everything the child does reflects back on him and anything the boy learns he can use against one and all."

"I see. Then the boy can't be trusted," Stephon mumbled as the tickling sensations of desire, need, and intense attraction had his blood close to boiling.

"If he were to be free of his father, then I believe he could be an honorable man. Lord Basil's drones speak highly of him, but under his father's control, ultimately you are dealing with Rufus. Everything you tell the boy, expect Rufus to know," Maurice said matter-of-factly.

"Of course, you are right." Stephon tried to keep the discontented growl out of his voice. "I've changed my mind. I don't believe there is anywhere in this building I can find solace. Let's go to the chambers. I'll await the rest of the council there."

"Yes, my lord." Maurice nodded and let Stephon lead the way out of the library and down the hallway.

CHAPTER 13

Present Day

I WASN'T sure where Sandy would be traveling from, but she'd seemed nervous about coming to Lord Basil's home. It seemed contrary to Stephon and Grandfather's behavior—most vampires went to their beneficiary's residences or to their business offices when they met. They did not meet them in their home. It made me sad to think of such a great lady as Sandy feeling unworthy to come to my grandfather's house because he was a born vampire and she was a shifter. These would be tough attitudes to change, and it would probably take years, if not decades, before our two species could coexist on an equal status again.

I snuggled deeper into the crook of Andrew's arm. After meeting with everyone and coming up with a basic plan, they'd gone off to see the land that would be our territory. The two of us took the quiet time as we could get it and just dozed on the sofa in the sunlight streaming through the windows. When the intercom buzzed, it awoke us from our doze. I jumped to my feet, hoping Sandy had finally arrived.

"Lord Lance, there's a woman here who says her name is Sandy and that you are expecting her," Brenda said disdainfully.

I could tell she was not impressed. But I didn't care. "I'll be right there." I grinned at Andrew, who just shook his head. He had no idea why I had fallen for Sandy like I had, but he wasn't about to get in my way. He could feel the warmth filling me and my excitement, as I opened the door, rushed past the guard, and toward the entry hall, Andrew right behind me.

"Sandy!" I threw my arms around her in delight. She hugged me in return before pushing me back a little, to give me the onceover, confirming I was still in one piece.

"I approve," she said before sliding a finger over my necklace and winking at Andrew. "Congratulations!" She leaned forward and kissed me on the cheek, then moved to hug Andrew. "May you both have long, happy lives together."

"Thank you!" I couldn't explain my own excitement. I felt a connection to her, as if she were my mother, grandmother, and sister all in one. There were so many things I wanted to share with her about my experiences since I had last seen her that I was practically bouncing in place.

"We will, Matriarch! Thank you for your blessing." Andrew bowed his head and bared his neck, showing her the respect that I, in my exuberance, had forgotten.

"We aren't so formal, you and I. Please, Andrew, even your mate, pup that he is, senses the warmth of my feelings for you both. I've always had a special place for you in my heart, child." Sandy reached up and ruffled Andrew's hair.

"Thank you, Grandma Sandy." Andrew practically blushed under the woman's attention.

"Much better." She laughed and took my outstretched hand. "Okay, pup, lead on before you come unglued."

"Oh—Brenda." Andrew turned to the mousy brunette, who stood with her hands clenching with restrained irritation. Her face was drawn into a tight ugly frown, as if she had swallowed a bug. I suspected she thought aliens had taken over her once orderly home and more were arriving all the time.

"Yes... my lord?"

"Is Lord Basil in his library? I'd like to peruse his collection, but I don't wish to interrupt him if he's working there." Andrew was making an excuse to give me and Sandy some alone time, although he really was interested in the contents of the library.

"Lord Basil is in his private suite," Brenda stated coldly.

"Good, then I won't be disturbing him. Will you please let him know Sandy, our Matriarch, has arrived, but I'm giving her and Lance some time to themselves. I'll be joining them in about half an hour. If you'd please ask Tim and Lord Basil to join us at that time." Andrew noticed the creep of red rising on Brenda's cheeks as she steadily became more agitated. It was clear she considered us to be beneath her and disliked us intensely. For all I knew, my relationship with Andrew, as accepted as it was in paranormal society, rankled her. She was human, after all.

"Yes.... Lord Consort." She spat out the title as if it were a dirty word.

I scrutinized her every move, feeling the wolf rise in me. She had no idea who or what we were but her misguided belief that she was better than us was something I couldn't allow. "Brenda, this is your one warning. You will treat my mate with respect. If you do not, you will not remain a member of my grandfather's staff, and there isn't a vampire in this house who will keep you if you disgrace yourself and him in such a manner. You are not in my employ, but my grandfather's. What his punishment is for such rude behavior toward his family, I can only imagine." I watched as Brenda noticeably paled at the threat of Grandfather's punishment.

"I am a pureblood Prince of my kind, and Andrew is monumentally more important to me than you will ever be. Have I made myself crystal clear on this point?" I hadn't let go of Sandy's hand, I hadn't raised my voice, but the temperature in the room seemed to have dropped to near freezing. I let my eyes change to an eerie yellow green, and my fangs dropped from my upper jaw, extending farther than any vampire I'd met. Brenda seemed to have lost her voice and could only nod as she stared in abject terror. Having made my point, I let my visage return to normal and turned to Sandy. "I have so much to tell you. I'm so glad you came." I led her toward the stairs to our suite.

"Thank you, Brenda." Andrew, always his cordial self, had me practically rolling my eyes. He caught up with us before we passed the library and kissed me, then opened the large mahogany door and went in. I led Sandy up to the second story. The guard opened the door for us, letting us into the room.

"How are you holding up?" she asked.

"Surprisingly well, I think. So much has happened. It's really overwhelming when I think about everything that's happened from the beginning and how different I feel."

"Well, give me the highlights first." Sandy patted my hand as we walked to the sofa. As we relaxed, I filled her in on all that had happened in the past couple of weeks since I'd last seen her. "Wow, child, you have been busy."

"Grandfather's meeting with Stephon and a vampire named Quinn. I guess he is one of the benefactors controlling our family. They are meeting later this morning and want to introduce me to him."

"Quinn is my benefactor. He is young in comparison to Lord Stephon and Lord Basil, but he has been good to us."

"Grandfather believes he will support us as well. He wants to draw together all of my supporters so we can present a united front to the vampire council."

"Is he planning on introducing you to more than just Quinn?"

"Yes, if there is time before we are summoned." I gave her hand a gentle squeeze. "Have you heard anything from the royals? Grandfather seems to think we should have had an answer by now from them."

"Unfortunately no. It's strange, but I haven't had much luck lately reaching the Gray family. I'm not really sure what's going on. It isn't like the court to be unavailable to a matriarch." Sandy's frustrated growl took me by surprise, as I had never heard anything like that come from her before.

"I don't know what we are going to do if we can't get the royals to acknowledge us."

"Let's not cross that bridge until we end up there." Sandy nudged her shoulder into mine.

"I am really starting to dislike meeting new people."

"Why is that pup?"

"Every time I meet someone new, I end up feeling like a circus sideshow." I cleared my throat, then pretended to sound like a ringmaster. "See the amazing pure-blood shifter. He will astound you by changing into whatever beast you can think of."

Sandy burst into giggles. "Oh it's not that bad, is it?"

"Well no, I guess not. Just frustrating that I am always having to prove myself. But I do understand the importance of it all. It just doesn't make it any easier." The words gushed out as I told her everything. She was my confidant, and I respected her opinion.

"My advice, relax and go with it for now." I rested my head on her shoulder. "I will continue to try and reach the royals. Usually, you contact the court and get a response right away." She shook her head. "I can't imagine what is causing this delay. The royal family, the Gray's, are a large, but not a very talented bunch. I know they held court recently, and Prince Drake Gray, the current head of the family, presided over the gathering."

"Well, wouldn't they have talked about my petition?" The whole idea of a mini-monarchy holding court unbeknownst to the majority of the world seemed completely ridiculous. Especially since they were evidently completely powerless and were the ruling family in name only, as they also had a benefactor controlling their every move.

"We should've been given some sort of directive as to whether they were going to see us or not. For some odd reason, everyone I know can't seem to get anyone from the family to respond. Nobody knows what's happened. It's like there is no head to the royal family, and everyone is floundering, without direction, but not saying anything." Sandy shrugged.

"Well, maybe Grandfather will have better luck. It's not like they can ignore the requests of a benefactor. Granted, he isn't my benefactor, but he is a born vampire. I just hate all this waiting around. I want to get it over with already." I stifled the urge to get up and pace about the room. It was undignified and would only upset Sandy. "I don't like this. With Brad getting away, we're all worried about the possibility of spies in the household. We're pretty sure someone here tipped him off that they were coming for him. I have my suspicions, but I haven't been here long enough to really know anyone. We're keeping our eyes open, of course."

"You are being careful?" Sandy glanced nervously about the room.

"We're all being very careful. Charlie's searched the private rooms and the library. She believes as long as we aren't overheard by staff, then we should be able to speak in private."

"Well, at least you have that. I'm so glad you have her. She is a very resourceful drone." Sandy patted my knee.

"She's going to be stuck at the farm for the next couple of days while Sam gets established...." A thud sounded. We both turned toward the empty stone fireplace.

"What's that...?" Sandy frowned.

Everything seemed to go in slow motion for me from that point. There was a strange metallic clicking sound, as if a pop can was dropped from high above, down a stone wall incline, then the scrunch of aluminum imploding and a popping hiss. Something had landed in the fireplace. I was just starting to rise to investigate when Sandy, myself, and the entire sofa were blown back in a deafening explosion.

The room filled with a hazy white gas. My control over my body was slipping. I rolled my head to the side until I could see Sandy lay about foot or so from me. She appeared to be unconscious, at least that was what I told myself. Breathing was becoming difficult. Gasping for air, but inhaling only noxious gas, had my mind reeling. The beast snarled. Somehow I managed to force myself to my feet and stumbled toward the door. My legs felt numb, as if lead weights anchored me to the floor. They refused to do my bidding. My knees buckled and I slid down the door. Gasping as darkness crept around the edges of my vision, I saw the steel security lock had been thrown. We'd been betrayed... again. I could hear the guards beating on the door, trying to break it down, but nobody would be getting through. *Andrew!* I screamed in my mind, panic replacing reason as my vision faltered and darkness fell.

CHAPTER 14

Stephon's Story—Vampire Council Chambers
Winter 1728

"THIS IS utter insanity! The shifters have done nothing to deserve this type of punishment. They are an honorable race and have surrendered gracefully. Leave them alone so they can lick their wounds and learn from their mistakes as we must learn from ours," Stephon hollered over the arguing members of the council.

"You are out of order, Lord Stephon. We all know you are a shifter lover. But most of us have lost loved ones to these beasts and find your 'slap on the hand' punishment to be far from satisfying," Lord Rufus snarled.

"Well, I find your recommendation to enslave a population to be ludicrous." Stephon regarded the three members of the council on the left and then those on the right where Rufus, Lord Basil, and one other member sat. "I for one will have nothing to do with it. You all, every last one of you, know my father would never allow this. And you of all people, Rufus, should know what it feels like to be a slave. I cannot believe you would condone this travesty."

"We wouldn't have to if you would just open the veil gateway. Then we could send the shifters through as we did the fae and we would have no further problems." Rufus threw his hands in the air as if this were the simplest solution.

"How many times do we have to go over this? That is not an option." Lord Basil slammed his fist onto the table. "It takes the blood of all four races to open the gateway. The dwarves told us that in the beginning. The last of the dwarves disappeared deep into their mines centuries ago and haven't been seen since."

"There must be a way. He"—Rufus pointed at Stephon—"knows them. He must know of a way."

"The day the gateway closed, locking away a third of their population—not to mention the fact that there aren't any fae on this side of the veil so we do not have any of their blood to add to ours—the dwarves withdrew and have had no dealings with any of the surface race." Basil threw up his arms in frustration. "What do you think he can do, magically make people who've been gone, locked away for centuries, just magically appear at will?"

"I am sorry. But the veil is simply not an option." Stephon sighed. "I have not seen any of the dwarves who were my friends since that fateful day. I do not know if they even exist any longer."

"Opening the veil is simply ludicrous. But even if it were possible, I would not vote yes to condemning shifters to the other side of the veil." Basil sat back in his chair, hands clutching the armrests as if to keep himself seated.

"But—" Rufus started before being interrupted.

"There is no other way unless you break the spell, which, in my limited understanding of the magical arts, is not possible," Stephon said and closed his eyes in exhaustion.

"Then the only other alternative is to control them and make sure nothing like this can happen again. If we dilute their bloodlines with other species, their abilities will weaken. Once they no longer pose a threat to our existence, we can release them from our care." Rufus smiled grimly as if he'd won the argument. "We can even put a clause in the peace agreement giving them the chance to earn back their independence from us."

"I do not like it, but over half my family was destroyed by shifters in this war," Lady Camila, a counselor from Spain, stated coldly. "I agree with Lord Rufus. If no way to contain them can be found, then our only alternative is to reduce their power until they no longer pose a threat to themselves or others."

"Lady Camila, surely you see the folly in this?" Stephon pleaded with her. "Without the very powers you are talking about decimating, most of us would not be alive today. We would have all died long ago at the hands of the fae."

"The fae are not here. The need for such violent and unpredictable power is past, and measures must be taken to ensure a safe future. We must make sure the shifters are not able to stand against us ever again." Rufus pounded on the table.

"I agree with Lord Stephon. This is a mistake," Lord Basil argued.

"That may be your opinion, but this is a council not a monarchy. I say we put it to a vote, shall we?" Rufus glared at Basil.

Stephon shook his head sadly. "All in favor of enslaving the shifter people, raise your right hand."

The vote was four to three. "That is a majority, Lord Stephon," Rufus sneered, sitting back and crossing his arms.

"So be it." Stephon sighed and sat heavily in his chair. "With this insanity, I deem this council to be reprehensible and no longer in my power to lead. I abdicate my seat on the council. I will not be a part of this folly, and I know for a fact my father—"

"Your father is dead, and his ghost cannot help you!" Rufus yelled.

"You will not speak of *my father*!" Stephon stood and released a power wave directed at Rufus. His fangs dropped from their sheaths. His eyes had darkened to blood red, and his long black claws resembling talons deeply gouged the wooden table Stephon leaned upon. "Do not challenge me, Rufus, you cannot win."

Rufus stared at the floor, his claws extended, at the ready if Stephon were to attack, but he didn't move.

Camilla rose from her seat to stand beside Stephon. "If you choose to leave, then we will have to vote in a new leader and take applicants for your family's seat. Be certain before you make this choice. Is this how Caius would want you to carry on his legacy?"

"Please, Stephon, don't make this decision so quickly. Think about this before you walk away." Lord Basil's council was sound, as was Camilla's but this argument was hardly new. It had been going on for some time, and this outcome had been anticipated.

Caius had always taught him a government only made good decisions when the men and women within were there for the people they served and not themselves. It was clear with this vote that the council was no longer serving the interests of the people, but he wasn't sure what currently motivated the majority. The day would come when Rufus's intensions were clear, and on that day, Stephon would kill him. Contemplating Rufus's death helped him to calm down enough to draw his talons and fangs back into his body. He could be patient.

"I have done nothing but consider my options regarding what I would do if this was the route taken by this council. You have truly left me no choice. This is madness. If you cannot see truth in my words, I am forced to show you how seriously I take this matter. I am leaving. With me I take my family's honor and withdraw the power of the eldest vampire from this council." Stephon viewed the members of the council from the Lord Master's dais for the last time. Some were friends. Others were just adversaries. "Ladies and gentlemen, I am truly saddened to say this has not been an honor, but a travesty."

Stephon walked alongside the table, the gathered elders sat in complete silence as he left the room.

Summer, 1729

STEPHON HAD intended to never return to the council chambers, but not even he could refuse a direct summons. He sighed as he walked into the sweltering-hot building. He felt the weight of the world resettle on his shoulders. The rumors had run rampant after he left the council. They said he had lost his mind when Caius had passed, that he had an illness affecting his mind, and that he was simply too old for rational thought. It was all ridiculous.

Of course, the idiocy, hypocrisy, and sheer ignorance that now ran the council sickened him. Rufus held the seat of head of council, and Lord Yuri had been voted in to fill the seventh seat. There had been a number of meetings and shifters parceled out like cattle to the born vampire families to manage and control their breeding. It was idiocy.

Stephon entered the courtroom and glanced around. The heat and humidity were stifling, and still they met in secrecy behind closed doors, regardless of the fact that they were situated in the tropics.

"First of all, before we begin and must see to the distasteful but necessary work before us, I have an announcement." Lord Rufus stood at the dais, surveying the filled auditorium of vampires and drones. "I would like to introduce my son, Quinn, who has come of age and whom I can officially name as my heir apparent."

Stephon's gaze roamed the room and locked on to the handsome young man who stepped up to the dais to stand beside his father. Quinn was the most attractive man Stephon had ever met, and it took everything he had to hold himself in his seat and keep from charging the young man and standing between him and the world.

"This is my son, Quinn. May he be a positive force in our society," Rufus said the customary blessing, and Quinn smiled, although it seemed he was not enjoying his coming out.

Applause answered the blessing, and Quinn nodded his thanks to the audience and returned to his seat.

"Now on to other business. The council calls Lord Stephon La'Fayette."

Stephon rose from his seat in the gallery upon being thus addressed. "Yes, Grand Master Rufus?" He nodded to the leader of the council of seven.

"Please take the stand before the council."

"As you wish, Grand Master." Stephon stepped from his seat in the gallery. As he went down the stairs, he was met partway by an escort of warriors, the guardians of the council. Just a short time ago the guardians would've been protecting his person, not seeing him as a possible threat to the safety of the council. Stephon took his place in the speaker's box, facing some of his biggest foes as well as his friends. Little had changed since he'd stepped down from the council.

"Stephon, what are you doing? You, better than most, know the consequences for refusing a mandate from this council." The Grand Master frowned. "You've been ordered to take over as benefactor to a number of shifter families, as have all born vampires. It is our responsibility to prevent a war from ever happening again. In order to ensure the safety of our race, this council has determined that careful monitoring and controlled breeding of the shifters will safeguard that future. Never again can they have the power to threaten the secrecy of our society, our existence, or their own."

"So that's what you tell yourself in order to sleep at night?" Stephon sadly shook his head. "I wondered how you justified such slavery. You're talking about shifters as if they're prize breeding animals. These are sentient beings, not so very different from us. They were our allies in the Blood Wars. If the veil falls and we're once again faced with the prospect of Seelie and Unseelie forces invading this plane, without the full strength of our allies, we will surely die."

"We've not seen the fair folk for more than a century. The council has determined the shifters are a greater, more immediate threat. There has never been an instance of the barrier's failure since it was erected. Therefore, there is no reason to believe it will happen in the future." The Grand Master held up a hand, silencing further debate. "This is all beside the point. These decisions have already been made and are not the reason you stand before us."

"I will not treat the children and families of honored friends and warriors as livestock. What you are doing is beneath you. You're supposed to be the moral backbone of our race, and yet you believe this is the proper way to treat a great people and an honorable ally?" Stephon pointed to the shifters, lined up against the wall in chains.

"Careful, Lord Stephon La'Fayette. Your words border on treason against your race." The Grand Master snarled. "If you will not take on the shifters as beneficiaries, then the beings assigned to you will be executed. You'll be allowed to watch their deaths before you yourself are put to death for treason. Is that truly the road you wish to take?"

Stephon shook his head, gripping the banister in front of him, hissing his frustration. He focused on the shifters, huddled to the side of the courtroom.

Against his better judgment, he was about to become responsible for them. There were some men, who were clearly soldiers, and women, tightly clutching their children. An infant bawled in the arms of a young girl who couldn't have been more than twelve. Altogether, there were some fifteen people whose lives would be forfeited if he refused to abide by the council's rules.

"What time frame are you proposing? We take on the families and care for them as if they were drones. But even drones are released on good behavior after a few decades. What of these people?" Stephon motioned to the people cowering against the wall.

"The peace treaty their leaders signed gave us complete control of their race for the rest of time. We've determined there are too few of them left to maintain a viable breeding pool. We've had to separate some committed pairs. They shall be bred with humans in order to keep their race alive." A sneer betrayed the Grand Master's contempt of the shifters. As if they were no more than filth beneath his feet, to be disposed of as efficiently as possible. Stephon searched the faces of the few remaining friends he had on the council, but most appeared too ashamed to meet his eyes.

"That is not, in the strictest sense true. The document signed stated that when a pure-blood shifter is found capable of leading their people, and they have—" Lord Basil, met his gaze, albeit with sadness and regret, as he was interrupted.

"The particulars of the Right to Rule clause are moot. There will never be another pure-blood shifter. There will be no shifters left to their own devices or living independently to create a pureblood of any family line. We have insured that by taking a census of all of the families and binding them to us. No breeding outside our control will be tolerated. All children discovered outside our control will be put to immediate death." Rufus smiled with evil glee.

Stephon closed his eyes and pinched the bridge of his nose in frustration. There was no winning this fight. He'd known it was lost before he entered the chamber, but at least he had gotten the chance to speak and let the people hear his view. He would do everything in his power to prevent the total annihilation of the shifters he was being forced to take custody of.

"I do this because you give me and them no other choice. They are welcome in my territory, and I will treat them as if they were my own. Know this, Rufus: a day will come when you and this council will regret what you do here." Stephon left the auditorium and walked around to where the prison section was located and where the shifters were being held. Maurice had caught up with him and walked quickly behind.

111

"I have the wagons ready, Lord Stephon," Maurice said as they walked down the hall of closed cell doors to where the warden sat at the end of the rows. The sounds of crying children and animals in pain, whimpering their distress, echoed down the hall.

"Thank you, Maurice. Let's try to make this as painless for these people as possible. These people are refugees in my eyes, and I want them cared for with dignity and respect."

"Yes, my lord."

"Warden, please release my wards, as I would like to return to my home. This has been a very unpleasant day," Stephon hissed at the drone holding the keys.

"Ummm, I'm not supposed to let them leave until Lord Rufus comes. He...."

"He wants to gloat. Well I don't care what Rufus wants. These people need care, and they are my wards and belong to me. So unless you wish to die, I'd suggest you start opening those doors."

"Yes, my lord." The drone practically leapt from his spot as Stephon had pushed a lot of his power in the drone's direction, ensuring the man would obey.

"You are very strong," a voice said from the shadows of a far corner. "I wondered if you would come down here yourself or send one of your drones. Lord Basil assured me you would see to their care yourself."

"I wouldn't leave something like this to anyone else. I may not agree with this, but that doesn't mean I will neglect these people because of it," Stephon said as Quinn stepped forward into the light.

"That was his assessment as well." Quinn appeared hesitant, but took another step toward Stephon. "I remember you from the library. You startled me and I didn't understand what was happening, but Lord Basil explained it to me. He told me that I am so attracted to you because you are my mate."

"Yes, I believe that as well." Stephon matched Quinn's movement, easing toward him.

"I am a bit overwhelmed by you. The power you exude is much greater than my father's, and he is head of the council." Quinn tipped his head to the side and smiled slightly.

"That is because I am older than your father. With age comes power," Stephon said softly, taking another step toward his seemingly skittish mate.

"I know that. I—"

112

"You're nervous. So am I. I've never met my mate before either, you know." Stephon took the last step, and Quinn stood within touching distance.

The young vampire reached out and touched Stephon's curly golden hair. "You're so beautiful," Quinn said on a sigh.

"I've never seen anyone as handsome as you." Stephon reached out and let his hand touch the shiny black floss that was Quinn's hair. "Your hair is darker than the deepest night."

Quinn cringed and hissed with pain, grabbing his temples. Stephon immediately knew what was happening. Rufus had figured out what was going on and was trying to stop Quinn from connecting with him.

"Come to me. Let me protect you." Stephon opened his arms, and Quinn dove into them. Stephon immediately threw up a mental shield, blocking Rufus from his son's mind.

"I can't stay. I have to face him and break free. I'm of age and a man. I can do it." Quinn sighed and snuggled into Stephon's chest.

"But you don't have to. I can protect you. You never have to return to him. Just come with me now and—"

"And never be a man. Always wonder if I could have stood up for myself. Please understand that I want to go with you, but I have to do this. I can't let him rule my life. Lord Basil has counseled me that I need to make a break from Rufus as soon as possible. I have been practicing, and it was my plan to do this long before I met you. Now I just have one more reason, and the best one of all, to succeed." Quinn leaned back, and Stephon was instantly lost. Quinn was his world, whether it was good or bad, Stephon couldn't say for sure. He knew that anything Quinn asked of him, he would somehow find a way to accomplish, even if it were the impossible.

"I do understand, but I don't wish to see you hurt." Stephon rubbed Quinn's back, savoring the feeling of having his mate in his arms.

"I know you don't, but I need to do this." Quinn smiled up at Stephon. "I will meet you at the lodestones at the equinox of spring, and we will bless our union in that holy place."

"My mate is a romantic." Stephon inhaled deeply of Quinn's scent, leaned down, and sealed his lips to Quinn's. Stephon pressed forward, darting his tongue along the velvety softness of his bottom lip, asking for permission to enter. Quinn opened to him, and he had the first real taste of his mate. It was exquisite and addicting. He wanted more, but the young man was already drawing back.

"If I let this continue, you'll get me to go anywhere and I will have to return and fight my father." Quinn sighed, squeezing Stephon tight against him.

"The lodestones, at the spring equinox." Stephon closed his eyes and tried to gather his nerves so he could let go of Quinn, even though his every instinct said to hold on tight.

"Yes." Quinn's voice was breathy and featherlight.

"Until then, my mate." Stephon stepped back and released Quinn, who flinched slightly at the intrusion of his father's mind back into his. He winked at Stephon, and was gone.

CHAPTER 15

I COULDN'T actually say I was conscious, at least not completely. My head was ringing and I felt sick to my stomach. I was cramped, cold, and in the dark. Andrew hovered on the edges of my mind. He was far away and getting farther by the moment.

I realized I was moving, and the pain that rippled along my bond with Andrew because of the increasing distance between us was so intense and sudden, it almost threw me back into unconsciousness. I fought against the darkness with everything I had.

Leannan! Thank the gods! Andrew's excited voice came through loud and clear, as if he were yelling in my ear. I forced my eyes open, for him. His relief that I'd woken was a balm to our straining bond.

Not so loud! Don't shout! Everything hurts! I practically wailed back at him. I didn't want to sound so whiney, but I truly hurt. Although I knew he hurt too, his excitement overrode his sense, and my inner bitch screeched. I carefully tried to stretch my aching limbs but soon met a cold, smooth, solid surface. I couldn't get any part of my body fully extended in any direction. I groaned and forced the pain to the back of my mind.

I'm sorry, Leannan. I've just been so lost without you. Where are you? Andrew pleaded for answers to the one question I couldn't answer.

No clue, love. But, as soon as I know, you'll know. I'm in some sort of metal shipping crate, I think. It's completely dark in here—I can't see anything. But it's definitely made of some kind of metal, and there are slits on the sides and top, probably for airflow.

Do you hear anything or smell anything? His frustration level was extremely high. He wanted to be with me now, if not sooner. Still, being able to hear me was an improvement over the silence of my unconsciousness.

115

I listened carefully, and I could just pick out the deep resonant rhythmic growl of a diesel truck's engine and tires thrumming on a paved road, and also a strange hissing noise. It didn't hit me what it was until a god-awful sweet scent surrounded me and my consciousness began to swirl again. Trying to hold back my own hysteria, I began pushing with all I was worth with my feet and hands against the cold metal, but it was no good. I felt Andrew's panicked attempt to force me to remain conscious, with him. As darkness encroached, I did the only thing I could think of.

I love you.... All went black.

AWARENESS RETURNED as more of a process this time. It was like coming out of a deep sleep in stages, with parts of me waking up before others. I hurt all over, and my stomach was so empty it ached, as if I hadn't eaten in days. My mind forced itself through the sludge-like miasma of nonexistence, grasping at something to hold on to. I took hold and clung to the pain, following it through to the other side, where another mind clung just as heartily to our stretched bond. It wasn't really consciousness, more like a dream of agony, but with it came the rest of my awareness.

I had no idea how much time had passed. My mind felt thick, and logical thought was almost beyond me. I could only guess it had been a long time. When I coughed, I could taste the sickly sweetness of the gas I'd been forced to breathe. I glanced around and discovered I was still in the box, but one end had been left open. My eyes itched and my throat was sore, as if I hadn't had anything to drink in a long time.

I reached for Andrew's mind and found him. He came back strong, but his thoughts were edged with panic. *Please, Leannan, don't go! I can't take it if you slip through my mind again and disappear.*

Well, it's not like I'm doing it on purpose, you know. If you don't quit screaming in my head, I'm so going to hurt you later when I get my hands on you. My response seemed to calm him a bit.

I'm sorry, but it's been so long and we haven't been able to find you. I've been going insane and, believe me, even my family has been trying everything to get me to calm down, but nothing's worked because the only thing I need is you. Andrew was going on and on, his mind rambling as if he continued just to keep the connection alive.

Take it slow. My head is pounding, and I hurt all over. I know you're trying to find me. It's only a matter of time, love. I'll try to stay with you, but if they gas me again, you have to keep it together until I come back. I could feel his eyes behind mine, staring at the metal sides, trying to find something that would lead him to me.

I'll do my best, Leannan. I promise. Can you let me see what's outside the box?

I leaned forward, slowly, toward the open end of the box. My wolf was hesitant. I could smell blood and lots of it. There was a dead man in the room. A dead shape shifter, if my nose was correct. I didn't know who it was, and the man smelled as though he'd been dead for quite some time, maybe days.

Stay with me now. I know it's awful. Just don't black out again.

Andrew, I'm not some wilting violet. Yeah, the man's dead, and it's gross, but that won't make me pass out. It was the stupid gas. I could almost hear him chuckle. Knowing he was goading me to keep me moving was irritating, to say the least.

My wolf wanted to transform, but I was afraid to. I wanted to be human first, if I could. I didn't know where I was, and I needed to be in control. I forced my aching arms and legs to move and made my way out of the box.

Oh my God! Andrew! I gasped in shock as I peered out beyond the steel crate. *What is your little sister doing here? Do you know who the boy is?* I questioned Andrew as I ran over to where Angela and a young boy were strapped to the wall. At first I was afraid to touch them. The boy was bloody, but Angela seemed uninjured. They were both breathing but unconscious. I felt Andrew's shock and relief that Angela was there, and his fear as well.

Mom and Dad called us shortly after you'd been taken, letting us know she was missing. We've been searching for you both and fearing the worst. Everyone is spread out, trying to find a scent to follow, a lead, some way to find you. We hoped to find one of you, but I never thought we'd be lucky enough for the two of you to be together.

I tried to free Angela, but I couldn't get the manacles that bound her to the wall off. I knew a certain wolf that could, though. There was nothing else in the room, other than the bloody body and the two kids.

Can you get the kids down? I've been going nuts without you, Lance. I mean truly certifiable. Grandfather and Stephon have been trying to help, but the only one who was able to reach me was Tim. Charlie has been out hunting for you since you disappeared. I don't think she's stopped moving for a second. Andrew's dismay was beginning to rise, just when he'd begun to calm down.

I'm here, Andrew. I'm not going anywhere. You can follow our link and find me... find us. I felt him relax a bit. *Tell me what happened? How long have I been gone?*

Sixteen days. It's been complete chaos. First we had to break into the suite. Someone tripped the emergency intruder alert, and the entire penthouse went into security lockdown. Charlie says security footage of the halls show everything locking up and the guards unable to get into the room. The system was meant to keep people out of the penthouse, but the guards' passcodes didn't work to get past the locks and into the room. Andrew's mind seemed to steady a bit as he explained.

Tell me Charlie knows who did this. I was furious. Anger was better than fear. It kept me from feeling helpless. I began to scan the room, we were brought in, but I couldn't find the door. The scent of blood obscured everything, and the walls appeared seamless. Brad had left me nothing, no tools I could use to get the kids down without shifting.

We don't have any proof, but Brenda is missing. Grandfather has contacted her family, and all they will tell him is that they haven't seen her for years. Grandfather said that's suspicious as she has told him often about family visits and friends she goes to see outside of her work at the penthouse.

I'm guessing Grandfather has never had her followed or verified any of her vacations? I wanted to rage and be spiteful, blame someone for this mess, but before I had come to Grandfather's house, he'd no reason to question her loyalty. The room was pretty much bare, I couldn't even be sure if it was above or below ground. The walls were cement, empty of any windows, writing or any indication as to what the room's original purpose had been. For all I knew it had been created just for me.

No. Grandfather said Brenda's private life was her own. She'd been thoroughly investigated as all of the humans are that worked in the penthouse. They came from families who knew about paranormals and had been given at least some education about us prior to being hired. Grandfather encourages the humans working for him to be as involved in the outside world as possible. The only stipulation is that everything that goes on in the penthouse stays there. They can't reveal our existence to those who are unaware.

Did they take anyone else? Was anyone hurt? How does Charlie think they got me out of the penthouse? I needed to keep him talking. It was helping to keep my agitation at bay. I had to be able to think. The walls were blank, the floor, unmarked, the lights were high, way out of reach and fluorescent. Nothing about the room hinted where it could possibly be located.

Sandy was on the floor unconscious when we got in the room. Nobody was hurt. We believe you were hauled up the chimney. There is the scent of strange drones all over the hearth and your scent among theirs, disappearing up the stack. They wouldn't let me follow the scent once it headed for the roof.

BLOOD TIES

Grandfather was afraid that once up there if I couldn't find you, I'd transform into a bird and fly away trying to find you.

He was right to keep you there. Who would find me if they had gotten you too? I tried to make my thoughts teasing, but the Andrew's trepidation was increasing instead of being calming. Controlling my frustration and making a conscious effort to keep my touch gentle, I ran my hands over his sister's body, examining it for injuries.

It took me and grandfather together to bust down the door. Every time I started to lose it, Tim would ask me if I could hear your heart. It's the only thing that keeps me going. I'd stop and listen and know you were still with me, still alive, even though you were unconscious. I tried to find you by focusing in on the sound, and I think, eventually, I will find you even if I only have your heartbeat to guide me, but I may not be sane when I do.

I'm here now. Please, Andrew, I know it's hard. You have to be strong for me, lover. You have to find me. We need you. I sent him all the emotion and strength I could. In my mind I heard his frustrated roar, and I heard people trying to talk to him—Max and Laura, Tim and Stephon, all trying to soothe my mate. *Please, Andrew, you are scaring your family. You must calm down and find us.* I pleaded with him.

I could feel him drawing in on himself as he forced the beast's instincts and frustration back, taking a grip on our humanity and centering himself, finding his focus, seeking me out. *If you can stay awake, I can track you faster. Your conscious mind is a stronger anchor than just the sound of your heartbeat.*

I had a sense that he'd begun moving as we spoke, narrowing the parameters of where I could be from the directions Andrew was giving his family, and they were all on their way. His tone had become sharp as he barked orders, telling people where he wanted them to go and what they needed to be doing. He was an alpha male. Command was part of his genetic makeup. He focused on it now to get them all where they needed to be.

Granted, I couldn't tell them much about my location, but our bond was like a piece of string, Andrew at one end and me on the other. Regardless of how far we were separated, Andrew could follow it directly to me. I just had to stay conscious long enough and keep both of us in control for him to do it.

I'd done all the checking of the kids I could while Andrew and I had been talking. Now to decide if I should shift, and hopefully get them out of the shackles before they woke up, or wait until they woke on their own. The problem was Andrew didn't know who the boy was, so if I shifted and the boy woke up to find a wolf trying to chew through his bindings, the kid would probably freak out.

"Your Highness, I hope you didn't mind the ride. We had to make proper arrangements for you. You see, now that you've killed Prince Drake, pompous moron that he was, your own people will be against you. All we have to do is get you blooded. I suppose you don't even know what that means, Prince...."

I-I think I hear Brad. Is that bastard there with you? Andrew snarled through our link, his rage as palpable as my own.

He's not in the room. His voice is coming over a speaker system.... Damn, it's loud. I tried to keep the whimper from my internal voice, but the enraged snarl I felt from Andrew told me I hadn't succeeded.

"Blooding means you go into a killing frenzy, from the overwhelming desire for blood. When you're starved and the smell of blood is strong enough, the animal that you are will take over and kill everything in reach. You may even suck the blood from your victims like the ancient purebloods did long ago. Perhaps you will prove that shifters are more like vampires than the tame lapdogs you've become."

What utter nonsense. Andrew growled in my mind. *He can't be serious. Our people were never blood drinkers like the vampires. We hunted humans as prey and for the adrenaline rush of hunting intelligent prey—but blood had nothing to do with it.*

Then he sure has his information wrong. Damn, but didn't Brad like to hear himself talk. Either the volume had regulated or whatever damage had been done to my head—concussion or drugs—was healing, because the echoing of Brad's voice was lessening to a normal volume.

"Don't worry, Prince, it won't take long. You've been starving and unconscious for two weeks already. The smell of blood in that room must be calling to the animal in you. The killing instinct must be maddening. I almost pity the tender morsels I've left for your first kills," Brad continued blithely on.

"The only thing calling to the animal in me, Brad, is you. I will kill... but it will be you I sink my fangs into," I growled, but Brad kept going as if he didn't hear me. He probably couldn't hear me or didn't care to listen to what I had to say. This was a game of torture, and he planned for me to suffer, along with these children, who he intended to become my victims. I sighed in frustration at his complete ignorance. Seeing the dead man and the blood already spilled did nothing for me except make me want to hurl. I was grateful the kids were still out cold and not being subjected to his nonsense.

I slid down the wall until I was squatting, leaning against it so I was at the same height as Angela. I guessed the boy was a year or two older than Angela, but he'd been brutally beaten. He was so small—fine boned and fragile. He had short brown scruffy hair. His head hung down and blood trickled from his mouth, and from the wounds on his back, arms, and legs. Brad must have tortured him, the sadistic bastard. Lance had known a few humans like him, men who got off on hurting the helpless.

Andrew, I'm going to shift and see if I can heal some of the wounds on the boy. He's a shifter, and I bet he's the kid Brad took from the farm. If the drones knew Brad was beating this child, I hope Grandfather treats them with as much understanding and mercy as they did this boy. I couldn't stop the snarl, and I was glad the kids were out so they didn't hear me. I didn't want to scare them.

I transformed. My clothes, or what was left of them, slid to the floor as the quicksilver molded my body like my hands shaped potter's clay. When I stood on four legs, I found myself at the ideal height to look directly at Angela's closed eyes. I gave my fur a shake and got to work. I carefully lipped the steel wrapped around her right wrist, edging my teeth into what I hoped was just the right position. I bore down, and with surprising ease, my teeth sliced through the metal as if there weren't any barrier at all. Evidently vampire bones are harder than steel. Who knew?

It took some maneuvering, but once I had the second handcuff off, I was able to slide her down the wall so she half sat, half lay on the floor. I did the same with the boy. His beaten back left a blood smear down the wall behind him as I eased him as gently as I could to the floor.

I couldn't prevent the flashbacks of my own beatings from taunting me. I remembered the sting of the leather as it tore at skin and muscle, the heat and pain as it sliced through nerves, and the exhaustion that came with trying to be brave, but still screaming until you were too hoarse to cry out, and finally the temporary bliss of unconsciousness. I pushed it all back; my own issues had to wait. I needed to focus—the child needed me.

I gently nudged his body with my snout and paws, trying to be as careful as I possibly could easing him from a sitting position against the wall, to lying on his stomach. The view of the hamburger someone had made of this child's back made me want to hurl, and at the same time rip Brad into itty bitty vampire bits… then pee on them… then set them on fire… then pee on them again. Okay, yes, the wolf in me was a vulgar beast, but there were times I agreed with him. The best I could do was to stop thinking about how the wounds had gotten there and focused on healing the boy. Once my saliva was in his system, he began to heal quickly, even in places I hadn't laved. I could tell from the set of his shoulders the pain was lessening, and within minutes, fresh pink skin covered his back and he began to twitch as he awoke.

He didn't cry out, but he was clearly terrified. His eyes were huge, and his mouth was open in a silent scream. I whined, crept slowly around him, and rested my head in Angela's lap as Brad's voice droned on. I wished he would shut up already. God, what a self-righteous blowhard. Deciding to see if I could wake Angela, lifted my head and gave her cheek a couple of quick licks, whimpering as I nuzzled her neck with my cold wet nose. It seemed to do the trick—Angela groggily sank her fingers into my fur and began to come around.

"Uncle Lance?" Angela's tears flowed freely down her face. She clutched me to her and buried her face in the scruff of my neck. "Where are we?"

I shook my head and huffed a bit. The wolf didn't want to shift back in case Brad had some further entertainment planned. I could shift quickly, but I didn't want to take the chance.

Andrew, Angela and the boy are both awake. I'm not sure what the kid's issue is, but he's terrified of me and he's not talking. I really don't know if he can speak.

Does Angela know where you are? The hope in Andrew's tone was unmistakable.

Unfortunately, no. That was the first thing she asked me. We both sighed with frustration. I kept my eyes on the boy, who'd drawn himself into a sitting position, his back to the wall. His eyes were glued to me, watching as I comforted Angela. Everything about the boy's scent told me he was a shifter child. Yet he behaved as if he didn't know what I was. The poor boy was frozen in fear.

I cocked my head to the side and inspected the boy intently, trying to figure out the puzzle of why I frightened him to the point of complete terror. He trembled and clutched his knees, staring at me as if I was death itself. I whimpered and nudged Angela again, and she seemed to get a hold of herself. She took a deep breath and sat back. She kept a hand tightly gripping my fur for reassurance. I tried to speak to her with actions alone by casting my gaze from Angela to the boy and back again. She understood quickly enough. Living with shape shifters, you tend to learn the shorthand of the significant glance at a young age.

"My name is Angela. This is my uncle, Lance." I stayed very still as Angela gave me a final pat and moved closer to the boy. He stared at me intently but did nothing other than watch as Angela scooted closer. "Are you okay? I saw when they brought you in. Your back was bleeding a lot, and you'd been hurt really bad." The boy said nothing as Angela mimicked his pose, pulled her knees up to her chest, and wrapped her arms around them. "My Uncle Lance is really good at healing. I bet it feels a lot better now than it did before." The fact the boy wasn't answering her didn't seem to deter Angela in the slightest. She just kept talking, loud enough for me and the boy to hear her. She completely ignored Brad's continuing monologue, droning on in what I realized now was a

122

continuous loop. "He and my brother are special that way. They can heal wounds like that." Angela touched the boy's arm. "You're cold."

He flinched but didn't move away from her. He reminded me of myself after my foster father beat me, flinching at every touch. I wanted to cross the room and grab my T-shirt from where I left it on the floor, but I was afraid to move lest I upset him further. Angela moved very slowly. She took hold of his arm and rubbed slowly up and down, soothingly. I had to admit, she was good. She had a natural instinct for what would help calm the boy, and it was working. He finally took his gaze off me and peered at Angela. He put his hand on her arm and began to rub it mimicking her movements. He seemed to relax a bit. He wrapped his little arms around Angela and she hugged him back.

How are things going, Leannan? Andrew's tone was tired but determined. I felt him take a firm hold of my thoughts, as if he were assuring himself I was still there.

We're doing okay for now. But Brad really did a number on this child. You remember how distrustful I was when we first met? I wanted Andrew to know exactly what he would be finding when they arrived, because it would only increase this child's trauma if he charged in here as some rabid predator, thinking he would find Brad.

Your eyes were so wild when we first met. The slightest thing would set you off running. You wanted to trust me, but everything you'd learned told you to trust only yourself. Those were very frustrating days, especially since I wasn't sure why I was so drawn to you at first. But I didn't want you to go, and all you wanted to do was run away. The love poured through our connection as Andrew remembered our beginnings.

Well, this boy's eyes are so haunted and full of fear… and, judging from the condition he was in when I woke up, I'm guessing his life hasn't been much different from mine. Only he's much younger than I was when the beatings began. I'm guessing he's maybe five or six years old. He's really small, terrified, and probably in shock. I tried to turn as much of my revulsion and emotion at the boy's treatment off. Now was not the time to get wrapped up in flashbacks of the past. These kids needed me, and I had to focus on now.

Move slowly. Don't push him. He has to come to you of his own will, or you'll scare him away from you.

I was so glad I could still hear Andrew. No matter what Brad did, he couldn't cut that connection. I wondered if he even realized Andrew was on his way and that he wasn't alone.

"Uncle Lance, I'm really scared. Do you think they're looking for us? Are Andrew and Daddy coming?" Angela started to cry.

I stood up. The boy watched me intensely. He was terrified by me, and after his treatment, I couldn't blame him for being scared. Thinking better of it, I lay back down on my belly and crawled very slowly, with my ears forward and my head low to the ground, trying to appear as friendly as possible. I even wagged my tail. Whimpering softly, I put my nose under her hand, and curled against her. There was no way to safely tell her yes or no in this form without anyone watching knowing the answer as well. I didn't know if Brad suspected or knew about Andrew's and my mental connection, but there was no way I was giving away that advantage if he was unaware. So I soothed her as best I could by rubbing gently against her.

"I think they are, but I don't think they'll hear you if you howl." Angela ran her fingers through my fur. "That bad man said nobody could hear us if we screamed. I can scream pretty loud, but nobody heard me."

The boy watched as Angela continued to pet me. He still hadn't said anything, but his eyes held a touch of curiosity and not just terror as they had at first. He no longer feared looking away from me. At the moment, the dead body and the blood surrounding it seemed to hold his attention before it refocusing back on me. The boy frowned, his head cocked to the side as his gaze locked on mine, a bad move if I'd been a wild wolf. Staring equals challenge in the wolf world, but I had a feeling he was just trying to figure me out. Finally, he reached out to Angela, touched her arm, and pointed from me to the body of the man.

"You think Uncle Lance killed the man?" Angela asked the boy, who nodded slowly, his gaze never leaving mine. "Uncle Lance, did you kill that man?" Angela's attention was riveted on me.

I raised my head slowly and shook my head distinctly "no."

At first there was shocked surprise: his mouth fell open and he started back a little. I wasn't really sure what caused it, though—the fact that I hadn't killed the man or that I had responded to Angela's question.

"Was he dead already when you woke up too?"

I nodded my head slowly "yes."

The boy's suspicions showed clearly in his squinted eyes, but he seemed a bit more relaxed as Angela had no problem believing the wolf was answering her questions. And still in the background, Brad's voice droned on.

"See, Uncle Lance would never hurt us. The bad man who hurt you probably hurt that man." Angela seemed to have the boy really considering the possibility our captors were the ones who killed the man.

"Ptchoo!" I sneezed so violently it shook me practically from nose to tail. The scent of blood was getting stronger. Only none of us were bleeding—it

124

wasn't our blood I could smell. The overpowering, nauseating stench of warm, dead, distinctly human blood was growing, but the body was long past the warm and bleeding stage.

Then I saw it. I had to close my eyes and give my head a shake, and check again to make sure it was real. It was sick and disgusting, something straight off the screen of a bad B horror movie. High up on the wall across from where the three of us sat, in the crease where the wall met the ceiling, blood was oozing. It wasn't a rush of fluid under high pressure, but it seemed to surge as if the blood were being pumped by a beating heart. The scent was so strong it made me gag. If Brad was trying to entice the animal in me to come out... he was failing miserably. I put a paw over my nose in a futile attempt to block some of the odor.

"What's that?" Angela mumbled. She followed my gaze and saw the blood.

She stood and started toward the wall for a closer look, but I rose to stand between her and the wall. I shook my head "no." I didn't want her going any closer. We didn't know where the blood had come from. It was gross enough from a distance. She didn't need a close-up visual.

"Is that...? That's just gross!" Angela scowled, wrinkling her nose. She folded her arms over her chest, and in a flash, I saw a replica of Laura when she was cross. In a fit of temper, she stomped her foot and then pointed at the wall. "And just what is that supposed to do, Uncle Lance? We aren't vampires. We don't get blood cravings." She threw up her arms in six-year-old exasperation, but allowed me to herd her back to the boy, where she sat.

I trotted over to the box and returned with my T-shirt, which I dropped in Angela's lap before lying back down at her side.

"Here, this is for you. My uncle doesn't need a shirt when he's wearing fur." Angela handed the boy the T-shirt. It wasn't much, but it would help keep him a bit warmer. He took the shirt hesitantly. "Go on. It's okay. Really," Angela encouraged the boy.

He didn't need to be told again. He pulled the shirt over his head and shivered.

I tried to check out the wall above us as carefully as I could from my position, with my head on Angela's lap. I didn't want to be surprised if it suddenly popped a blood vessel and began to bleed.

Angela wrapped the boy's arm in hers and snuggled close, leaning against his side, while I lay with my head in her lap. She'd drawn us so close together my nose almost touched the kid's leg. I sighed and closed my eyes until they were mere slits. I could watch the room, but I appeared to be asleep. The boy was relaxing, and curiosity about me was overpowering his fear. My apparent doze gave him the freedom to really study me without fearing retaliation—which I wouldn't have done anyway, but he needed the reassurance. I completely understood his mindset. It was an all too recent way of life for me. The boy reached out as if to touch me, but pulled back suddenly, some fear still holding him in check.

Angela rolled her eyes. "You can touch him, you know. Uncle Lance isn't going to hurt you. He already fixed your back."

He reached out again and froze. Angela took his hand in hers, gently placed his hand on my head, and stroked my fur back, the way you'd teach a very small child to pet an animal. His eyes suddenly got very large, not with fear, but wonder. I didn't move. It was clear he trusted Angela, so I let her help him. She was becoming this young boy's "Andrew."

She's becoming me, is she? Andrew was clearly amused by my assessment of his sister and the boy.

Well, he is choosing to trust her, and he's allowing her to guide him, even though he probably knows he shouldn't trust either of us. So yeah, in a way, she is becoming you… at least for him. The convoluted sentence practically had me rolling my eyes, but nothing would make me jeopardize the fragile trust being extended between the lad and Angela. I just wished we knew his name.

"Uncle Lance, do you think it'd be okay if we slept? My head really hurts, and he's exhausted."

I lifted my head, opened my eyes, and nodded. I shifted slightly onto my side so the two of them could curl against me, using me as a pillow.

Angela drew him down against me with her. She laid him down so his head rested over my heart, her arm draped protectively about him. Amazingly, he was asleep almost before I could curl myself around them, using my much larger body to try and keep us warm. I draped my big bushy tail over their backs like a blanket. It was all I could do.

It's the blood loss. He's just a cub, his shifter genetics will only help him so much before his first change during puberty. You can heal him, but Tim says it will take longer because he's exhausted. He has nothing to replenish what his body is using to repair itself and you can't give him blood. He needs food and fresh water, two things I'm sure your host didn't provide you with. He'll be fine, but it will take time. Andrew filled in the blanks for me.

Well, hopefully you'll get here before long and we can help him further. I was beginning to feel a bit groggy myself, now that the children were resting. I laid my head on my paws. Transforming was out of the question. My protective instincts were riding me hard to watch over these children. I'd never felt anything quite like it. The wolf claimed them as belonging to him—his pack, his children, his cubs—and nothing would interfere, or it would die.

I watched them sleep pillowed against me, their little hands clenching my fur. The desire to rub my scent all over both of them, proclaiming to any who opposed me that these cubs belonged to me and I would defend them... yeah the wolf was in control at the moment. Angela would understand. The boy would probably not handle a wolf rubbing its body against him very well. I couldn't imagine what Brad had told him to cause him to fear his own kind.

I've asked Grandfather if they've found anything about the boy and, so far, nothing. If we can't find his family, I asked him if we could send him home to my folks with Angela since you think he's attached himself to her.

I think that's a good idea. For some reason, he's terrified of me. I'm not sure if that's because I'm a shifter, or if Brad told him I was some sort of special type and more dangerous or something strange. It pissed me off to no end that Brad would try to use children against me. My fangs grew longer, and my mouth filled with venom. There was no denying I was completely capable of ripping open the first thing that threatened us. It'd be even better if that first thing were Brad. I'd welcome the chance for the last thing he saw to be my fangs coming toward his throat, knowing there was no eternal life at the end of my bite, unlike my grandfather's. I tried hard not to growl. I didn't want to wake the children.

Lance, you're exhausted. You need to rest. Andrew's voice sounded even more tired than I felt.

I gave my head a little shake in an attempt to keep sleep from taking over. *I'm the only one capable of watching over these kids. I can't sleep.* I yawned, my jaws cracking with the extreme stretch.

The wolf is more than capable of allowing you to rest, while the beast keeps an ear peeled for intruders. I know we're getting closer, but we're still a long ways off. There isn't an immediate danger, find whatever relief you can. You may need to fight later. Andrew's reasoning was sound, but I just didn't think I could sleep. Then I felt it, the slight shift of perspective that happens sometimes when we see through each other's eyes, or really any of our senses. I felt myself slipping into his relaxed body while he remained alert in mine. *Don't worry, Leannan. Sleep if you can. I'm here. I'll keep watch.*

I slept, my mind in his body and his mind awake in mine. Yeah, if it were anyone else, it would be creepy. As it was, I had no fear of being stuck swapped. It was just a bit unsettling. How do you explain being awake and asleep at the same time, because that's exactly what I was. A sliver of my consciousness stayed with the wolf and stayed awake with Andrew, while part of him remained with me in his body, sleeping. It was more than our bond holding the two halves of us together, more than the compulsion to be joined after a long separation. This was part of the two of us being one soul in two bodies.

Andrew inspected his sister and the boy, checking them over carefully so as not to disturb their rest. He wrinkled his nose in disgust at the blood that seeped down the far wall.

Late in the night, a fresh feeling of disgust flowed from Andrew.

What's up?

Evidently since one bleeding wall wasn't enough to throw you headlong into a blooding frenzy, he must believe two will do the trick. He's started with the wall to the left, behind the dead prince and the crate you were transported in, and he's increased the amount of blood that's flowing. Andrew's revulsion grew as blood wept down the walls in rivulets of red-black ghoulish gore.

Unlike Andrew, the wolf didn't seem even remotely disturbed by the scene. He was hungry—starved, in fact—but the scent of blood filling the room did nothing to entice him. He wasn't interested in eating humans or drinking blood. He was not crazed. Angry, furious, vengeful, most definitely. But he was not going insane and would starve to death long before hurting children. It was uncanny how absolutely positive I was about that fact, while Brad, who'd lived in this world of shape shifters, vampires, and drones for well over a hundred years, was so completely wrong.

I AWOKE in Andrew's body. I opened his eyes. Joe was driving the truck down some highway, through countryside I didn't recognize. The sun was just starting to rise. It was a relief to see the sun and feel it caress my... Andrew's skin. It wasn't meant to last. I was drawn away to my own body, and Andrew needed to return to his. For a brief moment, the two of us combined. Not enough. We were still too far apart to truly immerse in each other, but it eased some of the stress on our bond. I opened eyes that were my own and felt a sense of aching exhaustion and longing from the wolf. The missing half of our soul, Andrew's presence, was putting a greater strain on us than all the theatrics, threats, cold, and hunger combined. Andrew and I needed to be reunited soon, or we would both go just as crazy as Brad believed us to be.

I took a deep breath into lungs that were mine. It was a little disorienting, switching from one body to the other. At least it was morning and I'd gotten some rest, even though it really didn't feel like it physically. But I felt more awake. Andrew would sleep for a couple of hours to give himself a break, and the others would continue to change shifts, driving in our general direction as they searched for us. There was no doubt in my mind they were getting closer to wherever Brad had us hidden. They weren't nearby, but they were drawing nearer all the time. I rested my head on Angela's lap, my tail draped around the boy, the furthest length of it reaching as far as Angela's thighs.

The tone of Brad's voice changed. "Well, little prince, I see you have the kiddies all tucked in snug around you. I am surprised at your remarkable restraint. The information I was given said ancient purebloods were like newborn drones, blood-thirsty, mindless killers. Especially when they are new to their powers and, for some unknown reason, it's supposed to be worse immediately after mating. I would've thought the boy's bleeding wounds alone would have sent you over the edge. A drone would have been unable to keep from feeding. Why can't you just fucking die already!"

He's here, Andrew. I couldn't prevent the growl low in my chest, warning Brad if he were to give me the opportunity, even if it were in front of these children, I would kill him.

We're close, love. We just need a little more time. They weren't close, though, and I knew it.

"I was sure this horror show would be over by now. Well, I guess I'll just need to make it even more difficult. Let's see how you do with live prey." The sound of grinding gears and cement grating against rock was deafening as a part of the wall began to move. I began to get the feeling that this was a very old and seldom-used bunker from a bygone era. A bomb shelter like in the movies, built to withstand a nuclear blast, the walls and what now appeared to be a door on the right side of the room, would be impenetrable. Even to shifter claws. Brenda, my grandfather's secretary, was abruptly shoved into the room, and the door closed with a reverberating bang.

"You can't do this! I did everything you asked!" Brenda screamed in protest. "You promised me!"

Angela awoke, screamed, and tightly clenched my fur in her little hands. Brenda stared at us. The boy stood. Balling his little fists, he tried to get between me and Brenda. I rose carefully, drawing a trembling Angela with me, facing the person who was clearly a threat in the children's minds. Whatever Brenda had done, she'd now live to regret it tenfold. My snarl got Brenda's attention, and by her trembling reaction, she finally recognized me for who and what I was.

"Brenda's under the misguided belief that I can make her into a vampire drone. Which both you and I are fully aware is impossible as drones are not venomous, and I, unfortunately, will never be more than a drone. Father could have turned her, but her betrayal of his family has sealed her fate, and she's as good as dead. You see, she kept me informed of your activities of the last couple of days. She kidnapped Angela and beat the boy as proof to me she was strong enough to become a vampire. What a pathetic display of human logic. At least it was amusing and served a purpose." Brad's laughter was high pitched and strained, evil sounding—my fur stood on end. "Oh, by the way, I know he's stopped talking, so I'll let you in on a secret. His name is Henry Fenrir Fitz. After your appearance, I started checking through years of birth certificates at the Denver hospital, and guess what I found?" I could practically see the sneer on Brad's face that accompanied the hatred in his voice.

"Uncle Lance, does that mean he's your brother?" Angela whispered into my ear. I flicked it so she'd know I heard her but didn't take my eyes off Brenda.

I glanced quickly toward the boy and saw liquid brown eyes looking back at me, filled with fear. He'd moved back away from us, standing against the wall. I wasn't sure if it was because I was acting more aggressively and he was scared of me, or because he was terrified he could actually be my brother and that would make him a monster too. It'd taken months for me to come to terms with being part monster—or, actually, just not human at all, but something else entirely. Now the boy, Henry, was staring at me and seeing his future.

I gazed at Angela and humped my shoulders, trying to give her an "I don't know, maybe" answer. There really was no knowing how much to believe when it came to Brad. The boy was a shifter but just a cub. There was no way to judge the beast inside to know if he had strength similar to my own. Angela was too young to shift and tell me if his scent was similar to mine.

"I suppose Dr. Tim will be the only one who can answer that question." Angela nodded, thinking hard.

I nodded too. The boy needed to calm down. I needed him unafraid of me if I was going to protect them both. Angela walked over to where Henry stood and took his hand. She still wanted to help, and the trust she put in me to make sure they were safe with Brenda in the room filled me with a sense of pride and determination I'd never known before.

Brenda stood against the wall and pulled a knife from the waistband of her pants. She waved it about in her hands.

Seriously? What the hell does she think she's doing? I sent to Andrew. There was more likelihood of there being ice water in hell than of her actually succeeding in even scratching me with the little knife she held, even in my weakened, starved state.

I growled, shook my head, curled and drummed my claws so they clicked eerily on the cement floor. I wasn't worried about Brenda and her little knife. She wasn't worth my time. My fangs alone were longer than the knife clutched in her hands. I kept myself between Brenda and the children. She'd done enough damage to them, and I really didn't care to kill her in front of the kids.

For the time being, she seemed content to stay as far from me as possible, and I was good with that. Brenda was shaking so hard I wasn't sure she could've used the knife if she'd wanted to. If there was an award for stupidity, Brenda would be the winner—wait, there was: the Darwin Awards, given for the stupidest way to die. Brenda would now be at the top of that list. I pitied her, but it wouldn't save her. Brad was right. She would be dead soon, and most likely by the very fangs she'd wanted to make her immortal.

"Brenda's betrayal made it possible for me to kidnap you. It made me sick when she told me how my father... my father gushed over you. That sick old man! He's gone senile! Crazy in his old age and infirmity!" Brad ranted. "He should be hibernating, regaining his strength, because his mind has gone round the bend. It's unheard of for a born vampire of his standing and a member of the council to be fawning over a shape shifter! And not just any shape shifter! Oh no! He has to go nuts over a royal pureblood of the line that disgraced his only born son." Brad hissed. "I can save him and all of us. You're as big a threat to your own race as mine. I can prove it, and before anyone knows what's happened in my family. Then Father can sleep and I can handle things for him as I am destined to. I'm recording everything that happens in that room to show our world how vile and unstable purebloods really are. You'll be put down for the benefit of us all, and nothing will change. I will remain my father's heir apparent."

Now I understood. It wasn't just the greed and prejudice. He was jealous. Brad was used to being at the center of Grandfather's world. He was used to getting all the praise from Grandfather's ventures. And then I'd appeared and stolen his thunder, disrupted his carefully arranged world. He was going to fix it, save the entire paranormal world from the evil he saw me to be, and make himself the hero. Well, I had news for him—his great plan was backfiring. He didn't know me nearly as well as he thought he did. All this blood was just making me nauseous.

Spoiled rotten bratty man! Andrew seethed.

The worst part is I'd have given him anything he wanted if he would've asked. I didn't even know he thought I was taking things from him. How could I? He was attacking me before I even knew who I was. The whole thing seemed like a complete waste to me. All this hatred because of such an all-consuming selfishness—it was truly beyond my comprehension. I'd grown up with nothing, and now I couldn't understand how there couldn't be enough for everyone to share.

Through Andrew's mind, I heard the conversation with Grandfather. "...she was your leak. From what he's telling Lance...." Grandfather's snarls of rage were enough to make me rather pleased I wasn't Brenda. Her final fate would not be pleasant. Evidently the combination of her pleading and the fact she had disappeared after my kidnapping sealed her fate. She might have been suspected of a lot of things, but her date was now assured, once grandfather got a hold of her.

By the amount of peripheral information I was getting about Andrew's surroundings without even trying, I could tell that they were much closer. They'd begun a kind of circling pattern, narrowing my location down, using Andrew like a divining rod, trying to pinpoint our location.

To my utter disgust, another stream of blood began to ooze down the wall on the right. The scent intensified, and my stomach wanted to heave. If there'd been food in my stomach, I'd have vomited. So in a way, I was grateful I was starved.

"What the hell!" Brenda screeched as the blood poured steadily toward her. She watched the slow-moving stream and stepped away from it and toward us. I growled menacingly at her. She didn't want to be by the blood, but she was far safer dealing with something disgusting than getting any closer to me and my fangs.

The sight of more blood seemed to be the final straw for a haggard Angela. She began to sniffle, her little hands fisting and then rubbing her eyes. I shifted around so I could keep my gaze on Brenda but see Angela as well. It put me closer to her and Henry, who still had his back against the wall, but Angela needed me and I had to watch the enemy and the place on the wall where it became a door.

I whimpered softly, calling to Angela, and she veritably flew off the wall and threw her arms around my neck, bawling hysterically. I rubbed my head into her chest, trying to reassure her, to soothe her as she fell apart. That was when I felt him. The boy must have been moved by Angela's tears, because his hand rested very lightly on my hip as if to tell me he was there. He moved so quietly and slowly, I didn't dare move, afraid I'd scare him off. He came behind Angela and put an arm around her, the other clutching my fur as if to draw strength from me. She spun away from me and wrapped her arms around Henry, who let go of me and embraced her.

Get the twins on checking out Brad's story about this boy. I don't know if he's telling the truth, and I really don't care. After this, if he doesn't have a family, he will become my brother. The boy was clearly a shape shifter and traumatized, but if he really was my brother, I'd have yet another reason to destroy Brad.

"…Henry Fenrir Fitz. Brad said he was born in Denver, and Lance thinks he's maybe five or six years old. See what you can find. In fact, it probably wouldn't hurt to do a historical search of the hospitals in the area and see what if there are others…."

I heard Grandfather gasp at Andrew's words. The possibility that I had brothers or sisters out there, that he'd missed more than just me, would devastate Grandfather.

CHAPTER 16

BRAD HAD finally shut up. I wasn't sure if he'd left or was waiting for me to rip Brenda apart. Truth be told, I didn't want any part of her. I was leaving her for Grandfather. There wasn't anything I could do to her that would be more terrifying than what my grandfather would do when he arrived. I only hoped he'd have the restraint to allow me to remove the children before he took his revenge.

"Uncle Lance. Are you okay?" Angela wiped her eyes on her arm and hiccupped as she tried to stop crying.

I'd begun trembling as I contemplated Grandfather's vengeance. I took a deep breath and stilled my nerves. I nodded my head at Angela to show I was fine. It was hard knowing things and having no way of sharing them without shifting, but my being human would leave them vulnerable, so that was out of the question.

"Can you change into something different, Uncle Lance?" Angela's hand stroked my head. She stared at the strands and I could feel her fingers sorting one color of hair from another, picking at them lightly. "I like your wolf, but I want to see the other animals that everyone is always talking about."

She was trembling and kept glancing between Brenda, the knife she held, and the wall of blood. Then she'd stare at my fur and pick some more before her gaze would travel to the body and then back at my coat. She was a shifter and a strong little girl, but she was still just a cub and even though some of the things she might not have seen before, but had heard spoken of before, like dead bodies and blood. This was far beyond what her young psyche was truly capable of handling. She needed her parents. She needed a bit of normal and watching me shift as she'd seen her brothers and parents shift many times might help her keep her world just that much more in control. Although it might make Henry a bit more nervous, it all depended on what Brad or Brenda had told him.

I gave Angela a wolf grin, my tongue hanging out, before I gave her a slurping tongue-washing kiss on the cheek. She giggled a bit, which made me feel significantly better.

I eyed Brenda, who'd found a corner where the blood wasn't pooling. She trembled, clutching the knife to her breast. If I started shifting to larger carnivores, I'd probably frighten the human right out of her tiny little mind. My wolf barked in the back of my mind, liking the idea of showing Brenda exactly what kind of demon she thought she could betray. Henry shyly smiled and cocked his head to the side, curiosity clear on his face. I nodded and waited for Angela to choose.

"I've already seen the falcon, and this really isn't a good place for a bird. You can't fly in here."

I watched as Henry's jaw dropped open. I wasn't sure if it was because he never considered a bird or because I could fly. Either way, I'd have to ask him about it later, when there was more of an opportunity to show him what the possibilities were.

"How about the polar bear? Jack and Joe seemed impressed by him."

I watched Henry, who'd taken a step back. He'd gone a bit ashen at her suggestion, but Angela smiled at him and took his hand. I nodded and stepped a little way from the children and let the quicksilver take me, morphing the brown wolf, increasing my size, bleaching my fur. The change was so smooth and seamless, as if my entire body became liquid for a split second before reforming into the new shape. Where the wolf had previously stood, now an enormous polar bear took up over twice the space.

Angela squealed and clapped her hands. "You look like a giant white teddy bear!"

Sure, I could be a teddy bear for Angela and Henry, but for Brenda, I was her worst nightmare. Facing Brenda, I pulled back my lips and yawned, showing her my dagger-like teeth. When she started to cry, her fear became a palatable scent in the room. I enjoyed it.

Angela bounced over and began running her hands through my coarse white fur. "I could cuddly you all the time. Much better than my teddy, Uncle Lance. I bet you are warm in all that fur."

I gazed at Henry. He seemed nervous but not nearly as frightened as before. Curiosity was winning out as Angela continued to stroke my fur. I watched Brenda as Henry came to stand beside Angela and stroked my pelt. He laid his head against my shoulder and wrapped his arms around me as far as he could make them go. I felt the fingers of his right hand tap against my shoulder, beating out the rhythm of my heartbeat. He listened to my heartbeat, and I felt him smile slowly, as if it reassured him to hear it.

Angela trembled, and it seemed to run the length of her little body, but not because of fear. The temperature in the room felt like it was dropping. The children's breaths appeared as little puffs of white mist, proof of the warmth escaping their small lightly clothed bodies. If I didn't keep them warm, they'd die of hypothermia. Brad's death couldn't be gruesome enough or painful enough to atone for what he was putting these kids through. He could do what he wanted to me—I was an adult—but to hurt kids made him a truly horrible monster. I lay down and willed my fur longer. My bear was a much more massive animal than two children. If they would curl up with me, I could wrap myself around them, keep them warm, and still keep my eyes on Brenda, who seemed to have resigned herself to the death coming for her.

On my back, with my belly exposed and my front paws held open in invitation, I tried to make myself into a fuzzy polar-bear-shaped hot water bottle, inviting the kids to join me so I could keep them warm.

"It's getting cold." Angela sniffled and wiped her nose on her sleeve.

I nodded and wiggled my toes, waving the kids nearer. Henry, surprising both me and Angela, took her hand and drew her down beside me. He wrapped himself around her and curled against my side. I carefully wrapped myself around the two of them until little of the kids could be seen. I could only guess that Brad hoped to provoke me by messing with the temperature in the room. Well it worked, I was good and pissed off, but at the same time, I realized the longer he stayed, trying to mess with me, the greater our chances were he'd get caught here.

I nuzzled the top of Henry's head, reassuring myself as much as trying to soothe him. I could do this; I could keep them warm. They were safe. I was more than a match for anything Brad could throw at me.

LANCE! LOVE! You need to wake up for me.

I wasn't sure how long I'd been asleep, but Andrew's voice drew me from the fog. *Andrew?* I felt thick. Despite the fact that he was getting closer, I was starting to have a harder time drawing myself to consciousness. It wasn't that I was losing myself... exactly. I needed my mate, and I needed food. I was dying, and my mind was losing cohesion. The animal part of me was taking over. He'd never hurt the children. Brenda... well, she was another story. My anger with her would soon make her prey. I gave my head a shake, trying to clear the cobwebs.

136

You expecting someone else to speak to you in your mind? The love flowing through our connection was strong, even though he was teasing me. He was closer to me than he'd been in a long time.

A wave of longing struck so hard I wanted to rip through the walls containing me, and only the sleeping cubs curled between my paws held me in check. *Where are you, my mate? I need you so much. I feel like we are dying.* I tried not to whimper, but it was getting harder all the time.

Be strong, Lance. We're close. Andrew's tired sigh told me he was feeling as disconnected as I was. *The twins have worked their magic. They were able to find the birth certificate of Henry Nathaniel Basil Fenrir Fitz, born a year before my sister Angela. He's been in several foster homes, his experiences not all that different from your own. He's been labeled a hard-to-place child with emotional problems.* I could practically feel Andrew's growl through our bond. He despised the people I'd lived with. Even though I understood it wasn't their fault, I wasn't any fonder of them. Knowing the boy hadn't fared any better than I had didn't please me.

I nuzzled his head, allowing myself to hope for the first time that he might be my actual little brother. I didn't know what to feel other than an overwhelming seething hatred for Brad. *I... I have a baby brother. Andrew, I have a brother,* I stammered, trying to get my mind around the fact the boy between my paws was my own flesh and blood.

The twins are searching the hospital records and trying to see if there are any others. You could have a much larger family than we've even considered.

I continued to soak in the scent of the boy. The more I breathed of him, the more I felt he belonged with me, and absolutely nothing could take him from me now that I'd found him.

My control over the animal in me was becoming thin the longer I was separated from Andrew, but at the same time, his voice in my mind had been getting steadily stronger. He was getting closer; the pain of our stretched bond was significantly less. I just needed to hold out for a little longer, and my mate would be here to make everything right.

Despite the fact that there'd been little to do, exhaustion, starvation, and sleep deprivation were beginning to win, and I was losing the battle, and yet I wasn't. I knew even if the beast completely took over, the first thing I'd do would be to attack Brenda. As sick as it made me to think of it, I knew the beast in me would eat her without qualms. The protein I'd gain from that meal would keep me sane until Andrew arrived, but maybe not for much longer after that. I might not be human, but I do identify myself as mainly human in the sense of who I am. I didn't want to become a cannibal. I would hold out. I'd find a way. They were so close. I was sure Andrew would find me before I lost control.

In spite of myself, I yawned, my bear mouth opening wide, showing all my dagger-like teeth. I felt Henry watch me as I yawned a second time. He reached for my face. I lowered my head to where he could reach. He lifted my lip and inspected at my teeth, touching the huge fang that was longer than his hand. He wrapped his little fingers around the tooth in wonder at the size of it. His finger brushed my nose, and I sneezed. A smile lit his face, and silent laughter shook his little frame. I nuzzled his hand gently, and he petted my head and then ran his fingers over my rounded ears. He was warm and protected for possibly the first time in his life. I knew how it felt to be alone. It sucked, but my little brother wasn't alone anymore. When he was finished exploring my bear shape, he settled down alongside Angela, draped one of his arms over her back, and fell asleep.

I beheld the charges in my care and began to think about the battle to come. Even though I wanted to sink my teeth into Brad, I needed to protect these cubs more. *When you arrive, I'm going to need to move very quickly and I'll need to do it carrying the children. They've already been so traumatized by what they've been through. They don't need to see a battle as well. We need to get them to safety first, take revenge second.*

I could feel Andrew's reluctance to delay and possibly lose the advantage of surprise to the rescue of the kids, but he quickly let it go as he felt my resolve to save his sister and my brother. *We'll lose some of our advantage, and even getting them out of the room may not prevent them from seeing us fight to get to you. But I can appreciate wanting to protect them as much as possible.* Andrew's sigh was practically audible. I felt like he was almost in the room with me.

I need to be something large but fast. Any ideas? I wasn't sure what would be the best option. The bear was certainly large enough to carry both children, but not the fastest animal, at least not compared with a vampire. And although Brad was a drone, we didn't know who his reinforcements were. *A cheetah maybe?* I considered. I used the thought for just the right animal to distract both of us from the dull ache in our chests, from the feeling of being slowly torn apart.

A cheetah is the fastest land animal, but they have such a light frame, even if you reinforced the animal's natural form and made it heavier-boned than normal, I don't think it could hold both children. Andrew's logic was sound: the lightweight cat would never work.

I tried to think about every animal I'd ever seen for just the right beast. For a moment, an elephant flashed through my mind, and I smiled at the thought of trumpeting a charge and blasting my way out with the kids perched high up on my shoulders, out of the way of any possible attack. A cartoon elephant charging through cartoon walls filled my thoughts, and I chuckled softly.

Andrew's amusement at the thought was as clear as my own. *I still don't think your elephant belongs here, love. He would definitely be strong and fast, but you would never get out the door. Cartoon elephants may charge through walls, but living flesh doesn't go through cement very well, shifter or not. I think either the lion or the tiger would be your best choice. Even the bear is a bit large.*

The image of the bear trying to fit through the door with the children on its back and getting stuck in the middle almost made me laugh aloud. I was trying hard not to awaken them. They were asleep, and the more they slept, the more quickly time would pass. It also conserved energy, something none of us could spare.

THEY WERE here. It was close to morning, and it was overcast outside. My skin crawled with the need to touch my mate, who was very close. Seeing through Andrew's eyes, I could watch my family as they moved into position, surrounding a building. Grandfather, Laura, Max, Jack, Joe, Sam, Charlie, Tim, and the guard were about to attack. I drew back into myself, giving Andrew a mental hug before opening my eyes to my prison.

I glanced around the room and noted Brenda was still curled into a near fetal position clutching her little knife to her chest. She hadn't moved. If she was still there when the door opened, she would die where she lay.

I gently awoke the children, nuzzling them both until I had their complete attention. I stayed wrapped around them as I let the quicksilver take me. My fur softened, and black stripes covered my body. The muzzle on my face drew back, changing from the bear to a cat. My bones changed position and shape, into a narrower body style, that of my white tiger. I felt Henry stiffen and then relax. I'd transformed much closer to him this time than I had before, and there'd been no warning. I watched him carefully for his reaction, but he tipped his head to meet my gaze. He nodded and laid his head against my side, listening to the beat of my heart. It was as if he were checking to see if it sounded the same each time, reassuring himself that I was still me.

"Oh, Uncle Lance, you're magnificent. I really like this shape best of all."

I purred softly, thanking Angela. But we didn't have much time and I needed them to move. I had to get them ready for what was coming, and that meant I needed them on my back, ready to escape this room when the door opened. I looked at Angela and Henry, and then over my shoulder at my back, and growled softly.

"What is it?" Angela whispered.

I repeated the action, first at her, then at Henry, and then over my shoulder. I growled as I stared at the door. Henry caught on first. He took hold of Angela's hand and guided her up over my side as I rolled onto my stomach. She lay with her stomach over my shoulders, her arms draped over my neck, clutching at my fur. Henry climbed on behind her, lying a bit over her back, hands clutching at my fur, helping to hold her on.

With them settled in place, I modified my tiger's shape. I willed my legs longer and my chest and shoulders narrower. My body complied silently, making the small adjustments I needed to be able to get through the door with the kids astride. I willed my fur to grow longer and thicker, giving them plenty to hold onto.

The tiger lay very still, as if I were waiting to pounce. The door held my attention as I bunched the muscles beneath me, the tiger ready to strike, to charge the moment it opened. I focused momentarily on the near-comatose Brenda. She was curled in on herself in a fetal position against the wall. If she noticed my change or that the children were astride my back, she didn't show it. It had been quiet for a while now, the odds of Brad watching us beyond the door were slim, but whoever stood guard would soon regret their alliance with him. I doubted if anyone would be allowed to live for long.

Whenever you're ready, love, we're as ready in here as we're ever going to be.

The only answer I received was a roar both familiar and strange at the same time. Andrew was calling, but the animal he'd chosen was new. Screams came from outside the bunker. It was Andrew.

"Raaawww... ooo... ooo... ooo," I roared as I got carefully to my feet, with my charges clinging to my back. It served a dual purpose. I answered Andrew's call and kept Brenda at a distance. I might not be the one bringing her death, but I didn't want her to think I wasn't every bit as angry at her betrayal as Grandfather, and I was very willing to kill her if she pushed me. Andrew was just outside the door. I readied myself, steeling myself against my instincts to tackle my mate as he came in the door.

Screams continued; death was here, and the guards loyal to Brad were dying. If the drone remained, watching us, I had no delusions that Brad would be anything but dead. Something heavy was slammed repeatedly against the door. It flew open with a crash, and a couple of vampires and humans tumbled through, scrambling madly over each other in an attempt to get away from their pursuer.

Grandfather was fierce, truly an angel of death, as he strode gracefully into the room, a hand resting on the shoulder of a bristling, enormous, silverback mountain gorilla that practically dwarfed him. Yet the power emanating from Grandfather held me frozen in my tracks. He was every bit the vengeful bloodthirsty ancient vampire lord. It was terrifying to behold, and I was thrilled he was on my side. Grandfather's eyes were blood red with his rage, filled with the death he dealt without remorse or feeling. He was drenched in a miasma of black and red blood and gore that dripped from elongated fangs and claws, signs of death delivered.

My mate was just as enraged, though his beautiful sky-blue eyes remained the eyes I loved. His gorilla arched its back and roared, pounding his chest before returning to all fours. His fangs dripped with poisonous saliva. His bite would be a death sentence to any drone. He was powerful enough to rend a drone limb from limb and fast enough to catch them. I was very impressed. The silverback had easily gone through the door. Which was something I needed to do, even though I ached to pounce on the big monkey.

"Uncle Lance."

I heard Angela's fearful whisper. Both children clung desperately to me, and they leaned away from the vampires, from all of them, including Grandfather and Andrew. Angela didn't recognize her brother in this shape, and I couldn't tell her.

"Grandson, take your young charges from this place. Charlie is waiting for you beyond this door. There is nothing left alive in this building that will hurt you. Children, close your eyes and hold on tightly to Lance. He will take you out of the building, but keep your eyes closed." Grandfather's voice rang with power, and I felt the underlying compulsion press upon the kids. Willingly or not, they would keep their eyes closed and cling to me until we cleared the building.

I rumbled a thank you to Grandfather as I charged out the open door. It was all I could do to force myself from the room. The ache to touch Andrew was a physical pain, but I had to get the children out before Grandfather lost the composure that held him in check and the cubs saw something to further traumatize them.

As I slipped out the door, I was struck by the remains of the battle. It was grisly. There were the remains of drones, ripped apart, oozing black sludge-like blood and what appeared to be a human or two from the body parts that oozed red instead of black. It appeared that Brad had convinced more than just Brenda to his cause. Whether they were paid thugs or expected something else was irrelevant, they were dead. I took off at a run, down the hallway, up a flight of stairs, and outside before the screaming began again. The children, who still had human hearing, couldn't hear the pleading and terror in Brenda's voice as Grandfather took his vengeance. I had no pity for her, remembering Henry's condition and the merciless plan Brad had for these children. It was one thing to try to hurt me, but to try to make me attack children was beyond low. As I exited the bunker, I realized Charlie stood waiting at the door and my mate followed on my heels.

The fresh air of twilight hit my face, and Laura and Max appeared at my side. They swept Angela off my back and into their arms. They tried to get Henry to let go, but the boy clung to me as if his life depended on it. Tim stood back by the car. He held a pair of sweats for me. I glanced around the clearing and saw that the twins and Sam had taken over standing guard at the entrance to the subterranean hellhole we'd just emerged from.

Henry hugged my neck, his face buried in my fur. I could smell the fear radiating from his little body. He was surrounded by all these people, and he didn't know any of them. He didn't know who the monsters were and who he could trust. I understood his feelings all too well. I walked with Henry to Tim and took my clothes in my jaws, and then I wandered a short distance away from everyone. My mate and Charlie took up positions to watch me, close by but not too close.

They weren't about to let me out of their sight for long. But Henry needed some distance away from everyone. He needed a moment's peace before the strangeness began again. He lay upon my back, stiff and immobile, as if he were afraid to move, lest the monsters notice him and come after him. It struck me in that moment how small and young he really was. I lay down in the grass and began to purr softly, the vibration soothing, trying to tell Henry the only way I could that everything was all right.

Henry loosened his grip and raised his head. I peeked over my shoulder. He trembled as he took in our surroundings. He could still see the others, but they were far enough away that I hoped he would feel safe. It was the first time he was actually alone with me. He slid down from my back until he was sitting beside me, touching my side.

I let my transformation happen slowly. I didn't want to scare the kid, but there was no easy way to do this. When I was a naked man, lying on my stomach, I eased over onto my side and sat up.

"I'm just gonna get dressed, okay, Henry?" He watched me, his eyes filling with fear as I pulled on the sweat pants. I didn't bother with the T-shirt. I was more concerned with Henry's growing anxiety. I sat down beside him, and he tentatively reached out and touched my side, now completely bare of the fur that had previously covered me. He began to hunch his shoulders and withdraw, the fingers that touched me trembling. I had no idea what Brad had told my brother, but I had to ease his distress. I slowly opened my arms, then tapped my chest. "I'm still me in here. No matter what shape I take on the outside, Henry, I'll always be me."

Henry leaned back and stared deeply into my eyes before inching slowly forward and resting his head against my chest. When I felt him sigh and collapse against me, I wrapped my arms around him and held him tight.

"See, same heartbeat. I'm the same person, regardless if I'm a wolf, a bear, a tiger, or any other animal." I felt him rub his face against my chest. He was unconsciously marking me as his. He had no idea what he was doing, but I smiled nonetheless. My brother was accepting me. "Henry, are you okay?" I asked him gently, almost afraid he wouldn't respond.

He nodded slowly against my chest, then gazed up at me. His small hand reached up, and I felt his fingers slide along the necklace hanging round my neck. Sitting back a little, he picked it up, and carefully inspected the wolf and dream catcher. I cupped his face and drew his gaze to mine. His eyes were a soft gray, with little flecks of gold in them. He wrapped his arms around me and rested his head back against my chest. I stroked his short brown hair and snuggled him close, wrapping the T-shirt around him.

"It's going to be okay now. You're safe. Nothing will ever hurt you again. Not while I'm here." I rocked him gently, meaning every word. I felt him sigh, not in contentment but as if to say... buddy, if you only knew my life. I looked down into troubled eyes so much like my own. I almost laughed, because in that moment, I knew just how Andrew had felt when I'd done the same thing to him almost nine months ago. It was hard to believe so little time had passed. It felt like so much longer.

And as hard to believe as you found it then, I still managed to keep my word, most of the time. I felt Andrew's slight hesitation.

Don't you even start to think this was in any way your fault or your responsibility to prevent. Because of who I am, people will always be attacking me. It is going to be a fact of our lives. Our responsibility is in how we respond to the attacks and making sure we get back to each other as soon as possible. I would not put up with his blaming himself for Brad's actions even for one moment. The only one I would hold responsible was Brad, and he would pay dearly. *Everyone alright?*

Yeah. Grandfather is something else. I've never seen anyone quite as deadly as that man. Andrew emerged from the bunker, making his way slowly toward us.

"You know, I do think you're my little brother. I didn't know you existed. I wish I had." I rubbed my cheek against the top of his head. "Until about a year ago, I was in foster care too. We have a grandfather. He really cares a lot about us. He didn't know we were alive either. We have a real family, and Angela is part of that family. See, she's over there with her parents, Laura and Max. They're shape shifters, like us. We're a very proud, loving, and strong people."

Henry shivered but watched everything that was going on around us. He saw how Angela was being held and rocked by Laura, much like I was taking care of him. He snuggled back against me and patted my chest. Everyone continued to move about the clearing, preparing to leave, and he observed it all.

He wasn't as damaged as I'd been. He was scared, but he still wanted to reach out. I'd never have been able to reach out like that. Maybe it was hope opening doors for him. The damp trail of tears running down my chest was proof of his release of the fear. He, at least, felt safe enough to cry. I could only hold him and rock slowly back and forth, trying to soothe him. I began to softly sing. "When you feel afraid, when you lose your way, I'll find you. Just try to smile and dry your eyes. I will bring the moon back into your skies...." His tears covered my chest and I just held him until he cried himself out.

Andrew came up behind me. He couldn't stay away any longer. He leaned into my back, his arms coming around mine to hold both of us. *I... I'm sorry, Leannan. If I don't hold you both, I....* Andrew stuttered as his body trembled against my back.

It's all right. I understand. I need to hold you, too, but I can't just abandon my brother right now. He barely accepts me and Angela. He's terrified of everyone. The ache in our hearts from the separation was raw, and the compulsion to be together physically as well as mentally to reestablish our bond wouldn't be denied much longer. I felt the pressure of tears in my own eyes and knew soon I'd be forced by my very nature to abandon my brother, regardless of the damage it would do to our relationship. My bond with Andrew wouldn't be denied. The three of us rocked, and I stared up at the star-filled sky.

Henry startled a bit when he saw Andrew behind me, his chin resting on my shoulder, his arms wrapped around both of us, but he didn't shy away.

"This is my mate—my lover, Andrew."

Andrew tipped his head to the side and smiled softly. He reached out and ruffled Henry's hair very gently. "Hi, Henry."

"He was the gorilla. Did you get to see the gorilla?" I leaned back into Andrew. "He was magnificent."

Henry nodded, still eyeing Andrew with a kind of awed expression. He reached out a tentative hand and touched Andrew's arm. My stomach gave a loud gurgling growl, and Henry's eyes lit up with amusement as he patted my stomach. It was the opening I needed.

"Henry, I have to go hunt. I must eat. It's been too long since I've eaten, and any supplies the family brought won't be enough to feed the animal living inside me." I felt Henry stiffen and fear come back into his eyes. "Hey, now, no need for that." I rocked him back and forth, soothing the rush of anxiety. "I don't have time to explain everything, but I will. We don't hunt humans. There are plenty of deer, antelope, and elk in these hills. Andrew and I will go hunting. It'll take about half an hour or so, and then we'll be back."

144

Henry relaxed but didn't let go.

"Lance needs to eat. I'm sure you're hungry too." Andrew's deep voice rumbled from over my shoulder.

"Do you think you will be okay with our grandfather and Angela while Andrew and I hunt?" I felt him tremble and his slight shake of the head. "I think Angela's mom brought sandwiches and drinks. I know she makes really good cookies. Are you hungry?" His arms tightened around me. He wasn't ready to be separated from me just yet, and I didn't have time to get him ready. "Andrew, will you please go get Grandfather for me?"

I felt Henry's heartbeat begin to race and his breathing take on an almost hyperventilating pace. "Okay, it's okay, Henry. I just want you to meet him." Henry trembled violently, his little body shaking just from Grandfather's approach. "Grandfather is very important to me. He loved our mother and father very much. Please, just meet him for me." I stroked Henry's hair, trying to tell him with my actions as well as my voice that he was safe.

Grandfather settled on the grass beside us, his shoulder touching mine. I had tried everything to calm Henry but it wasn't working. Grandfather's soft deep voice spoke with kindness, and reassurance as if to back up mine. I was almost panicking myself as Henry gasped for air and shook, his panic attack increasing instead of quieting.

"Shhh, little brother. It's okay, Henry. This is our grandfather." I rubbed Henry's back. I babbled on, crooning, enticing, begging Henry to relax. "His name is Lord Basil, and he has the most wonderful green eyes. You can see straight to his soul through them. He loves us very much." I felt Henry's breathing slow a bit, and he leaned back and peeked up at Grandfather before shivering and closing his eyes and lying back against my chest. "He isn't a shifter like us. But he is a part of our family. He has very cool skin, and his heart is quiet. It doesn't beat as ours does, but if you listen very closely, you can hear it whispering that he loves you very much. Did you see him come to our rescue?" I felt Henry nod. "He was a little scary, I know. But he was there with Andrew. They were both worried about us and afraid for us. They fought to save us and get us out of there safely." I felt Henry take a deep breath as if to gather himself. He stared at Grandfather for what felt like an eternity, then Henry's trembling stopped and he relaxed. His grip on me eased, and his body went limp in my arms.

"Okay, Grandson, I'll take him now. You go and take care of yourself and Andrew. He will remain asleep until you are again able to handle him." Grandfather scooped Henry from my arms. "He won't remember falling asleep. I'll be able to get some food into him as, for the moment, he will do everything I tell him to."

"What did you do?" I was afraid Henry had fainted. He was limp in Grandfather's arms.

Grandfather shook his head, grinning sheepishly. "A dirty vampire trick. We have a very hypnotic gaze when we choose to use it. I simply put him to sleep. When he wakes up, you'll be there holding him just like now. He won't realize that you were ever gone." Grandfather swept a brown curl from Henry's forehead. "I'll hold him until then. Hopefully, he'll be able to accept me. Though I'm afraid the damage Brad's done this child may be too extensive. I'm afraid my little grandson won't be able to return my love."

"He'll be fine, Grandfather. We're a resilient family. It may take some time, so be patient. He's just a child and not nearly as damaged as I was when Andrew found me, even though my method of coping didn't include not talking." I arranged the T-shirt around my brother, tucking the material around him. "I couldn't love you more."

"Yes, but you were hurt by humans, not by a vampire." Grandfather shook his head, leaned forward, and kissed Henry on the forehead. "This may be the only chance I get to love my grandson, and I intend on enjoying the moment. Even if he doesn't know it."

Grandfather stood with Henry in his arms as if the child weighed no more than a sparrow. He extended a hand to me, and I stood slowly. I was a bit light headed. With Henry cared for, Andrew became my focus. We walked back to the group. Andrew had been discussing with his parents about allowing Angela to visit us at the penthouse for a couple of days while Henry adjusted to his new home. The idea held merit, but Laura and Max weren't sure they wanted her out of their sight. I could understand their trepidation. Brad still remained on the loose, and who knows what the drone would try next or who might get caught in the crossfire. There was also the worry of having a family member of Andrew's living at Grandfather's house. Angela was too young to be considered a fosterling. She wouldn't stay anywhere without a member of her family present.

I gave my head a shake. I couldn't think about this now. My thoughts were too muddled to concentrate or focus. I needed Andrew and I needed food, in that order.

His sentiment echoing mine, Andrew swept me into his arms and held me tight, as he'd been aching to do from the beginning. "I was so worried. I've never been so out of control. When you were unconscious, I went nearly insane. It was all Sam and the twins could do to hold me together long enough to get help."

Andrew began to babble, going on, but the adrenalin was still pumping through his system and he couldn't seem to stop. "Once Stephon arrived, he tried to restrain me, but for some reason, he really seemed to struggle. It was weird.

He'd always been able to overpower me before. I don't think he was really feeling all that well. The twins and Sam had to restrain me while Stephon tried to reason with me to get me to try to focus on finding you. But I just couldn't seem to focus on anything he tried to tell me. Tim finally convinced me to listen for your heartbeat." The shudder that went through Andrew's body traveled straight through my own.

He needed to get this out. To tell me everything that happened to him. So I listened. Yes, I could feel it for myself. Yes, I knew Brad wasn't among the drones they had killed in the bunker. Yes, I knew all the preparations they had made before attacking: how my guards had scoured the area checking for traps, for possible assassins hiding in the woods, and making sure there weren't other reinforcements waiting in ambush for them to attach the bunker trying to take them by surprise from behind. Yes, it was like having it happen to me, but this was just as important. It really wasn't about the event itself—he needed me to hear him, to listen to him, and to express himself about the event and what he'd gone through. Later, I'd tell him about my experience.

"When I finally listened for your heart, I realized I could feel it beating. I knew you were alive. I became a bit better. I was safer to be around. It was hard, but I could track you by sensing where I felt your heartbeat the most. Stephon left, saying he was going to see what he could find out from his contacts. We need to call him because I have hardly heard from him since he left. I've never seen him so haggard in my life. He seemed ill. I've never known him to be sick a day in my life."

Andrew nipped at my jaw between his sentences. His eyes would close and his body tremble as he clutched me tighter against him. "When you came to and said you were moving, I finally understood why I couldn't get a fix on you. I'd think I had it and we'd start to go in one direction, and then somehow would change and I'd know I was going away from you. God, I was so frustrated. But you were moving. We started investigating vehicles large enough to move you in that metal cage." Andrew sighed. He touched my hair, my face, and my arms. "It was torture when you blacked out. I practically counted the beats of your heart until you became conscious again. Just hanging on each beat, waiting for them to stop. But they didn't, and now I have you." He held me like I was the most precious thing in the world to him. I understood completely, because that's exactly what he was to me, my whole world in one man. "I love you."

I held Andrew's face and stared into his tortured eyes. "I love you too." I leaned forward and brushed my lips against his. "I'm in once piece, but I'm starving. You have to feed me, or I'll be unconscious again and you will have only yourself to blame."

Andrew laughed, but it was an unnatural, hysterical sound as he struggled to get a grip on his emotions. I felt them flowing through me. His adrenaline was wearing off. He hadn't eaten much more than I had in the last couple of weeks. He hadn't been able to stomach food.

"Come on, we both need to eat." I slipped out of the sweatpants and transformed into my brown wolf. Andrew smiled and became the white wolf. We took off running, with Jack and Joe giving chase. Their sandy wolves flanked us, and Sam's eagle screamed overhead, floating on the thermals above.

My first group hunt, I thought to Andrew.

Andrew's laughter, a rough bark, sounded much more like himself. *About time, don't you think?*

Our jumbled-up emotions would work themselves out while we ran. For the wolf, forward motion and thought worked together. Andrew ran alongside me, his shoulder brushing mine. Stride for stride, leap for leap, we ran completely in sync—two bodies, one mind. The snow crunched beneath our pads as we moved through the trees. It felt wonderful to be free, able to hunt. It'd been too long.

A flash of black at the corner of my eye had me hitting the brakes, with Andrew stopping a stride in front of me. As I stared into the trees, I saw Charlie and a small group of her strongest, fastest drones separate themselves from the woods. They were watching and would remain with us, guarding our flank, making sure our hunt was undisturbed. I let my tongue loll from my mouth in a wolf grin.

Charlie fingered the pummel of the sword at her hip. "Well, get on with it." She stated irritably.

Come on, you know she won't leave us alone. Very few things move as stealthily as a vampire drone. They won't ruin our hunt. Andrew's voice in my mind drew my attention to him, just in time to get a wet tongue slurp along my muzzle.

I could smell the elk down in the coulee among the brush in a dry washout, just ahead. We were above them and downwind from their location. They were resting in the undergrowth for the afternoon and would be up and about in an hour or two as the sun went down. We were too tired to make sport of them, and they were unaware of our approach. Our attack was fast, and the buck was dead before he knew what had happened. One snap of Andrew's jaws and it was all over but the venison feast. Jack and Joe had taken down a deer of their own just up the trail. When we howled our success, they joined in, and our wolf song filled the afternoon.

BLOOD TIES

Nothing but nothing had ever tasted so good in all my life. Yeah, as a runaway and an unwanted mouth at a number of tables growing up, I'd eaten a lot of crap to survive. I'd done the dumpster-diving thing behind fast-food restaurants and grocery stores. I'd found my way into locked areas around garbage bins and picked padlocks meant to keep people like me out. This... this was nothing like that. This compared more to a five-star restaurant than any dive, and I had no words to express how alive it made me feel. We didn't just take a few bites and leave, oh no. We bolted down pounds of the luscious stuff until we were both so stuffed I wasn't sure I could get back to the camp.

I flopped over onto my back, my stomach bloated with meat, my mate by my side, licking my muzzle, and his brothers playing in the setting sun. Right now at this moment, I could understand why my parents had chosen to become animals and remain that way. It was a very intoxicating way to live, especially after having survived a trauma or loss. Right now I was content to just lie here in the grass with my family around me. Yeah, it couldn't last. My little brother needed me desperately. But I needed this time to decompress or I'd be no good to anyone. So I enjoyed the brief reprieve for what it was, and for as long as I dared while Sam flew lazy circles overhead on the thermals, keeping watch over us.

CHAPTER 17

I WATCHED as Laura, Max, Angela, and the twins all piled into their SUV and headed back to the Reed farm. A couple of Charlie's guards followed in a separate vehicle, giving the family some space. I could feel Andrew's desire to go along and help his family; it mirrored my own. But our presence would only tie us to the family more and make them an even bigger target than they currently were.

Charlie sped about like a small tornado of activity. It would've been comical if the cause for her flitting about weren't so serious. For all her busy work, Charlie's eyes never really left Andrew and me. As she bustled about, seeing the Reeds were packed up and safely on the road with an escort in tow, she also directed others our way, making sure we had everything we needed. If Charlie could have split herself in two, she would have, just to make sure the Reed farm was completely safe. Instead, she did the next best thing and sent her most trusted men along with our family. With the severity of this last attack, she wouldn't leave our side. In fact, I'd be surprised if she would ever really leave me alone again.

"We could have hidden them for a while at Father's penthouse. My people have been through it, and there is no danger. Nobody would've realized they were there. They'd be safe while I hunted that idiot Brad." Charlie snarled angrily as we watched the family drive off.

"It doesn't work that way. Max and Laura won't be happy until they have their family back in their territory. Even knowing logically, as a person, that it may not be entirely safe—it won't matter to the beast." I shrugged my shoulders and tried to explain the instincts I felt deep inside. To Max, the thought of returning to the penthouse, which was my territory and not theirs, wouldn't have even been a consideration. Safe or not, with a threat to your family, the beast's instincts took over and logic was secondary. Their wolves demanded they return to their own territory, where the family would rally and defend itself. Intruders would be met with teeth and claws, no questions asked.

"The stupidity of letting a beast's instincts make the decisions when logic dictates a much safer path—no wonder animals become extinct." Charlie huffed and spun on her heel, moving off to get the rest of our people ready to leave.

Watching Charlie's frantic actions, a bad feeling settled in the pit of my stomach as I realized my crazy drone bodyguard blamed herself for what happened in the penthouse—my abduction—even though she hadn't been there at the time. And even if she had been, it happened so quickly, I doubted there would have been anything she could've done. *Remind me if I forget, we need to talk to Charlie. This wasn't her fault. I think she's blaming herself.*

Yeah, I was meaning to say something to you about that if you didn't catch it. Andrew's soft reply told me just how tired my mate really was as we walked to the limo. Sam held open the door. I bent toward the door and saw Grandfather already sitting in the back, with my little brother sound asleep in his arms.

"I'm going to ride with the others back to your territory. The twins said they'd join me after their folks were settled with the new guards and they made sure the ranch was secure." Sam placed a gentle hand on my shoulder. I stood turning to face him, meeting his eyes. "You all right? Really?" Sam asked as he gave my shoulder a reassuring squeeze.

"Just really tired. As long as Andrew and I are touching, everything else is tolerable." I gave him a tired smile. "Thanks for taking care of our territory, Sam. I can't tell you how much I appreciate the risk you're taking for us."

"Don't worry about it. Just be safe. We'll talk later." Sam patted Andrew's shoulder, and I climbed into the limo, Andrew following me.

I sighed as I sank into the soft leather of the seat. Andrew stretched out his long legs beside me. Tim and Charlie had chosen to ride in the front of the limo, with the driver, to give us some family time. Although I blessed them for their discretion where Andrew and I were concerned, because they always seemed to try to give us as much alone time as possible, I viewed the two of them as part of my family as much as Grandfather. I didn't like their keeping themselves at a distance, as if they were somehow less by being my vassals. They were family, and right now, I wanted them closer, but I was too tired to fuss over it.

The stress of our separation was finally beginning to abate, and with it went the last of the adrenaline that had been keeping me awake.

"Sleep, child. You are safe and fed, and your mate is with you. Nothing short of an act of the gods could wrench you from my grasp in this limo," Grandfather whispered, smiling as he met my gaze.

"I suppose you're right." I yawned, resting my head back against the seat. Andrew was already asleep, his head bobbed slightly with the motion of the car.

"Andrew hasn't really slept since you disappeared. I'm glad he can finally relax." Grandfather ran his fingers through Henry's hair.

"I don't think either of us is really much good without the other." I rested my head against the seat; it felt much softer than I'd ever realized a car headrest could feel... either that, or I was much more tired than I realized.

"I think you're wrong." Grandfather frowned slightly, his eyes a bit glassy, as if they were filled with tears he couldn't shed.

"Oh, how so?" I couldn't help but ask, even though my mind was already drifting and I was half asleep.

"Even though you were separated and in pain, your first priority was keeping the children safe and protecting them. He was driven to find you, but not mindlessly. When his parents came to him, saying his sister was also missing, logic still ruled his mind enough to pull him from searching the penthouse and the surrounding area to search his family's farm for his sister." Grandfather nuzzled the boy in his arms and inhaled deeply. I recognized what he was doing, marking my baby brother as part of his family and absorbing his scent, much as I'd done.

"Okay, so not completely worthless, just mostly out of it. It was kind of like I am right now. Part of me is already asleep, yet part of me is still conscious enough to talk to you. When Andrew and I were pulled apart, I felt like I was living in a nightmare. The part of me that is joined with him was stretched so thin it felt as if there wasn't enough of me in one place, the rest was scattered between us. I was thinking and acting, somehow, but it didn't feel completely real. Almost like it was happening to someone else... someone other than either one of us." I sighed as I felt Andrew draw me against him and I snuggled into his side. "But this... this is real. My mate." I mumbled the last as I drifted to sleep.

"HE'S WAKING up." I heard the words just as Henry was passed from Grandfather to me. The boy was stretched out so his head rested on my shoulder and his legs lay across Andrew's lap. I inhaled deeply, drawing myself awake. I felt the boy tremble slightly in my arms. He felt cool to the touch in comparison with Andrew, who I'd been snuggled up against. The reason Henry had stirred was immediately apparent: he was getting chilled from Grandfather's cool skin. Grandfather would have to wrap the child in a blanket or something next time he wanted to hold him for an extended period. I was sure there would be a next time. Grandfather exuded such longing to pamper Henry with all the love the boy could absorb. His only desire was to dote on him and cherish him.

"He's just a little chilled, Grandfather." I drew the boy more snugly into my arms, hoping to warm him, hoping maybe he'd be able to rest a bit longer.

152

"I'm an old fool. Of course he's cold," Grandfather grumbled as he flipped open a storage bin under one of the seats and pulled out a blanket, unfolded it, and wrapped it around Henry.

"He's fine." I smiled up at Grandfather as he fussed over tucking the blanket under Henry's legs.

"He reminds me of Nathaniel when he was this age, all legs and arms," Grandfather whispered as he sat back and stared at the two of us. I could tell it didn't matter to Grandfather that Lord Nathaniel wasn't Henry's biological father—of course, he wasn't mine either. To him, Henry was Nathaniel's son. Our actual biology had nothing to do with it. Our parents, Sasha and Prince Henry, were both mated to his son, Nathaniel, and that made us family. I could only hope Henry would be able to find a place for Grandfather in his heart, but the determined set of Grandfather's eyes told me regardless of how the boy felt, Henry would never want for anything in his life again. Grandfather would always be there to take care of him, as much as Henry would allow him to.

When Henry's sleepy gray eyes fluttered open and saw mine, he began to panic. In Grandfather's peaceful induced sleep, he was safe, and now the nightmare of his reality was crashing around him. Like a cornered animal, he both tried to hold on to me and to fight to get away at the same time, pushing and shoving at me. I held him snug against my chest. Cooing softly into his hair, we rocked back and forth as I tried to calm him enough to realize who I was and that he was safe.

"It's okay, Henry. I've got you," I whispered as he quit fighting and frantically clutched at my arms. "You're safe now. Nothing can hurt you. We're going home." I hushed him softly and rhythmically. His breathing began to slow as he relaxed. His arms slid around my neck, and he rested his head on my shoulder, his tears falling freely. Grandfather was right to do what he did. The boy had needed the sleep to put things right in his head, and I most definitely hadn't been in any condition to handle his fears and pain.

Andrew drew me against him as I held Henry, his arms going around the both of us as he nuzzled my shoulder and the top of Henry's head at the same time. Grandfather watched us, his eyes filling with longing. That was unacceptable. Henry would need to adjust, and the sooner he understood how this family worked, the better. I reached out and grabbed Grandfather's arm and pulled him into the seat beside me. Henry was stunned as the vampire slowly wrapped his arms around us too.

"There is a lot of love and caring in this car, Henry. There are so many types of family and love in this world I never knew existed until I found Andrew and became who I am, and now we are at the center of it. You'll never have to be alone again. You will always be cared for and loved. You will never have to stand alone because, regardless of what happens, I will always be your brother, and that will never change."

Henry pulled away a bit, viewing his surroundings. He noted Andrew, who rested his head against mine, one of his arms wrapped around my shoulders, the other wrapped around the both of us. He then glanced at Grandfather, who was on our other side. One of his arms had slid behind my shoulders, the other arm draped around the front of us both. We were in the protective center of the love of the two greatest men in my life.

Henry stared into Grandfather's clear green eyes. This time Grandfather met his gaze with love and just a touch of the fear of rejection. I rubbed Henry's back reassuringly, letting him go at his own pace, even though I wanted to hand him over onto Grandfather's lap and force the two together.

This can't be rushed, Leannan. Henry must decide to trust or not to trust at his own pace. You can't force it. Andrew's voice soothed my own ragged emotions.

I know. It's just I can see how much Grandfather wants to bond with Henry and... I hesitated as I felt Henry tremble slightly, let go with one hand, and his arm slide up toward Grandfather. Henry flinched and his hand returned to where it had been nestled against my neck. His eyes squeezed shut and he hid his face in my chest. I tried not to sigh with regret. I guess it must be too soon. I was asking too much of my little brother to expect his treatment at Brad's hands to just disappear and not be transferred to all vampires.

The fact that he reached for Grandfather at all was a good sign, though. Andrew's silent reassurance helped, but it didn't fix the problem. Andrew drew back, and I felt Grandfather's head rest against my shoulder and snuggle into my neck, much as Andrew had done on the opposite side. From where his chin rested on my shoulder, I knew Henry's hand was only inches from him. Andrew showed me Grandfather's eyes were closed. I could only guess Grandfather had seen Henry tentatively reach for him, then draw back. Henry was afraid to come to him, so Grandfather had placed himself within reach, still not pushing, allowing Henry to reach for him if he wished, hoping the boy's curiosity would coax him closer.

Grandfather didn't sleep. It was just something none of the vampires—drones or born vampires—did. So although Grandfather was relaxed and his eyes were closed, appearing to have dozed off with his head on my shoulder, nothing was further from the truth. If Grandfather's heart could have beat right then, it would've pounded faster than a marathon runner's at the end of a race for first place.

We were all waiting for Henry. I was almost sure Henry had fallen asleep when his little hand inched, ever so slowly, up toward Grandfather. Tiny fingers crawled, as if by moving so minutely he might not be seen or noticed. He froze for agonizingly long seconds before I saw through Andrew's eyes Henry take the last step and touch Grandfather's jaw with tentative fingers. Those little fingers were discovering some of the things that made Grandfather a force to be reckoned with. His face, like everything else about his physique, was cold, rock hard, and silky smooth. The flawless, timeless skin of a vampire. Grandfather remained still as a statue, eyes closed and completely relaxed, letting the boy do whatever he wanted.

Henry began to explore Grandfather's features. He ran his fingers up to Grandfather's cheekbones, across his temple, along his forehead, and down between his closed eyes. He stroked down Grandfather's nose and, when grandfather twitched his nose like he might sneeze, Henry trembled, but it was more a silent giggle. His confidence was growing in his exploration, and Grandfather's patience was paying off. Grandfather smiled slowly. When Henry's hand dropped away, Grandfather opened his eyes, then met and held Henry's gaze.

Andrew saw the connection click, just as it had with me. *See, everything is going to be all right.* Andrew's confidence made me smile. I'd felt so tense, and now... now I had a new little brother and a chance he would accept my grandfather. There was something about Grandfather's eyes. I wasn't sure if it was the ancient soul shining through them or the love they held that made trusting him exceedingly easy, but part of me knew Henry would never have a problem with Grandfather again.

Not to say there wouldn't be rough roads ahead. Henry was mute, and that disturbed me. Our people were resilient, and even after everything that had happened to me, I still had my voice. Somehow Brad had succeeded in taking away Henry's voice. Tim was going to have to check him out, and I was going to make Brad pay for his treatment of the children if it was the last thing I did.

Yes, he'll get his, but knock it off. If you start growling now, you'll mess up everything you've been working on building. Henry might misinterpret it as either you not wanting him close to Grandfather, or that Grandfather was doing something he didn't see. Andrew's sharp tone brought me around. He was right. I needed to focus on now, not my revenge.

With Henry's acceptance went the last of his resistance. He sighed and he closed his eyes, curled up in my arms, and used the drone of the tires under us as his lullaby as he fell into a natural sleep.

"We're almost to the parking garage at the penthouse," Grandfather whispered, sitting back in his seat, a big smile on his face.

Andrew reached over and tucked the blanket back around Henry. I was exhausted, and the relief I'd gotten from running with Andrew and hunting was already wearing thin. My mate and I needed some quality alone time. Our bond needed to be reaffirmed, and the mental link could only be refreshed when we merged our minds and bodies.

"He's going to be fine now. He just needs to sleep. Tomorrow we can start worrying about our next move." Andrew rubbed the muscles on the back of my neck. Even though I'd been trying to relax, nothing would make me feel better until we were united.

"Let me look after him." Grandfather reached over and scooped the sleeping boy from my arms. He winked confidently at me, and I realized Henry wouldn't need a bed this night—he'd sleep in Grandfather's arms. The ancient vampire didn't sleep, so he would watch over my little brother and help him through any nightmares he might have.

"If he needs anything...." I let the sentence drift. Truthfully, I'd be busy and everybody knew it.

"We'll be fine," Grandfather said in a singsong voice. "Go on up to your suite and relax."

I suddenly had a vision of Grandfather with an infant in his arms, the proud father adoring his newborn son. I had no doubt he made a wonderful father. He cradled Henry in his arms like an expert. I suddenly wondered if born vampire babies slept, or if their parents walked with them day and night.

The door opened and Charlie stood outside the vehicle. She kept herself absorbed in everything around her, never once seeing me. Even with her men surrounding us, she wouldn't let her guard down. It was exhausting to watch her.

"Good night." Grandfather nodded to Charlie and was out of the car with my brother and gone before I could wish him the same.

"God, I'm exhausted," I mumbled. "Can't we just curl up here in the car and sleep? The seats are comfy, and I'm sure there are more blankets hidden away somewhere."

"Our suite will be much more comfortable than this car, even though it is a limo. The bed will feel so good." Andrew encouraged me as he coaxed me to my feet and led me out the door.

"Shower... I have got to have a shower first. I can still smell all that crappy blood." I shivered and let Andrew lead me toward the elevator. Exhaustion rippled through me in waves, and when the elevator began to move, my knees buckled. Andrew caught me just before I hit the floor. I was emotionally and physically drained, all of my reserves gone. The adrenaline was long gone from my system, and I wasn't sure I could go another step.

"I've got you." Andrew swept me into his arms.

It was undignified and totally gave me a black mark against my street cred, but I really couldn't have cared less. It was a struggle to keep my eyes open at this point. My arms and legs felt like tingly wet noodles. I tucked my face into Andrew's neck and closed my eyes. The scent of my mate made everything all right.

I must have dozed slightly, because the next thing I knew, Andrew was sitting me down on the sofa in our suite. I glanced around the room, nothing seemed out of place. If I hadn't known for a fact that gas canisters had bounced down the chimney and noxious fumes covered everything, I never would have known to look at the place.

Grandfather and Charlie were extremely careful about having everything cleaned and the staff investigated for any connection to Brenda or Brad. Our guard is now half shifter and half vampire. They wanted to make sure you could feel safe before we returned.

Charlie and Tim were at the table, where he was fussing over what must have been seriously deep cuts at one point but, because of the speed of vampire healing, they were appeared pretty minor from my view on the couch. Still, Tim was thorough, and regardless of Charlie's protests, he was determined to take care of her.

"Charlie, give it up already. Tim won't be happy until you let him take care of you," I mumbled and managed to grin at the pair. "So just let him do it already."

Tim took hold of Charlie's arm. "He told you to let me help. So stop fighting me."

"Doesn't count when he isn't conscious," Charlie grumped, trying to pull away from him.

"I'm conscious enough for that," I growled and somehow managed to open my eyes a bit more and give Charlie a dirty look. Andrew chuckled softly and disappeared into our bedroom. "I know you can hear me, Charlie. Let Tim take care of you or else." Tim's laughter filled the room. It was a light, happy sound that made me smile despite the gruff authority I was trying to give my order.

"Damn it all! I have work to do! I need to check out this house from top to bottom. I don't have time to be fussing over small stuff that will heal on its own!" Charlie snarled, but I saw Tim hold open the suite door for her and motion her out into the hallway.

"Then the sooner you chill out and let me do my job, the more quickly you will get to your own." Tim closed the door behind them.

I jumped when Andrew settled beside me on the sofa. "Are you quite through taking care of everyone else, my love? Can I take care of you now?" Andrew sighed. His eyes were full of love and pain. This ordeal had been as exceedingly hard on him as it was on me. How he was able to keep going was beyond me.

"No, I have one more person to take care of." I smiled tiredly at my mate. The man was larger than life to me.

"Who else do you need? I'll get them for you." Pain laced his eyes as he gathered himself to stand.

I quickly reached for him, gently holding him in place. "You, of course. You're the most important person in the world to me, and you're just as exhausted as I am."

He settled back and leaned over and kissed me. "True, but I'm determined to sleep in our bed, with you safely tucked in my arms." He pushed up off the couch and then pulled me to my feet. The two of us stumbled arm in arm into our bedroom and fell onto our bed.

"I love you." I drew him up alongside me, and he pulled the blanket from the bottom of the bed with him, covering us both.

"I love you too." He fisted his fingers in my hair and laid his head on my chest, listening to my heartbeat. It was his focal point when searching for me, and he still felt drawn by its rhythm. Neither of us had energy for much of anything. We wouldn't be awake long. Just long enough to merge and heal the open wounds in our bond made by our long separation. With that came the chance to cherish each other.

"I could have lost you. I just found you and you were snatched from me," Andrew whimpered, childlike. He was torn up inside and none of this was his fault.

"In this life or the next, it doesn't matter. I will always find you and we will always be together," I reassured my lover. I ran my fingers through his short black hair.

"How about we just focus on staying together in this life?" He rubbed his face on my chest, marking me as his.

"I belong to only you," I whispered as he ran his hands over my body, reassuring himself and me that we were together and everything was finally all right.

CHAPTER 18

Stephon's Story—The Unbirthday Party—Part 2

STEPHON LED Quinn out of the maze and toward the dark colonial-style three-story house that was home to himself and his drones. He could hardly believe it. His mate was finally going to be inside his home. He wondered if he could coax the man into one of the rooms that didn't have any windows and lock him in so he couldn't leave. Stifling a sigh, he realized that would make him no better than Rufus. Besides, if his mate didn't want him, then there really was little he could do other than make the most of the time his mate did offer him. And wasn't that one hell of a kick in the teeth. Of course that didn't mean he wasn't going to try and seduce the vampire into staying by any means necessary. Stephon put a little swish in his step as he climbed the few stairs that led to the deck and the front door.

"God, Stephon," Quinn groaned.

Well at least he had his mate's attention. Stephon glanced over his shoulder and saw Quinn's eyes were locked on his ass. "You do not get in this ass until you explain what the hell has been going on for the last two hundred and seventy years."

"I guess I do have some explaining to do, but it isn't all that complicated."

"I'll be the judge of that." Stephon opened the front door and flipped on the entry light. "Welcome home, Quinn."

"Do you mean that?"

"What, that this is your home?" Stephon admired the rugged, quiet nature his mate seemed to have mastered. Quinn didn't take any comment for granted, but hope flowed easily from him and Stephon could work with hope.

"Th-that I am really welcome here. That this...." Quinn paused, standing in the shadow his expression hidden from view.

159

"Quinn. Wherever I am—regardless of the situation, or how long it has been since I have seen you—my home is always yours as well. You are my mate, the only one I will ever get, and the fates have put us together." Stephon held the door open. "Please come in."

"I don't know what to say." Quinn stepped into the light, his eyes bloodstained as if he were holding back tears that threatened to overwhelm him.

"We have time to discuss it. You'll explain it to me. It's going to be alright." Stephon hoped his words were true, because there was nothing he wanted to be more in this life than to be able to have his mate with him.

"I never meant to stay away. After I saw you in the library, I was so confused."

"Come." Stephon let the door close and led his mate into his office. Few people ever made it into this room. It was his private sanctuary from the rest of the world. The walls were covered in books, some ancient and bound in leather, some paperback, and, in jars, some papyrus scrolls written in languages long dead. After having met his mate in a library, he'd become rather fond of them. A large dark mahogany desk sat in the center of the room and a leather sofa sat against another.

Quinn had stopped at the door and stood staring at the portrait hanging over the sofa. "That's me. You have a portrait of me... in your office?"

"Yes." Stephon turned and scrutinized the canvas. The setting was imaginary, a simple meadow with mountains in the background and Quinn standing, gazing at the artist, smiling. But after he had moved here, it had struck him how much his surroundings resembled the background in the picture. "I painted that years ago, right after I met you. It made me feel like I was with you, like we were happy."

"It's beautiful. I envy you the talent. I can't do anything artistic."

"I doubt that very much. Maybe you just haven't found anything that interests you."

"Perhaps." Quinn swayed on his feet as if unsure of what he should be doing.

"Please." Stephon moved over to the sofa and sat, patting the seat beside him. "Make yourself comfortable."

Quinn walked over and joined Stephon, choosing to sit beside him instead of at the opposite end. "I'm not sure where to begin." Quinn frowned.

"Well, probably the beginning would be best."

"Alright." Quinn nodded. "You probably have figured out most of it."

"Maybe, but it would still be nice to hear it from you." Stephon did know much of how life had treated Quinn. He hadn't let the young vampire return to Rufus without making sure his contacts in Rufus's family were aware that he wanted the youth watched. Of course, spies aren't always trustworthy, and some of the information he received over the years was contradictory.

"Rufus knew immediately after you released me from your protection, all those years ago. As you can imagine, he was not understanding or accepting." Quinn's lips curled into a wry smile. "He hates you, and I became an immediate disappointment. What good is a gay son when you have a family line to consider? If we mated, there would be no children to continue his family line."

"He expected you to mate a female and have grandchildren for him."

"Yes. Well that was part of it, although I suspect any children of mine he would have eventually slaughtered, as he has my drones. He doesn't trust anything he can't directly control." Quinn shook his head sadly, the pain of loss clearly in his eyes.

Stephon offered his hand to his mate and was thrilled when Quinn accepted it, lacing their fingers together. "Why?"

"He felt threatened by them. As long as he is in control, then you have nothing to worry about. But the minute they were strong enough to break free, some horror always befell both his and my own drones. It took me a while to understand that father was killing his own children. But when a very good friend of mine, Jacque, had his one hundredth birthday and his partner Dane encouraged him to break the bond with Father so they could be together. I was happy for him. When he succeeded, I was there to help them celebrate their union. Jacque moved out of the house and into a little cottage near Father's home where they could have some privacy and live together. Dane was an independent drone from a different family line, and I never did find out who he belonged to, but they were both killed."

"What happened to them?" Stephon asked, giving Quinn's hand a reassuring squeeze.

"Jacque was my butler. After he moved out, he would come daily to do his job. I hardly even noticed a difference from when he was living at Father's house and later when he was commuting. One day he just didn't come. I asked around, but nobody would tell me what happened. A new drone just took on his duties. When I finally got free from Father's grasp, which took one hundred and fifty years from when I left you, I learned Father had Jacque and Dane murdered, along with every drone he's ever created who had dared to break away from him. Later, when I had my own drones go missing, I knew without asking what was happening. I just quit creating them. There was no point if my own Father was killing them."

"That sadistic bastard." Stephon growled. He couldn't believe what Quinn was telling him. Dane had been one of his drones. He'd been so happy for his son when he had voiced his request to be independent of Stephon. Caius had taught him a drone breaking away from a parent was a right of adulthood. It was something to be celebrated. Rufus was twisting the bond. He'd taken something sacred, a form of love and caring between parent and child, and twisted it into a shackle of control. The bond for even the most violent of drones usually only lasted forty years or so. The fact that Rufus had kept Quinn bound for one hundred and fifty years was unheard of.

"In the beginning I challenged him every year, and of course I failed. He is a very old vampire even if he isn't as old as you are, but the power he exudes is great. When I figured out that he was killing the drones that did break free, I became terrified of him and quit trying to break free. Gauging my power against those who succeeded so I would know when I was powerful enough to get away and defend myself against anyone he might send after me."

Stephon seethed but kept a lid on it. He didn't want to frighten his mate now that he had him here. He had carefully probed the edges of Quinn's mind and had found no connections, no drones or any sign of a lingering connection to his father. The separation had relaxed him a great deal, but it also had concerned him. A vampire was not meant to be so solitary with their thoughts.

"That's why it took so long. You needed to not only be able to mentally separate from your father, but be strong enough to stop any assassins that might come after you." Stephon hoped his tone would soothe Quinn and keep him talking.

"Yes. The battle to free myself was brutal and physical. When I told Rufus I wanted to be free of his control, he attacked me. He said I was betraying him. That he thought I had understood when I'd quit challenging him." The sadness in Quinn's eyes had him wanting to snuggle his mate close, but Stephon was afraid he would be rejected. It would be enough that he was holding Quinn's hand. "He said I was useless. A burden to him."

"You aren't useless or a burden." Stephon gave in to his desire. He let go of Quinn's hand. Reaching out, he drew his fingertips along Quinn's jaw in a gentle caress before he wrapped them around his mate's nape. Then he gently drew Quinn's head against his shoulder, while his other hand gently massaged his mate's thigh. Quinn didn't struggle, just moved where Stephon put him. He was finally able to hold his mate, really have the man in his arms and Stephon's soul felt at peace for the first time in a very long time.

"The battle felt like it took forever, with him telling me how much of a horrible son I had become. But as I started to win free, I began pulling information from him that he didn't want me to know. My father has a master."

"Is this master another vampire?" Stephon couldn't imagine who would be strong enough among the vampires to be able to subdue a vampire lord, other than maybe Caius or himself.

"No, it's a shifter. A pureblood my Father met long ago, before I was born, before the start of the Great War itself." Quinn rubbed his face into the crook of Stephon's neck. The movement sent a thrill along Stephon's spine that ended in his balls.

"Pure-blood shifters can be very strong mentally, especially when they are motivated or have a mate. Then the power of their minds multiplies and become quite a bit stronger. Lance is very new to his powers, but he freed Andrew and his family from their mental bond with me. He felt practically nothing, and I ended up with a monster headache from the backlash that I wouldn't wish on anyone." Stephon stroked the silken strands of Quinn's jet-black hair with his fingers, marveling at its softness.

"I don't know if this shifter has a mate or not. I only know Rufus had hoped I was strong enough mentally to bond with him and break the hold the shifter has on him. I wasn't and had no desire to bond even more closely with my father. The shifter, when he discovered Rufus's plan, practically threw me out of my father's mind, snapping the last of the bond between me and Rufus." Quinn chuckled softly. "Father was so angry. But he hadn't really beaten me. The shifter had thrown me out. I think that is the only reason Rufus has let me live. I never really succeeded in beating him, so in his mind I'm no threat to him."

"That was one hundred and twenty years ago. Why didn't you come to me then?" Stephon nuzzled the top of Quinn's head.

"He told me… he told me if I didn't stay away from you that he'd kill you."

"He can't kill me. He's not strong enough. Just like the first time I held you in my arms. He wasn't strong enough to force past me then, and he's not strong enough to hurt me now." Stephon rubbed the tense muscles in Quinn's neck.

"Maybe not then, and if he was alone, he wouldn't be able to do it. But, Stephon, he's not alone. That shifter is stronger than any I have ever met, and I have never actually met him in person." Quinn tilted his head up and began kissing the underside of Stephon's jaw, nipping at his five o'clock shadow.

"Quinn," Stephon whimpered. "Stop, please."

"You don't want me?" Quinn stopped kissing and attempted to pull away.

"Oh babe, of course I want you. I wouldn't be holding you like this if I didn't want you. But I have got to understand what's going on before I can— God, I don't want to wait. I want to just take you to my bedroom and hold you.

Keep you here in my arms forever and never let you go," Stephon rambled as he ran his hand over Quinn's back in long, languorous strokes along his spine.

"He can control the shifter, sometimes. And when he does, vile things happen. People die in the most ugly ways. When the shifter takes control back, he takes revenge on my father. I don't know the number of times I've watched him beat a lover to death. Watched him kill his own drones. The shifter tortured them to death while my father pleaded with the shifter to stop. The shifter physically used my father's own hand to vivisect a drone, and all my father could do was watch, a prisoner behind his own eyes. You live because he hates you so much that the shifter won't let him kill you."

"That doesn't make sense, babe."

"Every day you live is a thorn in my father's side. You make his life harder, and the shifter uses that to humiliate my father." Quinn's hand came up to rest on Stephon's abs, his fingers moving in small circles over the terry-cloth robe.

"Shifters aren't like us, though, babe. This shifter that controls your father is not going to get stronger. He may become more adept at manipulating him, but eventually, as your father ages, he should be able to—"

"No. My father's own mental abilities aren't that great and haven't increased in strength since I've known him. The control comes from the shifter, not my father. Even the power he exudes doesn't come from my father, but from the shifter controlling him."

"So you stayed away because you feared your father would take over this shifter during one of the times he, for some unknown reason, becomes weaker or distracted and your father has the opportunity to control the beast. You think that during one of these moments Rufus will take his revenge and kill me, even knowing the price he will pay when the shifter takes back his power." Stephon groaned and shifted his hips forward as Quinn's hand slipped between the folds of material, his nails grazing the skin beneath.

"Yes. I may be young, but I will protect what is mine, even if I have to stay away from you in order to do it." Quinn sighed.

"But you aren't staying away now?" Stephon kissed the top of Quinn's head, drawing some of the hair into his mouth and running the strands through his teeth.

"No. I was there, at the lodestone. I've gone every year since I broke away from Father, watching you from a distance as you wait for me through the equinox. You are always so disappointed and upset when you leave that I follow you to make sure you get home alright," Quinn mumbled, turning his face into the terry cloth.

"You were there?"

"Yes. I am always careful to remain upwind and out of sight so you wouldn't sense my presence. I've wanted to come to you. But I couldn't put you in danger. I couldn't risk your life by being with you."

"So what changed?" Stephon's fingers stroked along the top of the waistband of Quinn's jeans.

"The damn party. All the naked men. I watched you walk into the yard that was orgy central. The thought of you fucking one of the many naked guys who were here for your pleasure. I-I just…." Quinn was breathing hard.

"What, Quinn?" Stephon knew he was pushing, but Quinn had to tell him. He couldn't just accept Quinn was feeling what Stephon wanted him to—imagined him needing Stephon as much as he needed Quinn. No. Quinn had to say it. Then Stephon could make it all better, and they would start their life together.

"All those men wanting you, when I wanted you more. I needed you more." Quinn growled and the bathrobe was abruptly pushed open. "You are my mate. Mine, and I won't share you." Teeth scored his abs as Quinn's fangs dragged across his stomach, his soft tongue laving the skin between.

"Do you want me, Quinn? Are you really sure? Because I won't let you go if you accept me, my mate. I'll keep you for eternity." Stephon bent forward, drawing Quinn's face up to his, wanting so badly to taste those lips. Quinn's irises were stained blood red with desire. His fangs had dropped, and his fingers were tipped with black talons. He'd made the younger vampire lose control. Even the whites of his sclera were changing from a light bloodstained pink to darker red as the blood in his mate's system pounded through his body.

"Oh God, Stephon. I want that so much. I want you to take me and make me yours forever. I want to bite you and have you sink your fangs into me." Quinn pushed himself back, flinging himself to the other side of the sofa.

"But?" Stephon asked, tipping his head slightly to the side as he watched his mate dig his claws into the leather. There would definitely be puncture holes left behind.

"I have to return. I can't let him kill you." Quinn shook his head, his hands gripping the leather spastically. "He may not be in my mind anymore, but if I don't return he hurts the people I care about."

"Babe, there isn't anyone or anything I can't face with you beside me. It's only when we are apart that we are vulnerable. We can stop him." Stephon watched the blood fade from his mate's eyes.

"I don't know if-if I can take that chance. You are th-the most important thing to me in the whole world. Every morning I wake up and I make it th-through the day because I'm doing it for you. All the pain I've endured and the humiliation, everything he's made me do, I do it so you don't have to th-asufthfer," Quinn slurred around his teeth. Stephon thought it was adorable.

"You are so used to doing this alone. Fighting for us, alone. But, Quinn, I am not alone. My drones are many and strong. I have incredible friends who care about me and will help us," Stephon pleaded. His life depended on it, because he wasn't sure he'd be able to survive if Quinn rejected him again, even knowing the reasons behind it were, in Quinn's eyes, for Stephon's own good. "Babe, I'm an old vampire. The oldest of our people. I am going to be very honest with you, sweetheart. You have kept me at bay for about as long as I can stand it and remain sane."

"I know. The longer I am here and the closer I get to you, the more I can feel just how fragile your control is. Mine is no better." Quinn shifted around so he was leaning toward Stephon, his weight on his arms, hands gripping the leather like his life depended on it, holding him in place.

Stephon growled, grabbed Quinn by the shoulders, and pulled him up against his body. His mate didn't struggle, didn't fight to remain separate from him. "If I take you now—make you mine—even if you do go back, everyone will know that you are mated, unlike now. If you leave now, my scent will wash off and nobody will be the wiser. If you stay and we sleep together, I will, without a doubt, claim you as mine."

"If I stay, you will never find out who the pure-blood shifter controlling my father is. He has plans that are truly vile, and my father is helping him. He wants to bring down the veil." Quinn leaned up and kissed Stephon.

"Your life is not worth losing just so we can find out who this shifter is. You've done enough. You've risked enough."

"And when the veil falls and the fae return? When there are no shifters left and no born vampires left because the fae have decimated us all, because we don't know who the enemy is or how to fight him? What will we do then, Stephon?"

"It won't matter because we will be dead as well. When I go insane because my mate has rejected me, yet again, how long do you think I will survive before my drones will have to restrain me and have my best friends destroy me? How long do you think you will live when you hear that your inactions, regardless of how noble, have killed your mate?" Stephon panted, trying not to hyperventilate. He could feel Quinn drawing back from him, gathering himself, preparing himself to leave.

"That's so unfair of you. Making me feel guilty for wanting to save our people and protect you." Quinn hissed but began nibbling on the rock-solid tendons of Stephon's neck.

"Just because it's unfair doesn't mean it isn't true." Stephon's grip began to loosen as he relaxed in Quinn's arms. His mate nibbling at his throat did him in. It felt so wonderful. He couldn't help but become putty in his mate's arms.

"I know. I'm going to fix it. I could never leave without you knowing exactly how I feel about you. There is nothing in this world I want more than to spend eternity with you. To get to know everything about you." Quinn bathed the place where Stephon's shoulder and neck met, the place most mated couple's left their mating marks. He glided down, sucking on Stephon's collarbone to his pectoral muscle. "I've studied up on you. I've read the transcripts of all the council meetings. I've memorized some of the things you've said, your beliefs and Caius's beliefs."

"You have?" Stephon moaned and fisted his cock as Quinn's tongue laved over his hardening nipple.

"Oh yes." Quinn chuckled softly. "Your father was a very intelligent man. I think he's given us the solution to finding out who this enemy is and keeping you from losing your mind in the process. But, my beautiful mate, you will have to trust me just a little longer, before you lock me away and throw away the key, because I have no doubt that is what you want to do."

"Na... huh?" Stephon knew he sounded confused, but if his mate wanted his trust, then he would have it. "Yes, I trust you."

"I know you do." Quinn struck. Sinking his teeth in over Stephon's heart, his fangs piercing the vital organ. Stephon screamed in agony as Quinn's saliva sank into his heart, the poisons sinking into the organ and temporarily stopping its beating. Quinn sliced open his wrist with his own fangs and shoved it against Stephon's mouth. "Drink, my mate, and be filled with my blood while you sleep. When you awaken, I will be able to be with you in every way, and I will never leave again. I am so sorry, Stephon. This is the only way I can think of to keep you safe and us sane."

Stephon's eyes burned, his body aching in ways it never had. He felt himself sinking into shock and knew he would go into an immediate forced hibernation in order to metabolize his mate's poison.

"Q-quinn this is un-unnecessary. W-We c-can...." Stephon's teeth began to chatter as he tried to speak. Under normal circumstances, a mating bite would never kill him. When a vampire's toxins are introduced into the blood of its mate, it bonds the two together, but introduced directly to the heart, it could kill him before the blood had a chance to neutralize the poison.

"Shh…. Don't fight it." Quinn pressed his bleeding wrist to Stephon's lips. "Please, I want us to be together. I want us to be bonded, and this is the only way I can keep you safe. Your drones will feel you fall asleep and come for you. They will hide you from everyone, even I won't know where you are." Quinn stroked Stephon's hair, kissing his forehead. Tears of blood slid down Quinn's cheeks.

Stephon swallowed his mate's blood. It was the only thing that might save his life.

"Sleep, my mate, and this will soon be over," Quinn crooned as he held Stephon.

Yes, it would soon be over, because when he woke up, he would no longer treat his mate quite so gently. Quinn had no idea the power he could wield, even though he had been repeatedly told. He would awaken much sooner than his young mate realized. Stephon felt his eyes close against his will. One day he would kill Rufus for this. He would also punish his mate for believing he was incapable of not only defending himself, but keeping Quinn safe as well. But it would not be today.

"I'm so sorry, Stephon, please forgive me when you wake," Quinn begged. It was the last thing Stephon heard before his mind slid into the nothingness of hibernation.

CHAPTER 19

Present Day

BRIGHT LIGHT winked through a slit in the curtain, drawing me drowsily from the depths of my exhaustion-induced sleep. I groaned and pulled the blankets over my head. Morning... damn. I hated to leave the peace that surrounded me, and the contentment I felt having my mate pressed against my back.

If the sun is in your eyes, it's not morning, but afternoon. Andrew's sleepy tone mumbled in my brain.

Morning, afternoon... who cares? I just want to sleep. I could feel his amusement as he nuzzled the back of my neck and sighed softly, as comfortable with the world as I felt at that moment. I relaxed into his embrace and closed my eyes, just basking in the moment.

That's when it hit me. "Aw, fuck!" I frowned and started to pull away from Andrew.

He held me tight, knowing as soon as the thought flowed through my mind what the problem was. *Relax. She's fine.* His soothing thought calmed me, even though my concern persisted.

"I should have thought to ask before now. I feel like such a shit." Sandy had been in the room with me when they grabbed me. "They didn't hurt her, did they?" I couldn't help but ask, even though he'd already said she was fine.

"I don't think they even touched her. They were more concerned with getting you out of the room before I could get here. They didn't have time to mess with her too." Andrew ran his hand through my hair as if he were petting me, trying to soothe the beast inside. The part of me that had claimed Sandy as a member of my pack wouldn't be satisfied until I saw her, but for now I was content to listen.

"What happened to her? I can't believe I wasn't concerned for her before this." I was a bit disgusted with myself for that. She was one of my own and I'd forgotten her.

"Don't be so hard on yourself. If she'd been missing too, I would've asked you if she was with you long before we rescued you. You have been a bit busy. We found her unconscious in our sitting room, untouched. She had a monster of a headache, and I'm afraid I was a bit of an ass to her. I behaved like a raving lunatic when she awoke, trying to get any information about your attackers from her." Andrew rubbed his cheek against my shoulder. "I was a complete idiot. I owe her a major apology, my love."

"I'm sure she understands, even if she was hurting at the time. We'll talk to her. It will be all right. She knows how we are when our mates disappear." I rubbed the arm that held me against him.

"I doubt she'll ever see me as the kindhearted kid she once knew. I've never been a violent person, but you wouldn't have recognized me if you'd seen me. I was nasty and hostile, attacking everyone and everything that stood between me and finding you. I wouldn't have hesitated to rip apart anyone in my way, and I didn't care who I hurt to do it." Andrew rested his forehead between my shoulder blades. A palpable sadness resonated from him, yet he didn't truly regret his actions, because it was obvious he would do it again if forced.

"They understand, and if they haven't already forgiven you... well, then your relationship with them will change, but I'm sure they don't love you any less." I felt him nod against my back, and although he knew I told him the truth, he didn't like people thinking of him as cruel. "It is who we are, love. Our mating has changed you more than they can really know, and the beast inside you has grown as well. I know it because we share that spirit, but the reality of your change may have just hit home for those who've known you all your life."

"You think they just thought I received abilities from our mating and never considered the downside? That the animal spirit is also stronger with the increase in those abilities? Not necessarily meaning I'm more violent, but the potential is there to be aggressive and react out of those increased instincts in a savage manner," Andrew mumbled, the words muffled by the blankets surrounding us.

"Yes. I wouldn't say either of us is inherently brutal in our normal, everyday actions. We're logical and passionate about our beliefs. But, like any shifter, we have an animalistic side that will bite when cornered." I squirmed until he loosened his grip so I could turn over. "We'd been attacked, and that animal was on the hunt, snapping at everything in its way. I believe they will be more understanding than you give them credit for."

He rested his forehead against mine. "I sure hope so. The hurtful things I said to Tim... to all of them, really."

"They are fine. You'll apologize and we'll deal. If we have to explain your reactions so they understand them, we will." I ran my fingers through his thick black hair and felt him lean into my touch, relaxing and finally letting go of what he couldn't change or control.

"Are you really okay, my love?" He stroked my face gently, as if I were made of glass. He raised my hand to his lips and kissed the inside of my palm.

"Yes." I smiled as he nibbled on the tip of my finger. "I have a little brother. I never dreamed I could actually have blood family. I mean, my parents have been out there somewhere for a lot of years being animals."

"Maybe we should get up and take a shower, then get something to eat and check on how your little brother is adjusting to his new life. I think he came 'round to Grandfather last night. But you never know what the light of day will bring." Andrew pushed up, leaned over me, and pressed me against the mattress, kissing me senseless before sitting up. Stunned, I watched him strut into the bathroom. If he'd been in his wolf form, he'd have been wagging his tail, he was so happy to have me with him.

"You are so asking for it!" I laughed, glad his mood had improved, and ran after him into the en suite.

Remember what Sam brought with him that day? Andrew's tone was full of mischief as I slid into the bathroom. My handsome mate was standing beside the shower, adjusting the temperature of the water. He winked at me over his shoulder.

I groaned, my mind going completely blank of everything but the naked golden skin in front of me. I wanted to lick every inch of his body. I wanted... I shivered at the aggressive desires clawing their way into my mind. I'd never considered topping my mate. Andrew was my alpha, my lover, and the best friend I'd ever had. I enjoyed giving myself to him and belonging to him. Yet there was a part of me that wanted him to belong to me, but I wasn't sure it was something I could do, regardless of how much the beast craved Andrew bent over in front of us. It wasn't something I could do now. If—and it was a big if—if I were to ever top my mate, it would be done slowly and with all the love I could give. Not a little slap and tickle in the shower. I shoved the thought deep down for later consideration. I had no doubt Andrew would mention it. There was no way he didn't catch the picture in my mind, but now I needed to go play with my mate and get ready to see my brother, not hide away in our suite, lost in Andrew, even though nothing would make me happier.

I stepped into the shower. My mate took my hand, put me in front of him, and reached for the shampoo. He began to wash my hair as I grabbed a washcloth and body wash.

Nothing would make me happier than for you to make me yours. I think I want and need it as much as you do. The thought quietly slid into my mind as Andrew's hard cock pressed between my butt cheeks. *But not before you're ready for it. I find that with you, I can be a very patient man.*

"Thank you for understanding. I do want you. I crave your body wrapped around my cock and my teeth marking you...." I trembled under his hands and felt his teeth graze my neck.

"We'll get there when you're ready and not before," Andrew whispered into my ear. He nipped at the lobe, sending a sharp pain running down my spine like electricity. "But if you want to go see your brother instead of fucking our brains out, you have to stop picturing me bent over with your cock in my ass before you drive me out of my mind."

"God, you make it hard to think of anything else when you're rubbing against me like that." I moaned and turned around to face him. I tipped my head back and let the water run down my face, rinsing the soap from my hair. Our hard cocks rubbed against each other as he pressed me back against the shower tile. I wrapped my arms around him, and he lifted me up. My legs clung to his hips, angling my pelvis toward him. His fingers found my hole and, as we rubbed off, he played with my ass.

I will be in you again and soon, my love. The thought was a sensual caress. As his teeth, not his human but his wolf's teeth, sank into my shoulder, I shuddered my release.

"Andrew!" I screamed and shot cum all over our abs.

Mine! I heard him shout in my mind as his seed joined mine, briefly, before being rinsed away by the water. The release was a quick and temporary relief that would take the edge off so we could both comfortably spend time with our family. Our beasts were satiated for the moment, with me marked and smelling more like Andrew, but we wouldn't be complete until we were one.

I relaxed and let my rubbery legs slide to the ground. Andrew held me up, pressed against the shower wall, laving his bite with a lazy satisfaction. It was time to get out and we needed to get dressed before we had company. Best of all, there were jeans and T-shirts waiting for me to wear. I didn't have to wear khakis or dress pants. Call me obsessed, and I might be a prince, but I'd be a prince wearing jeans.

"You may want to rethink that, love. I believe Grandfather is probably contacting Stephon and Quinn so they can come see you today. Probably to counter my actions from the last time they were supposed to come here." Andrew began to draw away from me. I couldn't have that. I tightened my hold on him.

172

"What happened?" I found my legs and spun us so I had his back against the tile and my weight holding him there. Not that he couldn't just pick me up and move me if he wanted, but he stared at the ceiling and shook his head.

"They were supposed to arrive after your talk with Sandy. Stephon was waiting downstairs in the living room with Sam and the twins when you were abducted. They heard my scream, and when Grandfather came up to find out what was going on, they followed him."

"So they saw you break down the door in a rage...."

"I was freaking out, more animal than man. Your mind was gone so suddenly from mine because the gas had knocked you out. If I could have remained calmer, instead of the instant freak out, then we might have been able to track you right away. Instead... I...."

"You were clearly upset, and I'm sure nobody will hold that against you." I could really only hope I was telling the truth. I didn't understand the born vampires enough to know if they could relate to what the two of us were going through. Andrew remained silent for a while as I began to wash first his body and then my own, letting him work through his feelings.

"You would have been amazed. I still haven't decided if Stephon was really brave or the stupidest man I have ever known. He moved so fast. I didn't know he could move that fast. But it was stupid. I was raving."

"You were distraught. I'm sure he would—"

"No, they were all pretty much terrified of me." He shook his head, and I leaned back, taking one of his hands and leading him from the shower. "They were all talking... yelling... and I... well, I pretty much attacked anyone who tried to touch me."

I handed him a towel and let him talk. He needed to get it out, to explain it to me and himself, because he had a hard time reconciling his reactions and violence with the person he believed himself to be.

"I could have hurt him. In those moments, I didn't really see him, just someone standing in the way of finding you. Somehow he got past my claws. He had me in his arms, holding me from behind." It was killing Andrew that he'd been unable to tell friend from foe in his panicked state. But I understood all too well how fight or flight instincts worked.

"Andrew...."

"I heard him, but I didn't.... He kept repeating so softly, 'Poodle, you won't hurt me and I know it. Calm down, pup. We'll find him.' He said it over and over. At first, I fought him. I have no idea how Grandfather got all the damage we did to the walls in the hall fixed. If Stephon hadn't had me from behind, I'd have killed him. But he never let go, no matter what I bashed the two of us into. He held on until I gave up. We slid to the floor and I cried. I screamed and howled for you."

I took the towel he still held and began to dry him off. My mate had been so strong through all of this. Andrew's pain just made me want to kill Brad all the more for putting him through all of this for no reason whatsoever. The idiot didn't even know what he was doing. Yes, he tortured us, but not because of any of his stupid blood crap. No, he hurt us by simply separating us from each other.

"I hurt Stephon, I know I did. When I finally started to get a grip. I don't know how. Maybe Stephon was right, and part of me did realize who he was… but Tim was brilliant. He brought me your bowl, the one you'd made and I love so much, with the wolves carved into the edge. He put it in my hands and told me to focus on the bowl and listen for your heartbeat. He asked if I could hear it, and when I did, he said, 'See, you know he's alive. Now we just have to find him.'"

I'd finished drying him off and led him into the bedroom. I understood then that of the two of us, this ordeal had been harder on him. Yes, I'd been abducted and left in a bloody room with children I'd been expected to kill. But I'd been kept unconscious for two weeks while Andrew went out of his mind trying to find me by my heartbeat alone. I found his restraint remarkable, and I knew my mate to be a strong-willed and resilient man, regardless of what anyone else thought.

"That day, Grandfather called and made our apologies to Quinn. He told him once you were back we would contact him to reschedule our meeting. Stephon stayed with me for as long as he could even though he was in sick or possibly recovering from an injury. He left once we started following you. I tried to apologize, but he told me all he needed was rest and that I wasn't responsible for his condition. I still don't believe him, but I don't know how banging him around could have hurt him that badly. He left, but there really wasn't much else he could do. He kept in touch, calling and checking on me, making sure I didn't lose it entirely. Making sure we found you."

"So call him." It seemed completely logical to me.

"What?" Andrew appeared a bit startled at my comment.

"Phone calls work both ways. You said you wanted to call him earlier. So do it. He was sick. You think hurt him. Everything has calmed down now. So call the man and make sure he's alright. I know you want to." I wanted to hear Stephon's voice as well. He hadn't been there when Grandfather and the rest of the family had attacked the bunker. Andrew had to be right that he was not well or I couldn't imagine our friend not being there, glued to Andrew's side every second of the time I was missing.

"Really? You think it would be alright?" Andrew glanced around the room, trying to find his cell phone.

"It's in the bedroom on the dresser. Yes, I think it's exactly what you need to do."

Andrew took the towel from me and wrapped it around his waist, tucking the end so it would stay on its own and walked out into the bedroom. I followed him out and sat down on the edge of the bed to listen as Andrew picked up his cell from the dresser and dialed.

"Poodle."

"Hi Stephon."

"So nice to hear from you. I was thrilled when Basil called and let me know the two of you were reunited. How is LB doing? Are the two of you alright?"

"Yes, we're well. I just wanted to check on you and to say thank you. I don't know what would have happened if you hadn't been here...I-I—" Andrew stammered.

"Hey, now. What are friends for. The two of you are like family to me and I will always do whatever I can to help you."

"I know. But how are you? Stephon you were so sick. I never should have been able to manhandle you that easily. Yes, I'm stronger now that I'm mated, but I'm not the born pureblood. Stephon, something happened to you?"

"I'm fine. Getting better every day. To look at me now, you wouldn't even know that I'd been ill."

"Ok, but what happened?"

"Something wonderful."

"What?"

"My mate claimed me. He believes that he's incapacitated me. He fanged me in the heart, which threw me into hibernation."

"He bit you in the heart. But you're alright?"

"Yes. His venom, which is usually introduced into the bloodstream of a mate to tie us together, was injected directly into my heart. It acted as it is designed to, as a poison. But since he is my mate and my body recognized him, his poison didn't have a lasting effect and instead of killing me it only put me into hibernation for a short time. I'm fine. The bond between us has begun and he won't be able to stay away for long." Stephon chuckled over the line.

Ask him who it is? I sent to Andrew. Impatient to get to the good stuff.

"May I ask who the lucky groom to be is?" Andrew couldn't stop the grin that spread across his face. "And if I need to hurt him just a little, for hurting you?"

"Ah, unfortunately I am not quite ready to give up that secret just yet, Poodle. And no, you will not hurt him once you know who he is. We've already suffered enough. But tell LB not to worry, the man is gorgeous and I have him and his Unbirthday Party to thank for bringing me and mine finally together."

"So you are really alright?"

"Yes, Andrew. I'm fine. All you gave me were a few bumps and bruises. Your hysteria was nothing I haven't seen before in my life time. I was healed from our skirmish before I even got back to my home in the mountains."

"Ok. I was really worried."

"Relax. Kiss your mate and try not to lose him again."

"Thanks a lot." Andrew chuckled sheepishly.

"I'm off to see if I can track down my mate and surprise him with my benevolent presence. Ta-ta for now, children. I'll call you when I need you."

"Bye, Stephon." Andrew disconnected the call.

"I guess he isn't coming over today. I told you he would understand." I walked across the room and rose up on my tiptoes and brushed a light kiss across Andrew's lips.

"And if the others don't understand?"

"I really don't care if they get it or not. It's a fact of our existence. We're one being in two bodies with separation issues that may or may not go away with time. I almost think it's better if they don't understand entirely." I walked away toward my trunks, eyeing the one that held several pairs of blue jeans.

Andrew cracked a smile, his mood having been lifted by the phone call and my familiar frustration with all fabric other than denim. "I love how you look in jeans." He turned to his own wardrobe to find something to wear. "You know, I love being connected to you. I wouldn't change it if I could. These past couple of weeks have been horrendously painful, but I've gotten much more enjoyment out of our bond than suffering from it."

"Me too. But the fewer people who know how different certain aspects of our lives are from the rest of our kind, the better." I opened the trunk with hardly a glance, I grabbed a pair of well-worn jeans and a dark brown T-shirt. Stepping into the jeans and pulling the cotton over my head was the next best thing to being in Andrew's arms. It just felt right.

When I turned around, Andrew was standing at the foot of the bed in a pair of tailored black pants and a sky-blue button-front shirt. He'd left it open at the throat, showing off his mating necklace, displaying to the world that he belonged to me as I did to him. *You know, there are still moments when I look at you and can hardly believe that you belong to me. I'm just a....*

Don't go there. You have never been just anything. You've been lost is all, and now you're home, and you have a family who loves you and a mate who adores you. So just accept it already. There are other things to rebel against. Stephon would say those things are plaid and paisley....

I burst into laughter, but he was right, of course. I had much bigger things to concern myself with than my human past.

"Let me brush the tangles out." Andrew had my comb in hand and motioned to the bed. I took a seat, Andrew behind me, and he made quick work of my hair. He was almost finished when we heard a very soft knock at the main door of the suite.

"Henry?" Andrew asked.

"That would be my guess." I grinned, excited to see my little brother.

Andrew rose, handing me the comb so he could get the door. "Hi, kiddo." Andrew swept the boy into his arms and gave him a big hug before putting him back down and pointing to our bedroom door.

The soft thud of small running feet was my only warning as Henry appeared in the door, spotted me, and smiled so huge it crinkled his eyes. "Henry!" I held out my arms, and he bounded into the room and leaped at me with arms outstretched. I caught him and pulled him onto my lap and hugged him tightly, rocking a bit until he began to squirm.

"Have you been having fun with Grandfather?" I loosened my hold, thrilled that he stayed in my lap, as Andrew joined us on the bed, taking up his spot behind me and picking up the forgotten comb to finish brushing out my hair.

Henry nodded.

"I'm really glad you're getting along." I heard footsteps out in the sitting room. Andrew had left the door open, and the hall guard must have admitted someone.

"Good morning," Grandfather called.

"Good afternoon, Grandfather. We're in the bedroom. Come on in," I answered, hearing Grandfather's rather tentative footfalls toward the open door.

Seeing Andrew combing my hair while Henry sat on my lap, Grandfather grinned. "Just look at the three of you. How I rate such handsome grandsons, I will never know." He walked over to the bed and placed a hand on Andrew's shoulder while the other mussed Henry's hair. "And how does the day find you?"

"Very well. Thank you." I reached up and took Grandfather's hand. I drew him down onto the bed beside me. He angled himself on the end so he could face all three of us.

"Hungry," Andrew amended as he leaned forward and gave me a kiss on the cheek before handing me my comb, having drawn my hair back into a snug queue at the nape of my neck.

"If you're hungry, then order something already. The kitchen around here is dying to feed you. They only get to actually cook when you're here to feed. Grandfather let all the other human staff return to their families until we are sure Brad is taken care of." Charlie stood at the door. She huffed and grumbled, as if we were all just too much trouble. She would have pulled off the disgruntled-employee mood too if I hadn't caught her smirk as she disappeared into the living room.

"Hungry?" I asked Henry.

He nodded.

"Enough for three, Charlie, please." I didn't have to yell for her to hear me in the other room. All vampires had exceptional hearing, and even with the door closed, she probably could have heard us had she wanted to. It was just considered poor manners to listen in on other's conversations when in the same household. Not that it didn't happen. You just didn't talk about it or, like Grandfather, you installed a lot of soundproofing to make everyone feel better. With the door open, the point was moot.

"Good morning, Tim. Come on in," Andrew called as I glanced over my shoulder at him. It was hard to miss when Tim was hovering just outside the open bedroom door, not knowing if he should come in or not. He stood in the opening so he could see in and be seen, yet not be in the bedroom itself.

"Timothy, I will say this only once more and you will listen and obey me," I snapped.

Tim dropped immediately to one knee. He was startled and completely confused, as I'd never raised my voice to him or even been stern like this, but I was tired of his skittishness. He was family, dammit, and he was always welcome.

"Yes, my lord." Tim stared at the carpet.

"You will look at *me* when I speak to you," I snapped again.

"A vassal is not allowed to look his lord in the eye." Tim's voice was soft but strained and his eyes stayed rooted to the ground.

"I'm sick of this crap from you, Tim. I want my friend, not a servant. If you can't be both, then I won't have the servant. Have I made myself clear? You and Charlie are family to us. We care about you. If you can't get it through that thick skull of yours that your place is always beside us. That you are a part of this family regardless of who else joins it, because you think your damn station is that of a servant—so help me, I will fire your ass right this instant!" I was so done with being gentle and trying to convince him he had a place in my family. If he needed an ultimatum, I was giving it to him.

Tim shook his head and stood, chuckling. He lifted his head and met my gaze. "Thank you, but please don't fire me. You'd have to behead me, and I'd really rather keep it attached to my shoulders." Tim smiled wide. "I do appreciate that you want me to be part of the family, and I am always your friend. You also have to understand there are times I must observe my place as vassal. To me, it's an honor to be your vassal and I take it very seriously."

"But you seem to make it one or the other. Tim, you are both, and having a familiarity with us, and being part of the family doesn't discount what you do for us." Andrew gave my shoulder a squeeze. It was probably the best we were going to get from Tim. He wouldn't concede completely, but then again, he couldn't, and I would never have him killed.

Tim glanced to the left toward where I suspect Charlie stood waiting for the kitchen to deliver the meals, by the outer suite door. "Okay, how about this." Tim swiveled back toward us. "When it is just us: you, Andrew, Henry, Father"—Tim peeked over his shoulder again—"and Charlie, I will relax and join in. If there are others around, then I really need to keep to my position, and not just for you, but for me as well. In some circles it would be considered criminal for a vassal to become too familiar with their lord. I could be severely punished, and there would be nothing you could do about it."

"Not in my house." Grandfather frowned at his son.

"Yes, even here. For instance, if Quinn were to object to my familiarity and report me to the council, whether they agreed that a shifter should have a vassal or not, would not be a consideration. Just the protocol of my behavior would be suspect. You know they could bleed me or have me beaten as punishment for almost any infraction. The only thing they can't do is order my death, as my life is not my own, but Lance's." Tim closed his eyes for a moment. He seemed sad as if he were contemplating the eventuality and preparing himself to deal with it, before taking a breath to continue. "He would be right in doing so, because I am much closer to you than I should be and my perspective is all askew. Hardly that of a vassal who is always supposed to have an objective, impartial point of view so he can give the best advice."

"I'd rather you had my best interest at heart and told me the truth in all things than were you to be an objective outsider," I told him.

Nodding his head, Tim sighed. "I do my best to always be honest with you and, just so you know, I do care about you too."

"Charlie...." I called. She had to know she was part of this. Just because she was my bodyguard did not exclude her from being part of my family.

"Yeah, I know. Me too. Got it, and all the mushy stuff too," Charlie grumbled, but it was no good. I could hear the smile in her tone even though I couldn't see it.

"Good. Now that we have that settled, is lunch here yet?" I nuzzled my cheek into my little brother's hair. He was beginning to take on just a bit of familial scent, but my wolf still wanted to mark him further as ours. "I believe we're hungry." Henry's eyes got big and he nodded his head vigorously.

"He can't be hungry. We just ate not a couple of hours ago." Grandfather frowned, but the crinkle at the corners of his eyes belied his teasing.

"Young shifters eat a great deal. They have very high metabolisms." Andrew winked at Henry and stood, opening his hand for Henry to take, which he did, hopping off the bed.

"Ah, but of course. That must be it." Grandfather laughed and stood, letting me get up as well so we could all go out to the table and chairs in the lounge.

"Lunch should be up any time. Why don't you relax a bit and catch up. I'll go see what's taking so long." Charlie disappeared out the door.

"And you say I'm the one with issues." Tim smirked and dropped down onto the sofa.

"Her turn will come." Andrew smirked, taking a seat at the table with me and Henry, while Grandfather leaned against the back of the sofa.

"So, where do we stand? Do we have company coming to visit today?" I asked. I wasn't really nervous, but to be honest, I didn't feel ready to be put on display just yet.

"First, how are you feeling? Are you all right?" Grandfather asked. His concern was genuine and he had a legitimate reason. My mate had gone ballistic when we were separated, and I had no desire to relive that separation anytime soon.

"Getting better. We're still a bit on edge. Better now that I know everyone is being cared for and I have all of you around me." I couldn't stop the sigh that escaped. "Andrew and I are still putting ourselves back together. I may never let him out of my sight again for as long as I live."

"He was...." Grandfather paused, as if trying to figure out how to say something, and afraid it might not come out quite right.

180

"I explained that I really wasn't myself, while he was gone. I know I owe everyone a huge apology. You all must have thought I'd lost my mind, the way I practically attacked everyone within range. All I can say is—"

Grandfather held up his hands, cutting Andrew off. "We understand, me especially. I'm separated from my Illiana every day, but at least I know where she is. I can touch her, hold her, and even though she is unconscious, I can venture into her dreams. Our bond remains strong. When I leave, I still feel the need to return to her. My desire for her is no less than it was on the day we met." Grandfather paused and appeared to be lost for a moment, and Henry let go of my hand, got up and moved to stand in front of Grandfather, whose hand he took. "Things are hard because she sleeps, so even though on one hand we are together, we also remain apart." Grandfather reached down and picked Henry up, gave him a big hug and snuggle, and tickled him until you could see the silent giggles shaking the boy from head to toe. "Thank you, Henry. I'm better now."

"Still, I am sorry...." Andrew began as the intercom buzzer by the door sounded.

Charlie stepped into the room. "Yes?" Charlie said into the intercom.

"I just received word from Sam at the farm. Jack and Joe Reed are on their way to the penthouse. They have news for the family," a male voice replied.

"Please alert us when they arrive and send them up to Lance and Andrew's suite." Charlie told the guard over the intercom. Even surrounded by my family, she was on duty. "Just so you know"—Charlie spun round to face us, before pointing to the top of the fireplace where it met the roof—"I've placed cameras up on the roof, and the chimney is now grated off in a couple of places before opening out into that large hearth. There will be no repeats of your previous abduction. Nobody will be getting in or out of this room through the chimney ever again."

She wanted to destroy the fireplace, but I didn't think you would want her to do that. It is the one thing in this room that really reminds me of our home, Andrew thought.

I'm glad you convinced her to leave it here.

I didn't convince her of anything. When I said no, Grandfather told her to stuff it and just fix it. I'd never thought to see the day where Charlie appeared as if she'd like to rip Grandfather a new one, but she did what she was told. Andrew silently chuckled in my mind.

"Thank you, Charlie," I tried to reassure her and keep the laugh from my voice, but she was having none of it.

"I won't fail you again." Charlie growled, and was out the door before I could stop her.

"This can't go on. I won't have her beating herself up over something that happened when she wasn't even here," I yelled toward the door, knowing full well she could hear me and was refusing to acknowledge me.

"Give her some time." Grandfather carried Henry over to the table and sat him down in the chair he'd been previously seated in. "Her pride has been wounded, and by her brother. It's not just the fact that she wasn't here that is bothering her; it's his betrayal as well. She's angry and hurt by his actions as we all are, but I think she feels like she should have seen it coming and she didn't. I think she feels like she should have been able to prevent all of this."

"She may be a drone, but nobody can predict another person's actions. Charlie had no way of knowing Brenda was being used. Sure, none of us liked Brenda and she had an attitude, but that doesn't necessarily prove ill intent." Andrew sat back in his chair. "I can understand her feelings, but none of us saw it coming... well, none of us other than Stephon."

"Speaking of which, I spoke with him earlier before the two of you awoke. We decided you'd earned a few more days' rest. So he suggests we have our meeting at the end of the week. With a death in the shifter royal family, I'm sure they will be occupied with funeral arrangements. They may still contact you directly, as I suspect they will want to crown you the next prince."

"Please tell me it isn't a real formal coronation?" I could feel everything in me rebelling against the idea of the pomp and circumstance of the royal to-dos I'd seen on TV.

"Yes, it is a formal affair, but probably not in the way you've ever seen it done," Andrew said. "It's an outdoor ceremony, rain or shine. Done under a full moon, of course, in the meadow of the lodestone. It's a very sacred site for both our peoples."

"Well, originally it was a sacred place for three of the four paranormal species that inhabited this earth. But because of a tragic accident, when the fae were banished behind the veil, the dwarves—who lost a third of their population, trapped behind the veil—are now gone as well. They disappeared into their caverns beneath the earth and haven't been heard from since. Leaving only we two species, vampires and shifters." Grandfather put his hands on the back of Henry's chair, my brother frowning up at him with questioning eyes.

"Wait a minute...." I was thoroughly confused too.

"I've mentioned this all before. The Blood Wars with us against the fae." Andrew grinned. "There's so much to tell. I was sure we'd talked about it. The story of the lodestone was one of my favorites when I was a child."

Tim stood and walked over to the one of the bookcases on the far wall that I'd yet to have time to investigate. "I do believe…," he mumbled as he ran a finger along the spines.

"The story of the first prince was tragic. But the ballad was actually a set of instructions on how to keep the gate between the planes in place. If I remember correctly, it also holds a rather maudlin warning about the gate falling." Grandfather watched Tim as he pulled an old leather-bound book from the shelf and brought it back to the table, turning carefully the yellowed parchment pages.

"Here." Tim placed the book on the table open to a page of handwritten calligraphy.

Grandfather began to read aloud.

"Ballad of the Lodestone

The blood of two houses must unite,
To keep the gate closed infinite.
On the day of firsts, the chosen bleed,
The power, the dwarven stone to feed.

Blessed is the mother,
Her babe blooded the stone.
Blessed is the clan,
Their Lord bled for the throne.

Each innocent babe, born of blood,
Cries tears of reddest rosebud.
Of nature's meld of wild, raw and true,
Pureblood must sacrifice, shed to imbue.

Blessed is the mother,
Her babe blooded the stone.
Blessed is the clan,
Their Lord bled for the throne.

With this blood, the gate is sealed,
The veil is sure, the fae repealed.
Guard well the Vale of the Lode, my kin,
Heed my warning, when the veil is thin.

Blessed is the mother,
Her babe blooded the stone.
Blessed is the clan,
Their Lord bled for the throne.

The black pool sees and the veil shines bright.
A brother in need you will have to fight.
The veil doth rent and fall away,
Choose death, my kin, before the fae."

We all sat silent for a moment before Charlie opened the door and let in the kitchen staff. Tim grabbed the book and cleared it off the table as platters of meat and potatoes, salads and iced tea were brought in. Somehow I wasn't quite as hungry as I had been. The warning in the ballad hung heavy in the air.

Once the staff was gone, Charlie stayed with us but still hovered by the door.

Grandfather broke the silence. "I don't remember it being quite that foreboding."

"The person who wrote that... he basically told us to commit suicide if the fae regained entry back into this world. Why would he do that?" It went against my nature to just give up. Never once, even when I had thought myself a murderer, had I ever given up. I ran away. I lived by my wits and instincts. I fought my way through life in the human world just to survive, and not once had it even occurred to me to just stop running and kill myself. I couldn't explain why it didn't—it's not like I'd known I had Andrew then to live for. It just wasn't in me to throw my hands up in the air and say, "Oh poor me, I can't take it anymore, fuck it" and off myself. Yes, my inner voice was being crass again. I knew that was incredibly simplistic and emotionless, and that there are good people who've chosen to take their lives because of obstacles they felt they couldn't surmount. But for me... I can't express enough how much it had never even been a consideration.

BLOOD TIES

"The Blood Wars were unlike any other. If it hadn't been for the kings working together the way they did hand in hand with the council, this world would be very different." Charlie leaned back against the wall.

Andrew sat forward and passed around the platter of cold cuts, bread, and cheese for sandwiches.

"The fae are of two factions. They fight each other as much as everyone else. They believe themselves to be descendants of the gods and that it is their right to conquer and take whatever they want. They are the Seelie and the Unseelie. The Seelie are the fae of light—they are tall and lithe, beautiful to behold. Their hair is long and gossamer fine and they are always blonde and blue-eyed. Their powers are mainly mental, telepathy and illusion. They can make themselves appear to be anyone, and by reading your mind, they can behave as you know that person would. They see themselves as a force of good and that their rightful place is to rule over us as gods under their benevolent care." Grandfather scoffed.

"Oh, you mean kind of what vamps have done to my race?" I snapped. Grandfather was indignant at the idea of another race ruling over them, yet they'd subjected my own to exactly what he was describing.

"Touché." Grandfather smiled and shook his head, then sat down at the table beside Henry and helped the boy add mayo and mustard to the mound of sliced roast beef, cheese, and a single lettuce leaf that was more garnish than an actual vegetable, to his sandwich. "The Unseelie are as dark as the Seelie are light. Dark hair, dark eyes, and gray skin tone, and they too have the same mental abilities, speed, and agility as their brethren. Only they don't care to rule. They just want to feed. They do as they please whenever they want and try to manipulate everyone around them simply for their amusement. They don't have any higher aspirations for the greater good of anybody but themselves. In fact, they take great pride in their greed. Both factions of the fae, if they were to return, would seek vengeance—the Seelie wanting to punish for our daring to go against a god and the Unseelie just because they can."

"So the three species betrayed the fae, but something went wrong and the dwarves got stuck behind the veil along with them. And according to the ballad, as long as we do what we're supposed to, we've nothing to worry about." I could barely believe what I was hearing.

"Yep, pretty much." Charlie frowned and must have noticed I wasn't eating. "Eat the damn sandwich. It's not that bad. You've watched TV more exciting than that ballad," she grumbled at me.

I wanted to laugh at myself. She was right. Nothing was going to happen right now. We were just talking about it. It was just an old ballad that kind of explained some of the more formal traditions of our people. I was letting things get to me way too easily these days.

"Grandfather, I know you were against the beneficiary system, but after hearing that warning and the history of the Blood Wars, I don't understand how your people could enslave others."

"Centuries had passed between the time of the Blood Wars and when the Great War between the shifters and the vampires took place. What can I say, people forget. Even those of us with very long lives and very long memories don't always remember or appreciate what others went through so we can have the lives we now lead." Grandfather ruffled Henry's hair as the boy took a bite from a sandwich that I was sure he would have to unhinge his jaw in order to get his mouth around it. "Others probably thought the blood ceremonies and magic of the stone was unnecessary, that after so many centuries of feeding the power, it had become self-sustaining. Or that the fae and dwarves are dead on the other side of the veil and we've no cause to fear them any longer."

"Okay, so war stuff aside, I take it the coronation will take place at this lodestone, and for part of the ceremony, I have to be a sacrifice?" It was a bit confusing because I wasn't sure how I could be a sacrifice—I had visions of being tied to stakes or slabs, allowing my body to be slashed so my blood ran until I was dry—and still live to lead the council afterward.

"Yes. But not in the way you are thinking. You basically have to cut your hand while swearing an oath to lead your people to the best of your ability. The blood from the cut falls on the lodestone. The Matron of the royal family's house then crowns you king." Andrew rubbed my back as I stared at the turkey sandwich I'd put together, unsure if I could take a bite.

"What's that part about a baby that cries blood?" I reached for the potato chips and placed a few on my plate, still not hungry but making a good show of it.

"Born vampire babies cry regular tears when they are first born. But as they get older, their vampire nature begins to take over. Usually within the first six weeks after their birth, their first set of fangs drop and they cry tears of blood as they begin to crave it. The first tears are a light pinkish red, like a rosebud. Those tears are the infants blooding tears, signifying when it has the hunger and requires its first blood meal. The amount necessary is truly small, a mouthful every two to three months when the child cries pink tears, which get darker as the child gets older, until he or she is able to speak and tell you when the craving is upon him or her," Charlie said before pushing off from the door, walking over to the wall of windows, and stalking the length of the room to the door that led out onto the veranda and back area.

"Our people haven't seen a birth since the hibernation sickness began decades ago. Which is why I have such hope that, with your arrival and with Tim's extensive research, we'll be able to discover why our mates sleep and how to awaken them." Grandfather picked up a potato chip and delicately nibbled it, then frowned. "You really like these greasy, salty things?" He wrinkled his nose at Henry, who avidly nodded. "Ish, to each his own. But I think we need to broaden your pallet. I can guarantee you there are much more—appetizing things to eat than potato chips. Caviar, for instance, or that lovely artichoke salad the chef was talking about sounded amazing." Henry's turned up nose and scrunched-up face said more than a thousand words.

"He's going to be mainly a carnivore until he's about forty years old." Andrew laughed outright at Grandfather's forlorn expression. "If you prefer vegetables or lighter protein meals, feel free to have the cook make them. It doesn't hurt to have him try them, but be prepared for him to object. He's just a cub after all. Even Lance is going to prefer a diet much heavier on protein than what you are used to, although he is much more flexible than most."

"Well, yes, I suppose you are correct. It has been a long time since I've had cubs about in quite this fashion, and vampire children this age prefer vegetables and very light proteins, their diets being about fifty-fifty, blood to solids."

I phased out a bit, thinking about the lodestone as the conversation ran on around me, and I ate my sandwich. If the royal family hadn't had a pureblood heir since the Great War when the family bloodlines were mixed with human blood, and no vampire children had been born during that time, what, if anything, was sustaining the veil? Was the veil even still there? Maybe they were right to think the fae and dwarves dead. Maybe the warning was from a frightened man who'd seen too much death, and although a valid concern at the time, his warning was no longer necessary. Somehow I doubted we'd be that lucky.

"You coming?" Tim asked, standing at the door.

Focused on my empty plate but not really seeing it, Tim's voice startled me out of my reverie. I sat back, scanning the room, and noticed everyone was leaving. Charlie, Grandfather, and Henry had already left the room. Andrew was standing halfway between the table and the door, while Tim held the door open.

I really was scattered. I'd finished eating and hadn't even realized it. I pushed back from the table and rose. *What are we doing? Sorry, I was kind of lost in my own thoughts there.* I followed Tim and Andrew out the door.

Henry is showing us his playroom. Grandfather decked out one of the rooms at the end of the hall for Henry to play in while he's here. He also has his own bedroom attached to the playroom Tim said was to be Illiana and Grandfather's child's nursery. Grandfather wanted Henry to have it while he's here.

"Oh my, is he sure. I mean...." I stammered. Grandfather and Illiana had been and still were expecting, once she awoke from hibernation. Sadly, Henry could be an adult by the time Illiana awoke if things didn't change soon for her, as there was no telling when they would have a cure for the hibernation sickness.

"Yes. Just accept it and let him fuss. I haven't seen him this happy or alive in years." Tim smiled as he stood in the doorway, watching his father, my grandfather, down on his hands and knees involved in a wordless conversation with my brother as the two played together with Legos. My brother was clearly instructing Grandfather in the finer art of Lego construction. It was wonderful to behold.

EPILOGUE

I WAS awake. I had no idea why, but there I lay, staring at the ceiling. It was unusual for one of us to be awake and the other asleep, but Andrew softly snored behind me, his face in my hair and an arm around my middle. I was restless.

I carefully eased out from under his arm. I slid one pillow under it in my place and the pillow I'd been lying on under Andrew's nose. It didn't work.

Where are you going? His half-conscious question floated into my mind.

Bathroom. Go back to sleep.

Okay. I felt his mind retreat into the netherworld of dreamless sleep. He wasn't completely gone, but then again neither of us was ever completely alone. I stumbled into the bathroom and closed the door before turning on the light so it wouldn't disturb him. Squinting against the bright lights, I made my way to the toilet and relieved myself. I was washing my hands when I felt what had awoken me in the first place.

The touch on my mind was light and small, filled with curiosity. I reached for the mind, not sure if it was my brother, Henry, discovering a new power or maybe another shifter in the building who didn't know we were here. He was so quick—yes, I was pretty certain the touch was that of another male, but not my brother—that as I reached for him, he retreated, but when I eased back, he sought me. My wolf was intrigued by the game, and since I was awake anyway, I decided to hunt down the mind-playing games at this time of the night.

So, continuing the game of cat and mouse, I followed the touch out of the bathroom and out of the bedroom, then into the hall. My guard frowned at me as I stood in the center of the hallway, staring down the hall to where I expected to go, but feeling the draw into the room straight across from my own. Those were my grandfather's suites.

"Where's my grandfather?" I asked the guard.

"He is in your brother's room, watching Lord Henry sleep."

I bit my tongue to keep from sighing audibly at the title. The kid was too young to be a lord. Hell, I was too young to be a lord. I gave myself a shake. "Please tell him I need to see him immediately and I'll be waiting for him in his lounge."

I knew I was taking a liberty by entering my grandfather's rooms without his express permission, but I was afraid there was an intruder in the house—it had to be a very young and very small trespasser, a child would be my guess. I wasn't going to tell the guard there was a prowler and scare the kid out of his mind, not when we needed to find out who this child was. I'd yet to get any real words or language from him, just impressions and feelings.

"Yes, my lord," the guard replied. He started running down the hall as I opened the door and flipped on the light switch. I continued into the room, and although the mind-playing cat and mouse with me was just behind the next door, I wasn't prepared to go any farther without Grandfather present. That door, if this room mimicked my own suite across the hall, led to Grandfather's master bedroom.

There was no reason Grandfather would have a young child in his bedroom, at least none that I could come up with, but I wasn't about to violate the man's privacy. Especially when he'd given me so much and asked for so little. I would not enter his bedroom without him. Besides, it wasn't as if the kid was in distress. He just wanted to play. So I waited, the little mind dancing about mine, pressing against the barriers I'd erected but not really trying to get past them. It was more of the same game.

I could feel the confusion washing off Grandfather in crashing waves of energy as he opened the door and rushed into the room. The little mind retreated as if cold water had been thrown on it. I quickly spun from Grandfather to the direction of the bedroom as the mind retreated. I closed my eyes and envisioned the mind as a child running and saw myself wrapping my arms around him, placing a mental barrier around it, trying to protect it, but from what I didn't know.

"Ah!" Grandfather cried out, grabbing his temples. "Lance, stop! Please! Why are you trying to separate me from Illiana?"

"What?" I dropped the barrier and the little mind disappeared altogether as I turned to Grandfather in confusion. "That tiny mind I felt reach out to mine, that's Illiana? No way." I was completely confused. "Grandfather, that mind did not come from a female."

Grandfather's eyes flew open and he stared at me with such hope. "Did you say the mind you felt was male?"

"Yes, I'm positive. He's been playing cat and mouse with me for the last half hour as I figured out where in the house he was. It's odd, though. I'm sure it's a child. I thought it was Henry because he doesn't seem to have any use of language, but that's not true of Henry. He understands language. He just doesn't speak. This child doesn't even seem to really understand language. It's more emotion and instinct driven."

"Lance, the only person beyond that door is Illiana, my mate, and our unborn child. I can reach her, but I've never felt the child." Grandfather came to stand beside me, his hands trembling. "I wasn't even sure if the infant survived. None of the elders I've spoken with have ever known of a pregnant female going into hibernation before."

I put a hand on Grandfather's shoulder. "You have a son, and I suspect that you have been so intent on reaching your mate that the infant is afraid of you. He was here, playing, until you came in the door. Then he retreated, and when I tried to shield him, you said I was cutting you off from Illiana."

"You really felt my son?" Grandfather started to stumble, and I guided him to the sofa.

"Yes. I really think if you ease back, he'll come back out to play. You're so used to your connection with your mate, but he's connected to her too. And they're sharing a body, but not necessarily a mind. Her body is all he knows, but he's conscious and can tell we're out here. He just can't come out and play." A grin and joy like I'd never seen lit up Grandfather's face. "Now, ease back. I know you're excited, but draw back from her slowly and gently, as if you were caressing her face and stepping backward from her at the same time." I coached him, softening my tone, kind of poking around the edges to see if I could stir the kid's interest. But Grandfather's happiness infused the room, and when the main part of your day is feeling the emotions of others around you, good feelings are attractive, especially in this stress-filled household.

"Oh!" Grandfather exclaimed as his son began to feel around the edges of his consciousness. Not really invading, just feeling Grandfather out. The warmth on his face as he began to play the same cat-and-mouse game with his son as I'd been playing was priceless, and I have never been so happy that I could give such a gift to him.

"I'm going back to bed. You two kids enjoy yourselves." I yawned and stretched as I glanced over at the door.

Grandfather turned around and drew me into a hug. "I can't thank you enough for this. I finally have proof my son is alive, and I will never be able to repay you for bringing us together."

"You're my grandfather. My family. If it's in my power to do something, I will always try. I may not always succeed, but if you don't try, you've already lost."

"Will you come and meet Illiana tomorrow? I realize it's a long shot, but maybe your wolf will see what Tim and I are missing."

"Of course I will. I'd love to meet her." I hugged grandfather back tightly. "Couldn't Tim tell you if the baby was alive?"

Grandfather let me draw back from him. "Tim believed the baby was alive and suspected it might be hibernating. But a pregnant female has never in our recorded history ever gone into hibernation. We've taken some chances. Normally a mate would need to feed its hibernating partner only once a lunar cycle. Illiana needed to be feed much more often. We inserted a feeding tube into Illiana's stomach and colostomy and urinary catheter as well. The child needs more nutrition and produces more waste as it grows—even though the growth rate is extremely slow—than she would while hibernating and ingesting my blood alone."

"So all of the extra feedings and nutrients that are flowing through her body, is that why she almost wakes?"

"We really don't know. It might be, or it might be the onset of labor and she's trying to wake up to birth the child. Tim can't tell and we have nothing to reference this against. We weren't even sure the child would be developing properly under these circumstances."

"You know I will do whatever I can to help."

"Thank you. You've already done more than I ever imagined. I have a son and he is alive."

"Yes, I have an… uncle?" I wasn't quite sure how to feel about an infant uncle. But grandfather was happy and that was all that mattered. "I need to go. Andrew will come looking for me if I'm gone much longer."

"All right. Good night." Grandfather reached once again for the child and found him patiently waiting to play.

I left and returned to my own rooms, to my warm bed and a mate who was now wide awake and waiting for me with open arms.

"That was a very nice thing to do for Grandfather. But next time you get up in the middle of the night to go to the bathroom, I swear I'm getting up with you," Andrew grumbled as he pulled me snug against him, spooned up against my back.

"Yes, dear," I mumbled, already beginning to doze off.

BREEDING CHARTS

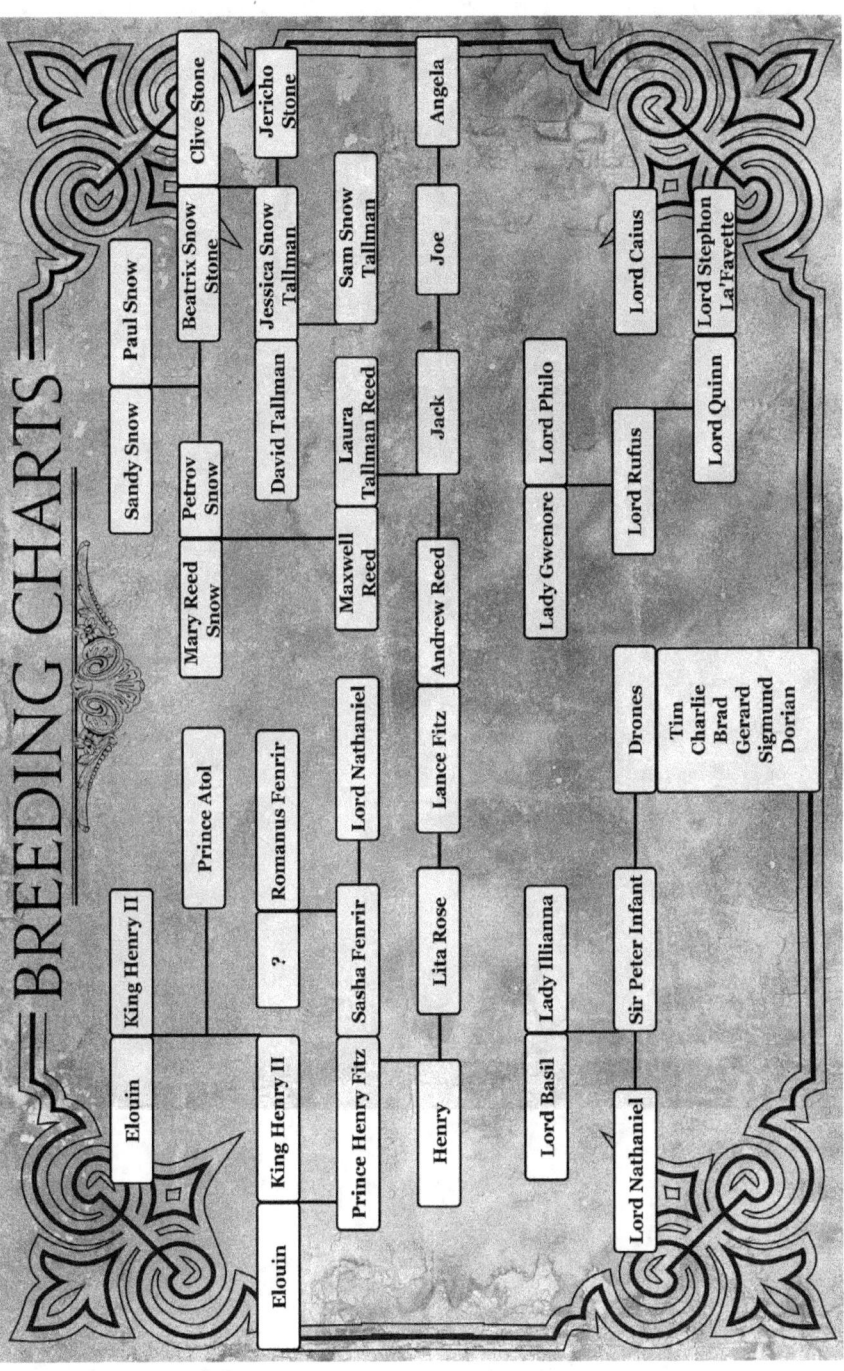

GLOSSARY

<u>Characters by family association</u>

Family Trees:

Sandy Snow—Matriarch of Snow Pack

Paul Snow—Sandy's Husband (deceased)

Maxwell Reed—Married into Snow Pack; Andrew Reed's Father

Laura Tallman Reed—Granddaughter of Sandy Snow; Wife of Maxwell Reed; Mother of Andrew Reed, Jack and Joe Reed, Angela Reed.

David Tallman—Grandson of Sandy Snow; Laura Tallman Reed's brother; Sam Tallman's father

Sam Tallman—Great Grandson of Sandy Snow; Son of David Tallman

Jericho Stone—Great Grandson of Sandy Snow

King Henry (the Gray)—First King of the Shifter Race

Queen Vesta Snow—First Queen and mate of King Henry

Prince Atol—Eldest son of King Henry and Queen Vesta, aka the Mad Prince; Mate of Ventall

Ventall—dwarf trapped behind the veil; mate of Prince Atol

Prince Henry II—2nd Son of King Henry and Queen Vesta; Becomes King Henry II—after murder of his father and his older brother is incapacitated by loss of his mate

Elouin—Mistress to King Henry II

Prince Henry Fitz III—Son of King Henry II and Mistress Elouin; Tri-Mates with Sasha Fenrir and Lord Nathaniel

Romanus Fenrir—Father of Sasha Fenrir; Helps to instigate the Great War between the Shifters and Vampires

Sasha Fenrir—Tri-Mates with Prince Henry II and Lord Nathaniel; Mother of Lance, Henry, and LitaRose

Lord Caius—Born Vampire; Lord Stephon's father

Lord Stephon La'Fayette—Born Vampire; Son of Lord Caius; Benefactor of Reed family

Stephon's Drones:

Victoria—Personal Assistant to Lord Stephon

Maurice—Chauffer

Lord Philo and Lady Gwenore—Born Vampire mates; Parents of Lord Rufus; Grandparents of Lord Quinn

Lord Rufus—Born Vampire; Father of Lord Quinn

Lord Quinn—Born Vampire; Benefactor of Snow and Tallman families

Lord Basil—Born Vampire; Vampire Council Member; Mate of Lady Illiana

Lady Illiana—Born Vampire; Mate of Lord Basil

Lord Nathaniel (deceased)—Born Vampire; Son of Lord Basil and Lady Illiana

Lord Basil and Lady Illiana's Drones:

Tim Carlson—Doctor

Charlie—Warrior

Brad—Former personal assistant

Gerard—Butler at Lord Nathaniel's estate

SUI LYNN is a born-and-raised Midwestern gal. She loves rock 'n' roll but can get a little bit country too. She has been writing for as long as she can remember and is always found with a book or pencil and paper in hand. She has two cocker spaniels who are the comic relief in her life. She loves orange soda, Dr. Who, and her computer, all of which she could not function without.

Sui received two M/M Goodreads Romance Group nominations: one for Best Paranormal Story of 2012 and the other for Best World Created for 2012. She has also been nominated for the Preditors & Editors Reader's Poll in the category of "all other" Novels.

Website: http://suilynn.com/
Blog: http://suidlynn.blogspot.com/
Facebook: https://www.facebook.com/sui.lynn.9
Twitter: http://twitter.com/#!/suidlynn
E-mail: sui.d.lynn@gmail.com

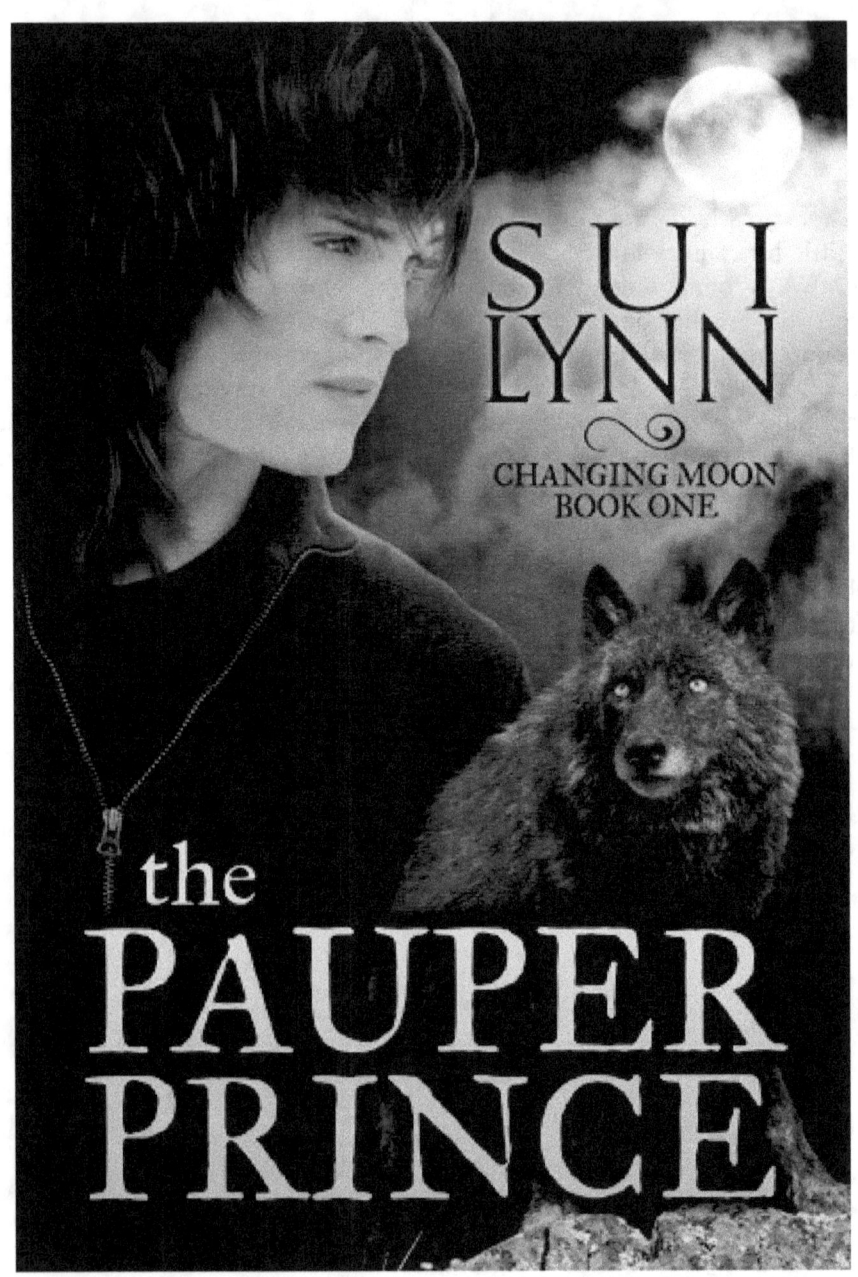

S U I
LYNN

CHANGING MOON
BOOK ONE

the
PAUPER
PRINCE

S U I
LYNN

CHANGING MOON
BOOK TWO

A ROYAL
BIND

http://www.dreamspinnerpress.com

SUI LYNN

ADEL'S
PURR

http://www.dreamspinnerpress.com

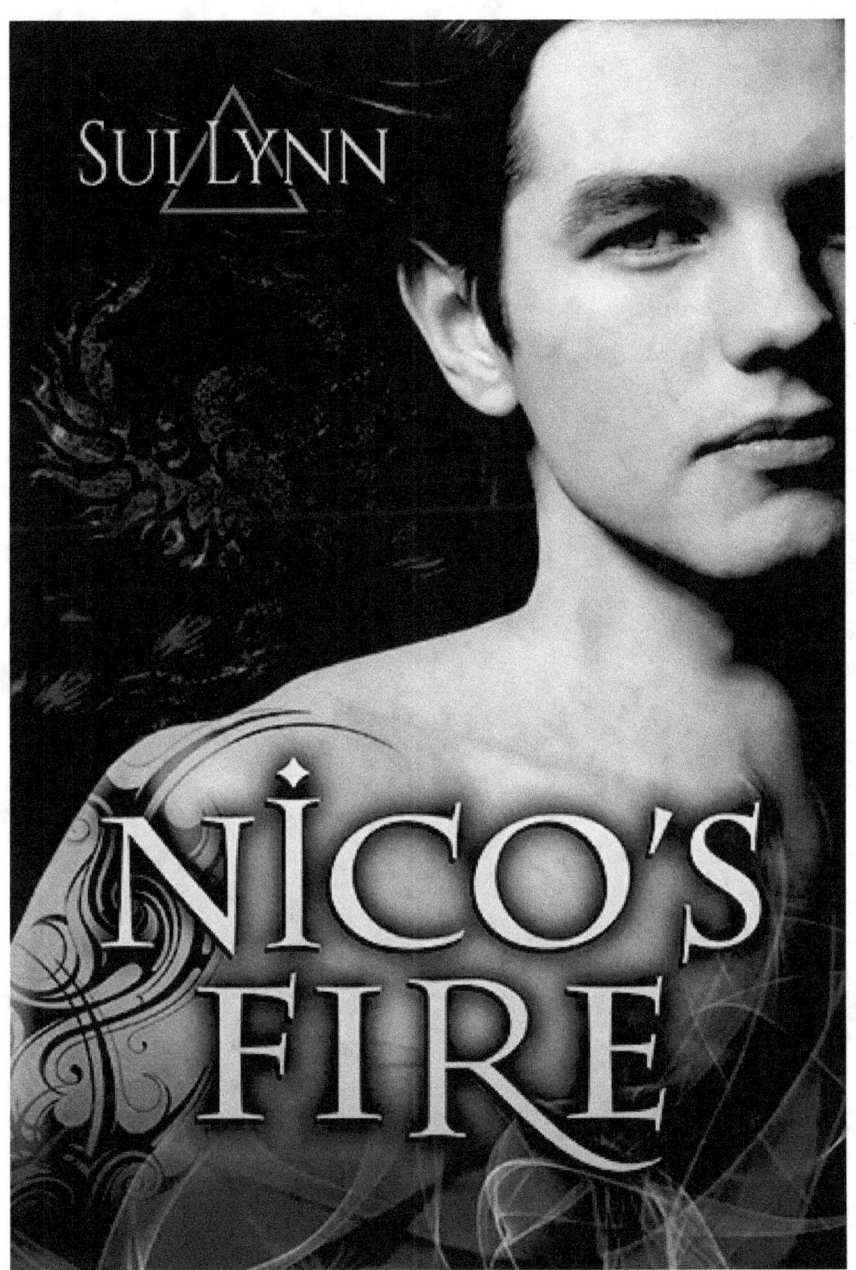

SUI LYNN

NICO'S FIRE

http://www.dreamspinnerpress.com

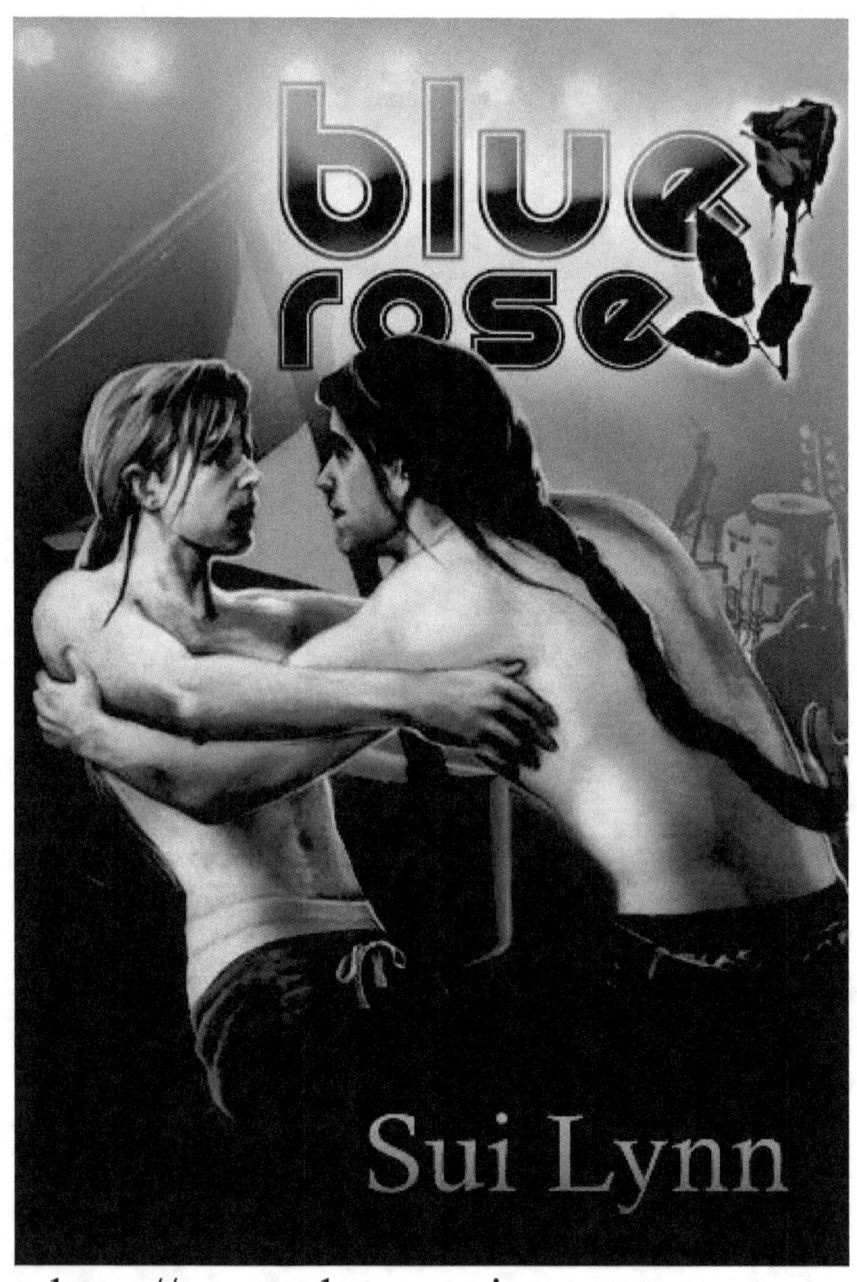

Sui Lynn

http://www.dreamspinnerpress.com

Book One of The Sleepless City

Shades of Sepia

Anne Barwell

http://www.dreamspinnerpress.com

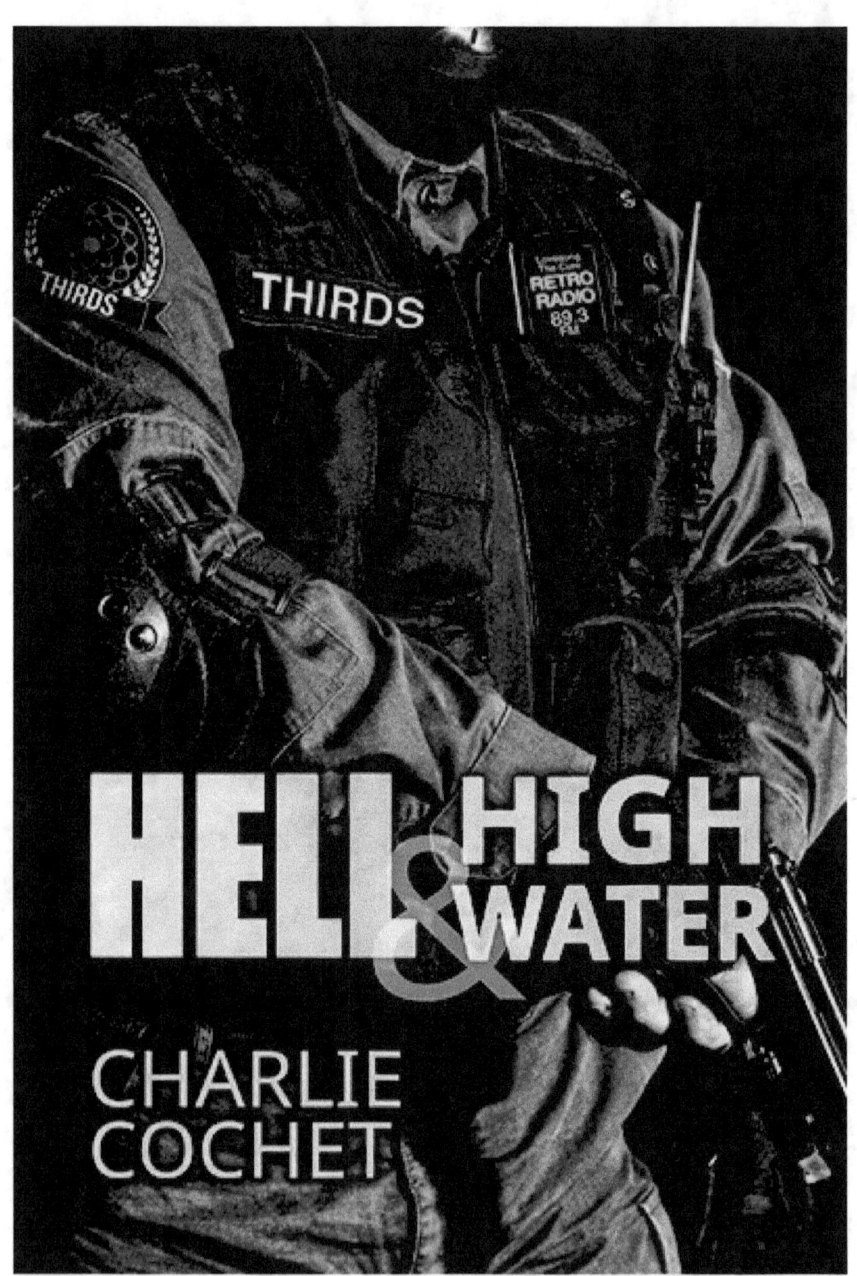

http://www.dreamspinnerpress.com

AN AMERICAN Lamb IN EUROPE

ROB COLTON

http://www.dreamspinnerpress.com